PUFFIN BOOKS
Editor: Kaye Webb

The House of the Nightmare

A little gooseflesh, a pleasurable shiver, may be all you get if you read these sinister, spooky stories by the fireside among your family, doors locked and windows barred and curtains drawn to shut out the night, but don't take the book to bed with you; don't read it alone.

Most of the stories aren't true, to be sure, but brilliant writers like Saki, Elizabeth Bowen, M. R. James, W. W. Jacobs, Walter de la Mare and Margaret Irwin can still give horrifying reality to imaginary ghosts, and you will never quite forget these tales of werewolves, the monkey's paw, the ancient Red Indian woman, the drowning woman's terrible curse, and the ghostly hand that animated the glove.

Kathleen Lines, who collected these eerie tales, is well known for her anthologies for children. In this book she has collected some of the classic nineteenth-century ghost stories and some in which modern authors have carried on the tradition, even including one which deals with a mysterious prediction made by a computer. Some true ghost stories are also to be found at the end of the book.

For readers of eleven and over.

Cover design by Madelon Vriesendorp

THE HOUSE OF
THE NIGHTMARE

and Other Eerie Tales

CHOSEN BY

Kathleen Lines

Puffin Books

in association with The Bodley Head

Puffin Books, Penguin Books Ltd, Harmondsworth, Middlesex, England
Penguin Books Australia Ltd, Ringwood, Victoria, Australia
Penguin Books (N.Z.) Ltd, 182–190 Wairau Road, Auckland 10, New Zealand

—

First published by The Bodley Head 1967
This collection published in Puffin Books 1970
Reprinted 1971, 1972, 1973, 1975

—

—

Made and printed in Great Britain
by Hazell Watson & Viney Ltd,
Aylesbury, Bucks
Set in Intertype Plantin

CONTENTS

FOREWORD

THE stories which make up the greater part of this book are by professional writers and storytellers. Possibly an incident, a rumour or a legend may sometimes have provided the initial idea, but it is the writer's imagination, added to his skill in the use of his craft and his power to create atmosphere, that enthralls the reader and gives to his story a horrifying reality.

Two stories are exceptions; no one knows who invented them nor exactly how old they are; they must have been *told* for many years before they were written down. In Shakespeare's *Much Ado About Nothing* there is a reference to the old English tale of *Mr Fox*. There is nothing supernatural about *Mr Fox*, but there is a good deal of concentrated horror, and the repeated sentences can sound as sinister as any rattling of bones or clanking of chains. The story of Grettir's fight with a very substantial ghost (in this connexion note that a real skeleton was left by M. R. James's horrid creature) is older still – it comes from Iceland, and though Grettir himself lived in the early eleventh century, the story was probably first written down around the beginning of the thirteenth century.

The 'classic' ghost stories seem to have been written from the mid-nineteenth century to the early part of this one, when the pace of life was more leisurely. Even those writers more nearly contemporary frequently set their stories in an earlier time and told them unhurriedly and at length. It would have been easy to have made a very fine selection set entirely in the past – though there would have been fewer stories. However, it is interesting to see how modern authors have carried on the tradition and to have in one book examples of strange stories which cover a con-

siderable period. W. W. Jacobs was born over a hundred years
ago; so was Ambrose Bierce, and he 'disappeared' in Mexico in
1913; the theme nearest to our own times is in that story by
Professor Dickinson which deals with the mysterious answer
given by a computer.

The short section at the end of the book contains a few true
and unexplained experiences. Many people believe in ghosts and
many quite ordinary people have seen apparitions or have experienced some lively manifestations of the supernatural, but it is
extraordinarily difficult (unless one is a member of an occult
society) to trace even the most modest tales of 'hauntings' to
their original sources. It is so often a case of 'Oh, yes, it *is* true,'
but it turns out to have happened to the friend of a cousin's husband's aunt, or to somebody else equally remote. The incidents
here are all connected *personally* with the writers. Only two
have been published before, and, except for *The Limping Man
of Makin-Meang*, which comes from an interesting and entertaining book, they have been told very simply, the bare facts
stated without any elaboration. Because they are so straightforward and because most of them are not frightening, they
are in a dramatic sense a 'let down' when compared with the
stories. But think for a moment: would not the sudden appearance of an extra person in the room beside one, the sight of an
apparently solid man walking through a definitely solid wall,
or of a man in fancy dress who wasn't really there, be just a bit
unnerving? And how many of us would like to walk alone on
remote Dartmoor, or be willing to spend the night in a desolate
and reputedly haunted house?

I should like to thank the authors (or their representatives
and publishers) who have allowed their stories to be reprinted
in this book, and I am especially grateful to Mrs Boston and to
Mr Bozman for so kindly sending me stories which have never
before been published. I should also like to thank Alice and Hugh
Kane, in Toronto, who told me about Mr Raddall's *The Amulet*;
the two friends who suggested stories by William Croft Dickinson and A. J. Alan; and those who allowed themselves to be persuaded to write their own true experiences.

Barnes, London S.W.13   KATHLEEN LINES

FROM IMAGINATION

THE HOUSE OF THE NIGHTMARE

Edward Lucas White

I FIRST caught sight of the house from the brow of the mountain as I cleared the woods and looked across the broad valley several hundred feet below me, to the low sun sinking towards the far blue hills. From that momentary viewpoint I had an exaggerated sense of looking almost vertically down. I seemed to be hanging over the chequer-board of roads and fields, dotted with farm buildings, and felt the familiar deception that I could almost throw a stone upon the house. I barely glimpsed its slate roof.

What caught my eyes was the bit of road in front of it, between the mass of dark-green trees about the house and the orchard opposite. Perfectly straight it was, bordered by an even row of trees, through which I made out a cinder side path and a low stone wall.

Conspicuous on the orchard side between two of the flanking trees was a white object, which I took to be a tall stone, a vertical splinter of one of the tilted limestone reefs with which the fields of the region are scarred.

The road itself I saw plain as a box-wood ruler on a green baize table. It gave me a pleasurable anticipation of a chance for a burst of speed. I had been painfully traversing closely forested, semi-mountainous hills. Not a farmhouse had I passed, only wretched cabins by the road, more than twenty miles of which I had found very bad and hindering. Now, when I was not many miles from my expected stopping-place, I looked forward to better going, and to that straight, level bit in particular.

As I sped cautiously down the sharp beginning of the long descent the trees engulfed me again, and I lost sight of the valley.

I dipped into a hollow, rose on the crest of the new hill, and again saw the house, nearer, and not so far below.

The tall stone caught my eye with a shock of surprise. Had I not thought it was opposite the house next the orchard? Clearly it was on the left-hand side of the road towards the house. My self-questioning lasted only the moment as I passed the crest. Then the outlook was cut off again; but I found myself gazing ahead, watching for the next chance at the same view.

At the end of the second hill I only saw the bit of road obliquely and could not be sure, but, as at first, the tall stone seemed on the right of the road.

At the top of the third and last hill I looked down the stretch of road under the over-arching trees, almost as one would look through a tube. There was a line of whiteness which I took for the tall stone. It was on the right.

I dipped into the last hollow. As I mounted the farther slope I kept my eyes on the top of the road ahead of me. When my line of sight surmounted the rise I marked the tall stone on my right hand among the serried maples. I leaned over, first on one side, then on the other, to inspect my tyres, then I threw the lever.

As I flew forward, I looked ahead. There was the tall stone – on the left of the road! I was really scared and almost dazed. I meant to stop dead, take a good look at the stone, and make up my mind beyond peradventure whether it was on the right or the left – if not, indeed, in the middle of the road.

In my bewilderment I put on the highest speed. The machine leaped forward; everything I touched went wrong; I steered wildly, slewed to the left, and crashed into a big maple.

When I came to my senses, I was flat on my back in the dry ditch. The last rays of the sun sent shafts of golden-green light through the maple boughs overhead. My first thought was an odd mixture of appreciation of the beauties of nature and disapproval of my own conduct in touring without a companion – a fad I had regretted more than once. Then my mind cleared and I sat up. I felt myself from the head down. I was not bleeding; no bones were broken; and, while much shaken, I had suffered no serious bruises.

Then I saw the boy. He was standing at the edge of the cinder-path, near the ditch. He was stocky and solidly built; barefoot, with his trousers rolled up to his knees; wore a sort of butternut shirt, open at the throat; and was coatless and hatless. He was tow-headed, with a shock of tousled hair; was much freckled, and had a hideous harelip. He shifted from one foot to the other, twiddled his toes, and said nothing whatever, though he stared at me intently.

I scrambled to my feet and proceeded to survey the wreck. It seemed distressingly complete. It had not blown up, nor even caught fire; but otherwise the ruin appeared hopelessly thorough. Everything I examined seemed worse smashed than the rest. My two hampers, alone, by one of those cynical jokes of chance, had escaped – both had pitched clear of the wreckage and were un-hurt, not even a bottle broken.

During my investigations the boy's faded eyes followed me continuously, but he uttered no word. When I had convinced myself of my helplessness I straightened up and addressed him:

'How far is it to a blacksmith's shop?'

'Eight mile,' he answered. He had a distressing case of cleft palate and was scarcely intelligible.

'Can you drive me there?' I inquired.

'Nary team on the place,' he replied; 'nary horse, nary cow.'

'How far to the next house?' I continued.

'Six mile,' he responded.

I glanced at the sky. The sun had set already. I looked at my watch: it was going – seven thirty-six.

'May I sleep in your house tonight?' I asked.

'You can come in if you want to,' he said, 'and sleep if you can. House all messy; ma's been dead three year, and dad's away. Nothin' to eat but buckwheat flour and rusty bacon.'

'I've plenty to eat,' I answered, picking up a hamper. 'Just take that hamper, will you?'

'You can come in if you've a mind to,' he said, 'but you got to carry your own stuff.' He did not speak gruffly or rudely, but appeared mildly stating an inoffensive fact.

'All right,' I said, picking up the other hamper; 'lead the way.'

The yard in front of the house was dark under a dozen or

more immense ailanthus trees. Below them many smaller trees had grown up, and beneath these a dank underwood of tall, rank suckers out of the deep, shaggy, matted grass. What had once been, apparently, a carriage-drive, left a narrow, curved track, disused and grass-grown, leading to the house. Even here were some shoots of the ailanthus, and the air was unpleasant with the vile smell of the roots and suckers and the insistent odour of their flowers.

The house was of grey stone, with green shutters faded almost as grey as the stone. Along its front was a veranda, not much raised from the ground, and with no balustrade or railing. On it were several hickory splint rockers. There were eight shuttered windows toward the porch, and midway of them a wide door, with small violet panes on either side of it and a fanlight above.

'Open the door,' I said to the boy.

'Open it yourself,' he replied, not unpleasantly nor disagreeably, but in such a tone that one could not but take the suggestion as a matter of course.

I put down the two hampers and tried the door. It was latched but not locked, and opened with a rusty grind of its hinges, on which it sagged crazily, scraping the floor as it turned. The passage smelt mouldy and damp. There were several doors on either side; the boy pointed to the first on the right.

'You can have that room,' he said.

I opened the door. What with the dusk, the interlacing trees outside, the piazza roof, and the closed shutters, I could make out little.

'Better get a lamp,' I said to the boy.

'Nary lamp,' he declared cheerfully. 'Nary candle. Mostly I get abed before dark.'

I returned to the remains of my conveyance. All four of my lamps were merely scrap metal and splintered glass. My lantern was mashed flat. I always, however, carried candles in my valise. This I found split and crushed, but still holding together. I carried it to the porch, opened it, and took out three candles.

Entering the room, where I found the boy standing just where I had left him, I lit the candle. The walls were white-washed, the floor bare. There was a mildewed, chilly smell, but the bed looked freshly made up and clean, although it felt clammy.

With a few drops of its own grease I stuck the candle on the corner of a mean, rickety little bureau. There was nothing else in the room save two rush-bottomed chairs and a small table. I went out on the porch, brought in my valise, and put it on the bed. I raised the sash of each window and pushed open the shutters. Then I asked the boy, who had not moved or spoken, to show me the way to the kitchen. He led me straight through the hall to the back of the house. The kitchen was large, and had no furniture save some pine chairs, a pine bench, and a pine table.

I stuck two candles on opposite corners of the table. There was no stove or range in the kitchen, only a big hearth, the ashes in which smelt and looked a month old. The wood in the wood-shed was dry enough, but even it had a cellary, stale smell. The axe and hatchet were both rusty and dull, but usable, and I quickly made a big fire. To my amazement, for the mid-June evening was hot and still, the boy, a wry smile on his ugly face, almost leaned over the flame, hands and arms spread out, and fairly roasted himself.

'Are you cold?' I inquired.

'I'm allus cold,' he replied, hugging the fire closer than ever, till I thought he must scorch.

I left him toasting himself while I went in search of water. I discovered the pump, which was in working order and not dry on the valves; but I had a furious struggle to fill the two leaky pails I had found. When I had put water to boil I fetched my hampers from the porch.

I brushed the table and set out my meal – cold fowl, cold ham, white and brown bread, olives, jam, and cake. When the can of soup was hot and the coffee made I drew up two chairs to the table and invited the boy to join me.

'I ain't hungry,' he said; 'I've had supper.'

He was a new sort of boy to me; all the boys I knew were hearty eaters and always ready. I had felt hungry myself, but somehow when I came to eat I had little appetite and hardly relished the food. I soon made an end of my meal, covered the fire, blew out the candles, and returned to the porch, where I

dropped into one of the hickory rockers to smoke. The boy followed me silently and seated himself on the porch floor, leaning
against a pillar, his feet on the grass outside.

'What do you do,' I asked, 'when your father is away?'

'Just loaf 'round,' he said. 'Just fool 'round.'

'How far off are your nearest neighbours?' I asked.

'Don't no neighbours never come here,' he stated. 'Say they're
afeared of the ghosts.'

I was not at all startled; the place had all those aspects which
lead to a house being called haunted. I was struck by his odd
matter-of-fact way of speaking – it was as if he had said they
were afraid of a cross dog.

'Do you ever see any ghosts around here?' I continued.

'Never see 'em,' he answered, as if I had mentioned tramps or
partridges. 'Never hear 'em. Sort o' feel 'em 'round sometimes.'

'Are you afraid of them?' I asked.

'Nope,' he declared. 'I ain't skeered o' ghosts; I'm skeered o'
nightmares. Ever have nightmares?'

'Very seldom,' I replied.

'I do,' he returned. 'Allus have the same nightmare – big sow,
big as a steer, trying to eat me up. Wake up so skeered I could
run to never. Nowheres to run to. Go to sleep, and have it again.
Wake up worse skeered than ever. Dad says it's buckwheat cakes
in summer.'

'You must have teased a sow some time,' I said.

'Yep,' he answered. 'Teased a big sow wunst, holding up one
of her pigs by the hind leg. Teased her too long. Fell in the pen
and got bit up some. Wisht I hadn't a' teased her. Have that
nightmare three times a week sometimes. Worse'n being burnt
out. Worse'n ghosts. Say, I sorter feel ghosts around now.'

He was not trying to frighten me. He was as simply stating
an opinion as if he had spoken of bats or mosquitoes. I made no
reply, and found myself listening involuntarily. My pipe went
out. I did not really want another, but felt disinclined for bed
as yet, and was comfortable where I was, while the smell
of the ailanthus blossoms was very disagreeable. I filled my
pipe again, lit it, and then, as I puffed, somehow dozed off for a
moment.

I awoke with a sensation of some light fabric trailed across my face. The boy's position was unchanged.

'Did you do that?' I asked sharply.

'Ain't done nary thing,' he rejoined. 'What was it?'

'It was like a piece of mosquito-netting brushed over my face.'

'That ain't netting,' he asserted; 'that's a veil. That's one of the ghosts. Some blow on you; some touch you with their long, cold fingers. That one with the veil she drags acrosst your face – well, mostly I think it's ma.'

He spoke with the unassailable conviction of the child in *We Are Seven*. I found no words to reply, and rose to go to bed.

'Good night,' I said.

'Good night,' he echoed. 'I'll sit out here a spell yet.'

I lit a match, found the candle I had stuck on the corner of the shabby little bureau, and undressed. The bed had a comfortable husk mattress, and I was soon asleep.

I had the sensation of having slept some time when I had a nightmare – the very nightmare the boy had described. A huge sow, big as a dray horse, was reared up with her forelegs over the foot-board of the bed, trying to scramble over to me. She grunted and puffed, and I felt I was the food she craved. I knew in the dream that it was only a dream, and strove to wake up.

Then the gigantic dream-beast floundered over the foot-board, fell across my shins, and I awoke.

I was in darkness as absolute as if I were sealed in a jet vault, yet the shudder of the nightmare instantly subsided, my nerves quieted; I realized where I was, and felt not the least panic. I turned over and was asleep again almost at once. Then I had a real nightmare, not recognizable as a dream, but appallingly real – an unutterable agony of reasonless horror.

There was a Thing in the room; not a sow, nor any other nameable creature, but a Thing. It was as big as an elephant, filled the room to the ceiling, was shaped like a wild boar, seated on its haunches, with its forelegs braced stiffly in front of it. It had a hot, slobbering, red mouth, full of big tusks, and its jaws worked hungrily. It shuffled and hunched itself forward, inch by inch, till its vast forelegs straddled the bed.

The bed crushed up like wet blotting-paper, and I felt the

weight of the Thing on my feet, on my legs, on my body, on my chest. It was hungry, and I was what it was hungry for, and it meant to begin on my face. Its dripping mouth was nearer and nearer.

Then the dream-helplessness that made me unable to call or move suddenly gave way, and I yelled and awoke. This time my terror was positive and not to be shaken off.

It was near dawn: I could descry dimly the cracked, dirty window-panes. I got up, lit the stump of my candle and two fresh ones, dressed hastily, strapped my ruined valise, and put it on the porch against the wall near the door. Then I called the boy. I realized quite suddenly that I had not told him my name or asked his.

I shouted 'Hallo!' a few times, but won no answer. I had had enough of that house. I was still permeated with the panic of the nightmare. I desisted from shouting, made no search, but with two candles went out to the kitchen. I took a swallow of cold coffee and munched a biscuit as I hustled my belongings into my hampers. Then, leaving a silver dollar on the table, I carried the hampers out on the porch and dumped them by my valise.

It was now light enough to see to walk, and I went out to the road. Already the night-dew had rusted much of the wreck, making it look more hopeless than before. It was, however, entirely undisturbed. There was not so much as a wheel-track or a hoof-print on the road. The tall, white stone, uncertainty about which had caused my disaster, stood like a sentinel opposite where I had upset.

I set out to find that blacksmith shop. Before I had gone far the sun rose clear from the horizon, and was almost at once scorching. As I footed it along I grew very much heated, and it seemed more like ten miles than six before I reached the first house. It was a new frame house, neatly painted and close to the road, with a whitewashed fence along its garden front.

I was about to open the gate when a big black dog with a curly tail bounded out of the bushes. He did not bark but stood inside the gate wagging his tail and regarding me with a friendly eye; yet I hesitated with my hand on the latch and considered. The dog might not be as friendly as he looked, and the sight of him made me realize that except for the boy I had seen no creature about the house where I had spent the night; no dog or cat; not even a toad or bird. While I was ruminating upon this a man came from behind the house.

'Will your dog bite?' I asked.

'Naw,' he answered; 'he don't bite. Come in.'

I told him I had had an accident to my automobile, and asked if he could drive me to the blacksmith shop and back to my wreckage.

'Cert,' he said. 'Happy to help you. I'll hitch up foreshortly. Wher'd you smash?'

'In front of the grey house about six miles back,' I answered.

'That big stone-built house?' he queried.

'The same,' I assented.

'Did you go a-past here?' he inquired astonished. 'I didn't hear ye.'

'No,' I said; 'I came from the other direction.'

'Why,' he meditated, 'you must'a' smashed about sunup. Did you come over them mountains in the dark?'

'No,' I replied; 'I came over them yesterday evening. I smashed up about sunset.'

'Sundown!' he exclaimed. 'Where in thunder've ye been all night?'

'I slept in the house where I broke down.'

'In that big stone-built house in the trees?' he demanded.

'Yes,' I agreed.

'Why,' he quavered excitedly, 'that there house is haunted! They say if you have to drive past it after dark, you can't tell which side of the road the big white stone is on.'

'I couldn't tell even before sunset,' I said.

'There!' he exclaimed. 'Look at that, now! And you slep' in that house! Did you sleep, honest?'

'I slept pretty well,' I said. 'Except for a nightmare, I slept all night.'

'Well,' he commented, 'I wouldn't go in that there house for a farm, nor sleep in it for my salvation. And you slep'! How in thunder did you get in?'

'The boy took me in,' I said.

'What sort of a boy?' he queried, his eyes fixed on me with a queer, countrified look of absorbed interest.

'A thick-set, freckle-faced boy with a harelip,' I said.

'Talk like his mouth was full of mush?' he demanded.

'Yes,' I said; 'bad case of cleft palate.'

'Well!' he exclaimed. 'I never did believe in ghosts, and I never did half believe that house was haunted, but I know it now. And you slep'!'

'I didn't see any ghosts,' I retorted irritably.

'You seen a ghost for sure,' he rejoined solemnly. 'That there harelip boy's been dead six months.'

From *Lukandoo and Other Stories* by Edward Lucas White (Dodd, Mead & Co., New York).

THE HAUNTINGS AT
THORHALLSTEAD

Allen French

This is an incident from a translation of the Grettir's Saga, one of
the most famous of the sagas of medieval Iceland. The original was
probably first written down around the beginning of the thirteenth
century by an unknown author.

A MAN named Thorhall lived at Thorhallstead in Shadyvale
of Waterdale. He had a large farm and much livestock, but the
place was haunted by a troll; cattle were taken away, and men
were hurt, and the shepherd and cowherds were so frightened
that they would not stay. So the place got a bad name, and
Thorhall could get few men to serve him; those who came stayed
but a little while, except one old cowherd that worked about
the barns.

At last one summer at the Althing Thorhall went to Skapti
the Lawman and asked what he should do for a shepherd.
'Well,' answered Skapti, 'I will send thee a shepherd named
Glam, a Swede who will not mind thy troll; but I warn thee
that he is an uncouth fellow, and not likeable.'

Thorhall answered that he would not mind that, if only the
man would stay by him. Then Skapti sent Glam to make the
bargain with Thorhall. Glam was a huge unkempt man, with
a shock of hair and great grey staring eyes, uncanny to look
on.

Thorhall asked, 'Wilt thou watch my sheep in winter?'

Glam said he would if he were pleased with the service and
not crossed in his ways; he asked what the place was like. Thorhall answered that the vale was haunted, and sometimes the
shepherds were hurt.

'I do not mind such little things,' said Glam. 'It will be less
dull for me.'

'Well,' replied Thorhall, 'I need such a man as thou.'

So they agreed on the terms, and Glam took up his work well. He was out in any weather, and brought all his sheep home at evening. He would speak with the goodman, but little with the others, and they liked him little. To the women he spoke roughly, and laughed when they sang pious songs, and scoffed when he saw them going to church; a rough and savage brute of a man he was, and but that he did the work as no one had before, he would have been sent away.

So the winter came on, and Glam lost none of his sheep, and when they asked him if he saw any strange sights he laughed and said there had been little to notice. Then it came to the day before Christmas, and at breakfast Glam called for his meat.

'This is a fast-day,' said the goodwife, 'for tomorrow is Yule-day.'

'I am sick and tired of such fooleries,' said Glam, 'and I see no way in which we are better off than when we were heathen. Now give me my meat, and stop this nonsense.'

So she brought meat for very fear of him, and he ate his meal and went muttering to his work. It was a stormy day, and men could not see far on the mountain side; they heard for a while how Glam whooped to his sheep to keep them together, and as the storm grew worse they looked to have him bring the flock home early, but he did not come. They went to church, and then night drew on, and still Glam was away. Then they asked whether they should not go out to seek for him and the sheep, but it was so late and stormy that no one went.

But in the morning, when the weather was clear and all had been to church, Thorhall sent his men to look for Glam and the sheep. Part of the sheep they found here and part there, some in the valley and some on the hills, till all were gathered together. Then the searchers came on a place which was trampled as if men had fought there, and there the feet of the fighters had moved great stones and hacked the frozen earth. And a little way from there lay Glam dead – a fearful sight he was, black in the face and as huge as an ox.

From that fighting place there led bloody footsteps, great and shapeless, away through the snow to cliffs above the valley, and the men were afraid to venture among the rocks to see what had made those marks. But it is true that since that time the troll that had killed Glam was never seen again, so that Glam must have been the death of him.

Now, though the searchers shuddered at the sight of Glam, looking more hateful in death than he had ever been in life, they tried to bring his body to the churchyard. But he was so heavy that they could not carry him far, and so went home, for night was coming on. In the morning they went with horses and a sledge, but even then they could get him but a little way. The horses could scarcely budge the sledge and at last they got so frightened of their burden that it was not safe to handle them, and so they were driven home.

Then on the next day the men went with the priest, who should exorcise the evil power that kept Glam from the church. But they could find the body nowhere, and at last the priest went home; and then the others found the body just where they had left it. So they took counsel with Thorhall, and at last buried Glam where he lay, with a cairn of stones over him to keep him quiet.

But soon after men came running into Thorhallstead at dusk, and said they had seen Glam walking on the hillside. Then on other days he was seen, and he was heard whooping up the valley, as if to call his sheep. He was seen close at hand by Yule-tide farers, and one man lost his wits at the sight, for the thrall was more big and fearsome than he had been in life. Then after Twelfth-night Glam was seen close by the outbuildings of the farm.

The serving men and women became frightened at that, for the troll had scarcely ever let himself be seen, but Glam's boldness meant much evil. So some fled away, and only the bravest remained.

At last one night there was a great creaking of the roof, and all knew that Glam was walking on it; he stamped so that they thought he would come through the thatch. After that he walked the roof nearly every night, and still others from the household fled the place. Glam became so bold that at last he was seen at earliest dusk, and almost until sunrise in the morning. Those that went up into the vale he chased, so that men scarcely ventured there, even by day. It was feared that the whole business of the farm would go to ruin, but as spring came on Glam was seen less, so that Thorhall knew he should have relief from the hauntings while summer lasted.

So Thorhall hired servants to stay with him for the summer, and it was hard to get them even for that season. He heard of a man who was looking for work, being just landed and without money. The man's name was Thorgaut; he said he was not particular what work he did.

'I need a shepherd,' said Thorhall, 'and I will not hide from thee that the place is haunted.'

'No ghost has scared me yet,' answered Thorgaut, and so they came to an agreement. Thorgaut went and watched Thorhall's sheep, and all went well through the summer, but when winter came then Glam was seen, and every night he came and walked the roof. Thorgaut laughed at that, and said the ghost must come indoors before he would be troubled.

And though one day the shepherd's dog was found dead with its back broken, Glam did not meddle with Thorgaut, and except for his noises he made no trouble until it came to the day before Christmas. Then that morning the goodwife begged the shepherd not to go out with his sheep. For that was the day that Glam was slain.

But Thorgaut laughed, and said to the mistress: 'I am not afraid of that. I shall return in spite of Glam.'

So he went out with his sheep, and was not seen all day, and after sunset had not come home. They spoke of Glam's death on that day, and feared the same death had come upon the shepherd; but when Thorhall wished to go out and search, no one would go with him while it was dark. So it was not until next morning that they went out and searched for the shepherd, and found the sheep scattered as before. And at Glam's cairn they found Thorgaut dead, terribly bruised and with his bones all broken.

They brought his body to the churchyard, and buried him there, and his spirit did not walk. But Glam grew worse than before, and began to slay the horses and the sheep which wandered up into the hills, and was often seen near the buildings, while every night he tramped the roof. Then all Thorhall's people fled to other places, excepting only his wife and an old cowherd that had been with them now for many years, who would not go because the work needed to be done.

But one morning when Thorhall came to the hay-barn he found the cowherd lying all doubled up, dead, with his back broken as if over Glam's knee.

Then Thorhall feared for his own life; he took his wife and his goods, and all the cattle that he could drive before him, and all the sheep that would follow, and went away out of the vale to a safe place. But Glam slew all the cattle and sheep that Thorhall left behind, and the hauntings grew less only when the spring came on.

Then Thorhall tried it once more, and got a few servants, and went back to his house. All went well for the summer; but when the long nights came on, then Glam was seen again, and at the first word of him most of the servants fled away. Glam was very bold and walked the roof nightly, and broke down doors and gates and walls, and men began to be troubled for all the lower valley, for Glam was to be seen upon the hillsides peering down upon the farms.

Now Grettir the Strong heard of the hauntings of Thorhall-stead, and thought that here was something at which he might try his hand. So Grettir went to Thorhallstead.

Thorhall welcomed him well and was glad of his coming, for none came that way in those days. He asked where Grettir was bound, and Grettir said he came to spend the night there.

'Guests are rare with me,' said Thorhall. 'Now I warn you that none come here without losing their horses, for Glam slays them all.'

'Well,' Grettir said, 'I can buy plenty more.' So the farmer put the horse in the barn, and made Grettir welcome in every way.

Grettir saw that the whole place was badly wrecked; there was not a door that had not been torn from its place, and the fences had been thrown down. Doors had been propped up at the house and barns, but everything else was in miserable order, and the farmer and his wife were there alone. But though there were all these signs of Glam through the night, there was neither sight nor sound of him, and when in the morning they went out to the barn, the horse was safe.

So Grettir stayed there another night and slept in peace, for Glam did not walk the roof, and he left the door untouched. But when in the morning they went out to the barn, there was the horse dragged from his stall, and all his bones broken.

'Now,' said Thorhall to Grettir, 'flee away from this place, or Glam will slay thee next!'

'Nay,' answered Grettir, 'in payment for my horse I must at least have a sight of him.' And though Thorhall still begged him to flee for his life, Grettir would not go.

So Grettir helped the farmer in his work about the place, and at night lay down in the hall, but the farmer went to his locked bed. Grettir lay upon a settle, and before him was a strong beam by which he might brace himself. He wrapped himself in his cloak and went to sleep. A light was set to burn there, and the hall looked miserably battered and pillaged.

It was not yet midnight when Grettir was waked by a great noise above his head as if the roof were falling in. He lay still and listened, and heard Glam tramping the roof, up and down the whole length of it; the rafters creaked under him, and the whole building groaned with the strain. For a long time Glam walked back and forth, but every minute it seemed as if the roof would fall.

Then at length Grettir heard how the thrall leaped to the ground and strode to the door of the hall. With one twitch he snatched the door from its place and flung it far away; there was a moon that night, and Grettir saw how the light streamed in through the door into the passage. Then the moonlight was cut off as Glam stooped before the door and put in his head.

Enormously tall was he, and horribly large of head; the hair was wild and the eyes were great and glassy. He came into the passageway and stepped softly into the hall. There he straightened up so that his head was at the cross-beams; he held with his hands to the beam nearest the passage, and rolled his eyes, staring about the hall.

Grettir lay quiet. Then when Glam's eyes were used to the dim light he saw Grettir lying like a bundle on the seat, and came up the hall with great silent strides to where he lay. He reached forth a long arm, and seized the cloak, and strove to pick Grettir up to see what he was.

Grettir braced himself by the beam at his foot, and Glam did not budge him. Then the ghost pulled harder, and still Grettir did not yield. A third time Glam pulled, and this time he raised Grettir from his place, but the stout cloak tore in two between them. Glam stood there stupidly peering at the cloth he held in his hand.

Then Grettir ran in upon him and seized him by the body, and tried to bend him backwards; but Glam stood stiff as a tree and Grettir could not move him. And Grettir saw that he had more on his hands than ever he had dreamed of.

Then he braced himself by the beam at his feet, but Glam gripped him and tore him away. Glam strove to break Grettir's hold about his waist, yet Grettir held fast, and tried again to throw him, but the weight was too great. Then Glam drove Grettir before him to crush him against the wall, but Grettir twisted about, and the panelling was broken as Glam lurched into it. So at last Glam put out his strength and by pushing or pulling he began to get Grettir away from the wall and towards the door.

That was a mighty wrestling, for Grettir did his utmost to save himself. He was no match for Glam in strength, but his skill was great, and he used every trick to stay the ghost, for once in the open he would have no chance. Then those two crashed back and forth across the hall, and broke before them seats and benches, and fell against the walls until the very timbers cracked. But ever Glam drew Grettir nearer the passage that led to the door, and at last he got him there.

Now Grettir fought for his very life, and tripped the thrall but could not throw him, and caught at the beams but could not keep his hold. Glam drew him along the passage, and at last made ready to bear him out of the door.

Then Grettir saw that his last chance had come, and as Glam stooped to grasp him closer, all the time pulling towards the door, then Grettir suddenly rushed against him with all his strength, and drove him backwards against the casing. They broke the lintel before them, and Glam's shoulders and head burst through the plate-beam and the thatch; then they both fell violently outwards from the door, and down upon the ground. Glam fell upon his back and Grettir upon him, and there they lay, breathless, and gasping, and spent.

There in the moonlight Grettir for the first time clearly saw Glam's face. So dreadful was the sight, with those huge eyes rolling horribly, that well nigh Grettir's spirit fled, and he had no thought to save himself.

Then Glam spoke, and said: 'Now have we measured our strength, Grettir, and now I lay my weird on thee. Thou hast only half the strength which would have come to thee had thou not put thyself in my way; now it shall never grow greater, though many will call thee strong enough. And now has thy luck turned, and whatever thou doest after this shall go against thee. Thou shalt be outlawed, and wilt dwell much alone; then often shalt thou see my glaring eyes, and shalt dread to be alone, and that shall be thy death.'

But when Glam had finished speaking, then Grettir roused himself, and drew his sword, and smote the ghost's head from his body, and laid it at his thigh.

Then Grettir called the farmer out, and showed him what he had done, and Thorhall praised God that his plague was gone at last. Then they made a great fire over Glam, and burnt him all to ashes, and brought those to a barren place, and buried them deep. And Glam never walked again, nor troubled anyone more, save only Grettir. For always after that Grettir saw strange shapes in the dark and all sorts of horrors disturbed his sleep, and he could scarcely bear to be alone in the night. And often he saw before him Glam's rolling glassy eyes.

From *Grettir the Strong* by Allen French (The Bodley Head, London, and E. P. Dutton & Co., New York).

HIS OWN NUMBER

William Croft Dickinson

'WHAT do you gain by putting a man into space?' asked
Johnson, somewhat aggressively. 'Instruments are far more
efficient.'

'But,' protested Hamilton, our Professor of Mathematical
Physics, 'an astronaut can make use of instruments which don't
respond to remote control. Also, he can bring the right instruments into work at exactly the right time in flight.'

'Maybe so,' returned Johnson. 'But what if he gets excited?
The advantage of the instrument is that it never gets excited. It
has no emotions. Its response is purely automatic.'

'Can you be sure of that?' asked Munro, from his chair by the
fire. And, by the way he spoke, we could sense that there was
something behind his question.

'If it is in perfect order, why not?' persisted Johnson.

'I don't know,' Munro replied, slowly. 'But I can tell you a
tale of an electronic computer that was in perfect order and yet
three times gave the same answer to an unfortunate technician.'

'Something like a wrist-watch which is affected by the pulse-
beat of the wearer?' suggested Hayles.

'Something more than that,' said Munro. 'A great deal more.
But what that "something" was, I simply don't know. Or can an
instrument have "second sight", or respond to forces that are
beyond our reckoning? I wish I knew the answer to that. However, I'll tell you my tale, and then each of you can try to explain it to his own satisfaction.'

As you probably know, when I first came here I came to a Research Fellowship in the Department of Mathematics. And, as
it happened, one of the problems upon which I was engaged

necessitated the use of an electronic computer. There were several in the Department, but the one which I normally used was quite a simple instrument: little more than an advanced calculator. I could 'programme' a number of calculations, feed them into it, and, in less than a minute, out would come the answer which it would have taken me perhaps a month to work out by myself. Just that, and no more. And I wish I could say it was always: 'Just that, and no more.' For here comes my tale.

One afternoon, being somewhat rushed – for I had been invited to a sherry party in the Senate Room – I asked one of the technicians if he'd feed my calculations into the computer, and leave the result on my desk. By pure chance the man I asked to do the job for me was called Murdoch Finlayson: a Highlander from somewhere up in Wester Ross. He was a good fellow in every way, and as honest and conscientious as they make them. I say 'by pure chance'; but perhaps it was all foreordained that I should pick on Finlayson. Certainly it seemed so, in the end. But, at the time, all I wanted to do was to get away to a sherry party; Finlayson happened to be near at hand; and I knew that I could trust him.

I thought, when I asked him to do the job, and when I indicated the computer I wanted him to use, that he looked strangely hesitant, and even backed away a bit. I remember wondering if he had been wanting to leave early, and here was I keeping him tied to his work. But, just when I was about to say that there was no real hurry, and that I'd attend to it myself in the morning, he seemed to pull himself together, reached out for my calculations, and, with an odd look in his eyes, murmured something that sounded like 'the third time'.

I was a little puzzled by his reaction to what I thought was a simple request, and even more puzzled by that murmured remark about 'the third time'; but, being in a hurry, gave the matter no second thought and dashed off.

My sherry party lasted somewhat longer than I had expected and, when I returned to the Department, I found it deserted. Everyone had gone home. I walked over to my desk, and then stood there, dumbfounded. Instead of the somewhat complex formula I had expected, I saw one of the computer's sheets bear-

ing a simple number. A simple line of six digits. I won't give you
the exact number on that sheet, but it was something like

585244

and underneath the number was a short note:

It's come for the third time.

I recognized Finlayson's handwriting. But what did he mean by
that cryptic statement? First of all, he had murmured something
about 'the third time'; and now he had left a message saying:
'It's come for the third time.' And what was that simple line of
digits, anyway? If it was supposed to be the answer to my series
of calculations, it was no answer at all.

At first I felt slightly angry. What was Finlayson playing at?
Then a vague feeling of uneasiness supervened. Finlayson was
too sound and solid to be playing tricks with me. I remembered
his hesitancy, and a new thought struck me: had it perhaps been
fear? What could that number mean? As a line of digits, a six-
figure number, I could see nothing unusual about it. It was a
simple number, and nothing more. Then, for a time, I played
with it. I cubed it; but I was no wiser. I added up the digits and
cubed the total; I multiplied by three and tried again; and so
forth and so on till I admitted that I was simply wasting my
time. I could make nothing of it.

Unfortunately I didn't know where Finlayson lived, so perforce I had to contain my curiosity until the next morning. Also
I had to contain that vague feeling of uneasiness which still persisted. But the next morning, as soon as I had entered the Department, I sought him out.

'This is an extraordinary result, Finlayson,' I said, holding out
the computer sheet which he had left on my desk.

'Aye, sir.'

'But surely the computer must have gone completely haywire.'

'The computer's all right, sir. But yon's the result it gave me,
and I'm no liking it at all.'

'The computer can't be right,' I persisted. 'And your note
seems to say that this is the third time you've received this result
from it. Do you really mean that on three separate occasions,

whatever the calculations you have put into this computer, it has each time returned this same number – 585244?'

'It has that, sir. And it's unchancy. I'm no liking a machine that gives me yon same number three times. I'm thinking that maybe it's my own number. And now I'm afeared o' it. I'm for handing in my papers and leaving, sir. I'll away to my brother's to help with the sheep. 'Tis safer feeding a flock of ewes than tending a machine that aye gives you a queer number.'

'Nonsense,' I retorted. 'There's something wrong with the computer, or with the way in which you set it and fed in the calculations.'

'Maybe aye and maybe no, sir. But maybe I've been given my own number, and I'm no liking it at all. I'm wanting to leave.'

I realized that I was up against some form of Highland superstition. Finlayson had been given a simple number three times, and that was enough for him. Maybe it was 'his own number' – whatever that might mean. I realized, too, that he had made up his mind to go, and that nothing I could say would dissuade him. Sheep were safer than electronic computers.

'All right,' I said to him, 'I'll speak to the Dean. And if it is any comfort to you, I won't ask you to operate that computer again.'

He thanked me for what he called my 'consideration', and went back to his work. I, in turn, went straight to the Dean.

'What an extraordinary business,' said the Dean, when I had recounted the circumstances to him. 'I wouldn't have believed it of Finlayson. I would have said he was far too intelligent to let anything like that upset him. There's surely something wrong with that computer. It's a very old instrument. Let's have a look at it.'

And, naturally, 'having a look at it' included feeding in the calculations which I had previously given to Finlayson. The computer quickly gave us the result. And it was a result far different from Finlayson's simple number, 585244. Although it would have taken me days to check it, the result was a complex formula like the one I had expected.

The Dean muttered something to himself and then turned to me. 'We'll try it again. I have some calculations of my own to which I know the answer.'

He went to his room, came back with his calculations and fed them into the machine. A few seconds later, out came the computer's sheet bearing the answer.

'Perfectly correct,' said the Dean, crisply. 'Finlayson must have been imagining things. Or else, for some unknown reason, he has three times fed a wrong programme into the computer. Even then, he couldn't get an answer like 585244.'

'I don't know,' I replied, slowly. 'He's too good a technician to make mistakes. And carelessness is no explanation. He's convinced he has received that six-figure number on the last three occasions on which he has used this machine. I'm beginning to think he did – though don't ask me why. But he's also convinced that there's some premonition in it. "His own number" has turned up three times. And "the third time" is a kind of final summons. Superstition if you like, but I'm beginning to feel for him. I think we should let him go.'

'Very well,' returned the Dean with a sigh of resignation. 'Have it your own way. I'll tell him he can leave at the end of the week. But you know as well as I do how difficult it is to get good technicians.'

We sought out Finlayson and the Dean told him that if he was determined to go he could be released at the end of the week. The man's eyes lit up at the news, and his relief was obvious.

'I'll away to my brother's,' he said, delightedly. 'He'll be glad of my help, and I'll be glad to be helping him. Not that I've been unhappy in my work here, sir. I would not be saying that. But I'm kind of feared to be staying. And if ye had not said I could go, I doubt I would have been going all the same. Though it would not be like me to be doing a thing like that.'

'Where does your brother live?' the Dean asked, quickly changing the conversation.

'In Glen Ogle, sir, on the road from Lochearnhead to Killin.'

'A beautiful stretch of country,' I put in. 'Do you know, I'll drive you there on Saturday morning if you like. It will be a lovely run. Where shall I pick you up?'

He accepted my offer with alacrity, and gave me the address of his lodgings.

I did not tell him of the two tests of the computer which the Dean and I had carried out.

The Saturday morning was fine and clear. I called for him at the address he had given me, and found him waiting, with his possessions packed into a large grip.

Once we had passed through Stirling and had reached the foot-hills of the Highlands, the beauty of the country siezed hold of me. Finlayson's desire to join his brother amid these browns and purples, golds, blues and greens, seemed the most sensible thing in all the world. The sun made the hills a glory; Ben Ledi and Ben Vorlich raised their heads in the distance; and, as we left Callander, the long-continuing Falls of Leny cascaded over their rocks by the side of the road. Finlayson's thrice-recurring number was surely a blessing and not a curse.

We had run through Lochearnhead and had entered Glen Ogle when, just as I was about to ask Finlayson for the whereabouts of his brother's farm, the car suddenly slowed down and stopped. I knew the tank was practically full, for I had just put in eight gallons at Callander. My first thought was carburettor-trouble, or possibly a blocked feed. I loosened the bonnet-catch, got out, raised the bonnet, and went through all the usual checks. But, to my annoyance, I could find nothing wrong. The tank was full; feed, pump and carburettor were all functioning properly. I gave myself a few minor shocks as I tested the electrical circuits. Nothing wrong there. Coil, battery, distributor, plugs, were all in order. I reached over to the fascia board and pressed the self-starter. The starter-motor whirred noisily in the stillness, but the engine did not respond. Once more I tested every connexion and every part. Again I pressed the self-starter, and again with no effect. Thoroughly exasperated, I turned to Finlayson who had joined me in this exhaustive check and who was as puzzled as I was.

'Well, and what do we do now?' I asked.

'I'll walk the two-three miles to my brother's,' he said. 'He has the tractor, and can tow us to the farm. Then maybe we can find out what has gone wrong.'

'Excellent!' I agreed. 'Off you go.'

I sat down on the grass and I watched him striding away until
he disappeared round a bend in the road. A little later I got up,
closed the bonnet of the car, and took a road map from one of the
door-pockets. Perhaps there was an alternative route for my way
back.

I had barely opened the map and laid it out on top of the bonnet when a car came tearing round the bend ahead. As soon as
the driver saw me, he pulled up with a screech of his brakes and
jumped out.

'For God's sake come back with me,' he cried. 'I've killed a
man, just up the road. He walked right into me.'

For a moment the shock of his words stunned me, and I stood
irresolute.

'Quick!' he continued. 'We'll take your car. It will save the
time of reversing mine.'

Without further ado, he jumped into the driver's seat of my
car, pressed the self-starter and impatiently signalled to me to get
in beside him.

So Finlayson was dead. Somehow I knew it was Finlayson.
Dead in Glen Ogle where sheep were safer than machines. He
had walked from my useless car to meet his death round the
bend in the road.

My useless car! With a sudden tremor of every nerve I realized
that the engine was turning over as smoothly as it had ever done.

Had the whole world turned upside down?

Mechanically I got in and sat down beside the man. He drove a
short distance round the bend and then slowly came to a halt. I
saw at once that my fears were only too true. Finlayson was dead.
The man had lifted him on to the grass that verged the road. I
got out and bent over him. There was nothing I could do.

'I saw him walking on his own side of the road,' I heard the
man saying to me. 'And I was on my own side too. But he
couldn't have seen me or heard me. Just when I should have
passed him, he suddenly crossed over. My God! He crossed right
in front of me! Do you think he was deaf? Or perhaps he was
thinking of something. Absent-minded. How else could he walk
right into me?'

The man was talking on and on. Later, I realized he had to

talk. It was the only relief for him. But I was not listening. Finlayson lay there, broken, still. Seeking life, he had found death. His 'number' had 'come up' three times. It was 'unchancy'. To hell with his number! What had that to do with this?

At the subsequent inquiry, the driver of the car was completely exonerated. In a moment of absent-mindedness Finlayson had stepped across the road right into the path of the oncoming car. The finding was clear and definite. Yet for me, I could not forget that the unhappy man had felt some premonition of mischance. He had decided to cheat mischance and seek safety amid the hills. And mischance and death had met him there. Yet what possible connexion could there be between 'his number', 585244, and his death?

At first I thought that Finlayson had possibly seen 'his number' on a telegraph pole, or perhaps on a pylon, and, startled, had crossed the road to look at it more clearly. I made a special journey to Lochearnhead, parked my car there, and examined every bit of the road from the place where my car had 'broken down' to the place where Finlayson had been killed. But I could find nothing to substantiate my theory.

And why had my car so mysteriously broken down and then so mysteriously started again? Could it be that the fates had decreed the time and place of the death of Murdoch Finlayson and had used the puny machines of man's invention for their decree's fulfilment? An electronic computer that could be made to give the one number, and an internal combustion engine that could be brought to a halt. And why that number? Why that number?

That one question so dominated my mind that it ruined my work by day and my rest by night. And then, perhaps a fortnight after Finlayson's death, I was given an answer; yet it was an answer that still left everything unexplained.

I had gone over to the Staff House for lunch, and had joined a table where, too late, I found an animated discussion in progress to the effect that members of the Faculty of Arts were too ig-

norant of elementary science, and members of the Faculty of
Science too ignorant of the arts. I was in no mood to join in the
discussion, though politeness demanded that occasionally I
should put in my word. The table gradually emptied until only
Crossland, the Professor of Geography, and I were left.

'Neither Science nor Arts can answer some of our questions,'
I said to him, bitterly.

'I know,' he replied. 'It must have been a terrible shock for you.
I suppose we shall never know why that computer returned the
one number to Finlayson three times. That is, if it did. And what
was the number, by the way? I never heard.'

'A simple line of six digits – 585244.'

'Sounds just like a normal national grid reference,' Crossland
commented.

'A normal national grid reference?' I queried.

'Yes. Surely you know our national grid system for map-
references. Or,' he continued with a smile, 'is this a case of the
scientist knowing too little of the work in the Faculty of Arts?'

'You've scored a point there,' I replied. 'I'm afraid I'm completely ignorant of this grid system of yours.'

'Probably you've been using motoring-maps too much,' he
conceded. 'But the grid is quite simple. If you look at any sheet of
the Ordnance Survey you will see that it is divided into kilometre
squares by grid lines, numbered from 0 to 99, running west to
east, and 0 to 99, running south to north. Then, within each
kilometre square, a closer definition is obtained by measuring in
tenths between the grid lines. Thus a particular spot, say a farm-
steading or a spinney, can be pin-pointed on the map, within its
numbered square, by a grid-reference which runs to six figures:
three, west to east; and three, south to north. A six-figure number, which is known as the "normal national grid reference".'

For a minute or so I digested this in silence.

'Can we go over to your map-room?' I asked.

'Surely,' he said, a little surprised. 'And see on a map how it
works?'

'Yes.'

We went over to Crossland's department.

'Any particular map?' he asked.

'Yes. A map of Western Perthshire.'

Crossland produced the Ordnance Survey Sheet. I looked at it almost with reluctance.

Taking out a pencil, I pointed to the place on the map where, as near as I could judge, Finlayson had met his death. 'What would be the grid reference for that particular spot?' I asked, and wondered at the strangeness of my voice.

Crossland picked up a transparent slide and bent over the map. I heard him take in his breath. He straightened himself, and when he turned to look at me his eyes were troubled and questioning.

'Yes,' concluded Munro. 'I needn't tell you what the grid reference was. But can anyone tell me why Finlayson was given that number three times on an electronic computer? Or why my car "broke down", so that he could walk of his own accord to that very spot?'

From *Dark Encounters* by William Croft Dickinson (Harvill Press, London).

GABRIEL-ERNEST

Saki

'THERE is a wild beast in your woods,' said the artist Cunningham, as he was being driven to the station. It was the only remark he had made during the drive, but as Van Cheele had talked incessantly his companion's silence had not been noticeable.

'A stray fox or two and some resident weasels. Nothing more formidable,' said Van Cheele. The artist said nothing.

'What did you mean about a wild beast?' said Van Cheele later, when they were on the platform.

'Nothing. My imagination. Here is the train,' said Cunningham.

That afternoon, Van Cheele went for one of his frequent rambles through his woodland property. He had a stuffed bittern in his study, and knew the names of quite a number of wild flowers, so his aunt had possibly some justification in describing him as a great naturalist. At any rate, he was a great walker. It was his custom to make mental notes of everything he saw during his walks, not so much for the purpose of assisting contemporary science as to provide topics for conversation afterwards. When the bluebells began to show themselves in flower he made a point of informing every one of the fact; the season of the year might have warned his hearers of the likelihood of such an occurrence, but at least they felt that he was being absolutely frank with them.

What Van Cheele saw on this particular afternoon was, however, something far removed from his ordinary range of experience. On a shelf of smooth stone overhanging a deep pool in the hollow of an oak coppice a boy of about sixteen lay asprawl, drying his wet brown limbs luxuriously in the sun. His wet hair, parted by a recent dive, lay close to his head and his light-brown eyes, so light that there was an almost tigerish gleam in them, were turned towards Van Cheele with a certain lazy watchfulness. It was an unexpected apparition, and Van Cheele found himself engaged in the novel process of thinking before he spoke. Where on earth could this wild-looking boy hail from? The miller's wife had lost a child some two months ago, supposed to have been swept away by the mill-race, but that had been a mere baby, not a half-grown lad.

'What are you doing here?' he demanded.

'Obviously, sunning myself,' replied the boy.

'Where do you live?'

'Here, in these woods.'

'You can't live in the woods,' said Van Cheele.

'They are very nice woods,' said the boy, with a touch of patronage in his voice.

'But where do you sleep at night?'

'I don't sleep at night; that's my busiest time.'

Van Cheele began to have an irritated feeling that he was grappling with a problem that was eluding him.

'What do you feed on?' he asked.

'Flesh,' said the boy, and he pronounced the word with slow relish, as though he were tasting it.

'Flesh! What flesh?'

'Since it interests you, rabbits, wild-fowls, hares, poultry, lambs in their season, children when I can get any; they're usually too well locked in at night, when I mostly do my hunting. It's quite two months since I tasted child-flesh.'

Ignoring the chaffing nature of the last remark, Van Cheele tried to draw the boy on the subject of possible poaching operations.

'You're talking through your hat when you speak of feeding on hares.' (Considering the nature of the boy's toilet, the simile was hardly an apt one.) 'Our hillside hares aren't easily caught.'

'At night I hunt on four feet,' was the somewhat cryptic response.

'I suppose you mean that you hunt with a dog?' hazarded Van Cheele.

The boy rolled slowly over on to his back, and laughed a weird low laugh, that was pleasantly like a chuckle and disagreeably like a snarl.

'I don't fancy any dog would be very anxious for my company, especially at night.'

Van Cheele began to feel that there was something positively uncanny about the strange-eyed, strange-tongued youngster.

'I can't have you staying in these woods,' he declared authoritatively.

'I fancy you'd rather have me here than in your house,' said the boy.

The prospect of this wild, nude animal in Van Cheele's primly-ordered house was certainly an alarming one.

'If you don't go I shall have to make you,' said Van Cheele.

The boy turned like a flash, plunged into the pool, and in a moment had flung his wet and glistening body half-way up the bank where Van Cheele was standing. In an otter the movement would not have been remarkable; in a boy, Van Cheele found it sufficiently startling. His foot slipped as he made an involuntary backward movement, and he found himself almost prostrate on the slippery weed-grown bank, with those tigerish yellow eyes not very far from his own. Almost instinctively, he half-raised his hand to his throat. The boy laughed again, a laugh in which the snarl had nearly driven out the chuckle, and then, with another of his astonishing lightning movements, plunged out of view into a yielding tangle of weed and fern.

'What an extraordinary wild animal!' said Van Cheele as he picked himself up. And then he recalled Cunningham's remark, 'There is a wild beast in your woods.'

Walking slowly homeward, Van Cheele began to turn over in his mind various local occurrences which might be traceable to the existence of this astonishing young savage.

Something had been thinning the game in the woods lately, poultry had been missing from the farms, hares were growing unaccountably scarcer, and complaints had reached him of lambs being carried off bodily from the hills. Was it possible that this wild boy was really hunting the countryside in company with some clever poacher dog? He had spoken of hunting 'four-footed' by night, but then, again, he had hinted strangely at no dog caring to come near him, 'especially at night'. It was certainly puzzling. And then, as Van Cheele ran his mind over the various depredations that had been committed during the last month or two, he came suddenly to a dead stop, alike in his walk and his speculations. The child missing from the mill two months ago – the accepted theory was that it had tumbled into the mill-race and been swept away; but the mother had always declared she had heard a shriek on the hill side of the house, in the opposite direction from the water. It was unthinkable, of course, but he wished that the boy had not made that uncanny remark about child-flesh eaten two months ago. Such dreadful things should not be said even in fun.

Van Cheele, contrary to his usual wont, did not feel disposed to be communicative about his discovery in the wood. His position as a parish councillor and justice of the peace seemed somehow compromised by the fact that he was harbouring a personality of such doubtful repute on his property; there was even a possibility that a heavy bill of damages for raided lambs and poultry might be laid at his door. At dinner that night he was quite unusually silent.

'Where's your voice gone to?' said his aunt. 'One would think you had seen a wolf.'

Van Cheele, who was not familiar with the old saying, thought the remark rather foolish; if he *had* seen a wolf on his property his tongue would have been extraordinarily busy with the subject.

At breakfast next morning Van Cheele was conscious that his feeling of uneasiness regarding yesterday's episode had not wholly disappeared, and he resolved to go by train to the neighbouring cathedral town, hunt up Cunningham, and learn from him what he had really seen that had prompted the remark about a wild beast in the woods. With this resolution taken, his usual cheerfulness partially returned, and he hummed a bright little melody as he sauntered to the morning-room for his customary cigarette. As he entered the room the melody made way abruptly for a pious invocation. Gracefully asprawl on the ottoman, in an attitude of almost exaggerated repose, was the boy of the woods. He was drier than when Van Cheele had last seen him, but no other alteration was noticeable in his toilet.

'How dare you come here?' asked Van Cheele furiously.

'You told me I was not to stay in the woods,' said the boy calmly.

'But not to come here. Supposing my aunt should see you!'

And with a view to minimizing that catastrophe Van Cheele hastily obscured as much of his unwelcome guest as possible under the folds of a *Morning Post*. At that moment his aunt entered the room.

'This is a poor boy who has lost his way – and lost his memory. He doesn't know who he is or where he comes from,' explained Van Cheele desperately, glancing apprehensively at the waif's face to see whether he was going to add inconvenient candour to his other savage propensities.

Miss Van Cheele was enormously interested.

'Perhaps his underlinen is marked,' she suggested.

'He seems to have lost most of that, too,' said Van Cheele, making frantic little grabs at the *Morning Post* to keep it in its place.

A naked homeless child appealed to Miss Van Cheele as warmly as a stray kitten or derelict puppy would have done.

'We must do all we can for him,' she decided, and in a very short time a messenger, dispatched to the rectory, where a page-boy was kept, had returned with a suit of pantry clothes and the necessary accessories of shirt, shoes, collar, etc. Clothed, clean and groomed, the boy lost none of his uncanniness in Van Cheele's eyes, but his aunt found him sweet.

'We must call him something till we know who he really is,' she said. 'Gabriel-Ernest, I think; those are nice suitable names.'

Van Cheele agreed, but he privately doubted whether they were being grafted on to a nice suitable child. His misgivings were not diminished by the fact that his staid and elderly spaniel had bolted out of the house at the first incoming of the boy, and now obstinately remained shivering and yapping at the farther end of the orchard, while the canary, usually as vocally industrious as Van Cheele himself, had put itself on an allowance of frightened cheeps. More than ever, he was resolved to consult Cunningham without loss of time.

As he drove off to the station his aunt was arranging that

Gabriel-Ernest should help her to entertain the infant members of her Sunday-school class at tea that afternoon.

Cunningham was not at first disposed to be communicative.

'My mother died of some brain trouble,' he explained, 'so you will understand why I am averse to dwelling on anything of an impossibly fantastic nature that I may see or think that I have seen.'

'But what *did* you see?' persisted Van Cheele.

'What I thought I saw was something so extraordinary that no really sane man could dignify it with the credit of having actually happened. I was standing, the last evening I was with you, half-hidden in the hedgegrowth by the orchard gate, watching the dying glow of the sunset. Suddenly I became aware of a naked boy, a bather from some neighbouring pool, I took him to be, who was standing out on the bare hillside also watching the sunset. His pose was so suggestive of some wild faun of Pagan myth that I instantly wanted to engage him as a model, and in another moment I think I should have hailed him. But just then the sun dipped out of view, and all the orange and pink slid out of the landscape, leaving it cold and grey. And at the same moment an astonishing thing happened – the boy vanished too!'

'What, vanished away into nothing?' asked Van Cheele excitedly.

'No; that is the dreadful part of it, answered the artist; 'on the open hillside where the boy had been standing a second ago, stood a large wolf, blackish in colour, with gleaming fangs and cruel, yellow eyes. You may think –'

But Van Cheele did not stop for anything as futile as thought. Already he was tearing at top speed towards the station. He dismissed the idea of a telegram. 'Gabriel-Ernest is a werewolf' was a hopelessly inadequate effort at conveying the situation, and his aunt would think it was a code message to which he had omitted to give her the key.

His one hope was that he might reach home before sundown. The cab which he chartered at the other end of the railway journey bore him with what seemed exasperating slowness along the country roads, which were pink and mauve with the flush of the sinking sun. His aunt was putting away some unfinished jam and cakes when he arrived.

'Where is Gabriel-Ernest?' he almost screamed.

'He is taking the little Toop child home,' said his aunt. 'It was getting so late, I thought it wasn't safe to let it go back alone. What a lovely sunset, isn't it?'

But Van Cheele, although not oblivious of the glow in the western sky, did not stay to discuss its beauties. At a speed for which he was scarcely geared, he raced along the narrow lane that led to the home of the Toops. On one side ran the swift current of the mill-stream, on the other rose the stretch of bare hillside. A dwindling rim of red sun showed still on the skyline, and the next turning must bring him in view of the ill-assorted couple he was pursuing. Then the colour went suddenly out of things, and grey light settled itself with a quick shiver over the landscape. Van Cheele heard a shrill wail of fear, and stopped running.

Nothing was ever seen again of the Toop child or Gabriel-Ernest, but the latter's discarded garments were found lying in the road, so it was assumed that the child had fallen into the water, that the boy had stripped and jumped in, in a vain en-deavour to save it. Van Cheele and some workmen who were near by at the time testified to having heard a child scream loudly just near the spot where the clothes were found. Mrs Toop, who had eleven other children, was decently resigned to her be-reavement, but Miss Van Cheele sincerely mourned her lost foundling. It was on her initiative that a memorial brass was put up in the parish church to 'Gabriel-Ernest, an unknown boy, who bravely sacrificed his life for another.'

Van Cheele gave way to his aunt in most things, but he flatly refused to subscribe to the Gabriel-Ernest memorial.

From *The Bodley Head Saki* (The Bodley Head, London).

HAND IN GLOVE

Elizabeth Bowen

JASMINE LODGE was favourably set on a residential, prettily-wooded hillside in the south of Ireland, overlooking a river and, still better, the roofs of a lively garrison town. Around 1904, which was the flowering period of the Miss Trevors, girls could not have had a more auspicious home – the neighbourhood spun merrily round the military. Ethel and Elsie, a spirited pair, garnered the full advantage – no ball, hop, picnic, lawn tennis, croquet or boating party was complete without them; in winter, though they could not afford to hunt, they trimly bicycled to all meets, and on frosty evenings, with their guitars, set off to *soirées*, snug inside their cab in their fur-tipped capes.

They possessed an aunt, a Mrs Varley de Grey, *née* Elysia Trevor, a formerly notable local belle, who, drawn back again in her widowhood to what had been the scene of her early triumphs, occupied a back bedroom in Jasmine Lodge. Mrs Varley de Grey had had no luck: her splashing match, in its time the talk of two kingdoms, had ended up in disaster – the well-born captain in a cavalry regiment having gone so far as to blow out his brains in India, leaving behind him nothing but her and debts. Mrs Varley de Grey had returned from India with nothing but seven large trunks crammed with recent finery; and she also had been impaired by shock. This had taken place while Ethel and Elsie, whose father had married late, were still unborn – so it was that, for as long as the girls recalled, their aunt had been the sole drawback to Jasmine Lodge. Their parents had orphaned them, somewhat thoughtlessly, by simultaneously dying of scarlet fever when Ethel was just out and Elsie soon to be – they were therefore left lacking a chaperone and, with their gift for putting everything to some use, propped the aunt up in order that she might play that role. Only when her peculiarities became too marked did they feel it necessary to withdraw her: by that time, however, all the surrounding ladies could be said to compete for the honour of taking into society the sought-after Miss Trevors. From then on, no more was seen or heard of Mrs Varley de Grey. ('Oh, just a trifle unwell, but nothing much!') She remained upstairs, at the back; when the girls were giving one of their little parties, or a couple of officers came to call, the key of her room would be turned in the outer lock.

The girls hung Chinese lanterns from the creepered verandah, and would sit lightly strumming on their guitars. Not less fascinating was their badinage, accompanied by a daring flash of the eyes. They were known as the clever Miss Trevors, not because of any taint of dogmatism or book-learning – no, when a gentleman cried 'Those girls have brains!' he meant it wholly in admiration – but because of their accomplishments, ingenuity, and agility. They took leading parts in theatricals, lent spirit to numbers of drawing-room games, were naughty mimics, and sang duets. Nor did their fingers lag behind their wits – they constructed lampshades, crêpe paper flowers and picturesque hats; and, above all, varied their dresses marvellously – no one could beat them for ideas, snipping, slashing or fitting. Once more allowing nothing to go to waste, they had remodelled the trousseau out of their aunt's trunks, causing sad old tulles and tarlatans, satins and *moiré* taffetas to appear to have come from Paris only today. They re-stitched spangles, pressed ruffles crisp, and revived many a corsage of squashed silk roses. They went somewhat softly about that task, for the trunks were all stored in the attic immediately over the back room.

They wore their clothes well. 'A pin on either of those two would look smart!' declared other girls. All that they were short of was evening gloves – they had two pairs each, which they had been compelled to buy. *What* could have become of Mrs Varley de Grey's presumably sumptuous numbers of this item, they were unable to fathom, and it was too bad. Had gloves been over-looked in her rush from India? – or, were they here, in that *one* trunk the Trevors could not get at? All other locks had yielded to pulls or pickings, or the sisters found keys to fit them, or they had used the toolbox; but this last stronghold defied them. In that sad little soiled silk sack, always on her person, Mrs Varley de Grey, they became convinced, hoarded the operative keys, along with some frippery rings and brooches – all true emeralds, pearls and diamonds having been long ago, as they knew, sold. Such contrariety on their aunt's part irked them – meanwhile, gaieties bore hard on their existing gloves. Last thing at nights when they came in, last thing in the evenings before they went out, they would manfully dab away at the fingertips. So, it must be admitted that a long whiff of benzine pursued them as they whirled round the ballroom floor.

They were tall and handsome – nothing so soft as pretty, but in those days it was a vocation to be a handsome girl; many of the best marriages had been made by such. They carried themselves imposingly, had good busts and shoulders, waists firm under the whalebone, and straight backs. Their features were striking, their colouring high; low on their foreheads bounced dark mops of curls. Ethel was, perhaps, the dominant one, but both girls were pronounced to be full of character.

Whom, and still more when, did they mean to marry? They had already seen regiments out and in; for quite a number of years, it began to seem, bets in the neighbourhood had been running high. Sympathetic spy-glasses were trained on the conspicuous gateway to Jasmine Lodge; each new cavalier was noted. The only trouble might be, their promoters claimed, that the clever Trevors were always so surrounded that they had not a moment in which to turn or choose. Or otherwise, could it possibly be that the admiration aroused by Ethel and Elsie, and their now institutional place in the local scene, scared out more tender feeling from the masculine breast? It came to be felt, and perhaps by the girls themselves, that, having lingered so long and so puzzlingly, it was up to them to bring off (like their aunt) a *coup*. Society around this garrison town had long plumed itself upon its romantic record; summer and winter, Cupid shot his darts. Lush scenery, the oblivion of all things else bred by the steamy climate, and perpetual gallivanting – all were conducive. Ethel's and Elsie's names, it could be presumed, were by now murmured wherever the Union Jack flew. Nevertheless, it was time they should decide.

Ethel's decision took place late one spring. She set her cap, in a manner worthy of her, at the second son of an English marquess. Lord Fred had come on a visit, for the fishing, to a mansion some miles down the river from Jasmine Lodge. He first made his appearance, with the rest of the house-party, at one of the more resplendent military balls, and was understood to be a man-about-town. The civilian glint of his *pince-nez*, at once serene and superb, instantaneously wrought, with his great name, on Ethel's heart. She beheld him, and the assembled audience, with approbation, looked on at the moment so big with fate. The truth, it appeared in a flash, was that Ethel, though so condescending with her charms, had not from the first been destined to love a soldier; and that here, after long attrition, her answer was. Lord Fred was, by all, at once signed over to her. For his part, he responded to her attentions quite gladly, though in a somewhat dazed way. If he did not so often dance with her – indeed, how could he, for she was much besought? – he could at least be perceived to gaze. At a swiftly-organized river picnic, the next evening, he by consent fell to Ethel's lot – she had spent the foregoing morning snipping and tacking at a remaining muslin of Mrs Varley de Grey's, a very fresh forget-me-not-dotted pattern. The muslin did not survive the evening out, for when the moon should have risen, rain poured into the boats. Ethel's good-humoured drollery carried all before it, and Lord Fred wrapped his blazer around her form.

Next day, more rain; and all felt flat. At Jasmine Lodge the expectant deck chairs had to be hurried in from the garden, and the small close rooms, with their greeneried windows and plentiful bric-à-brac, gave out a stuffy, resentful, indoor smell. The maid was out; Elsie was lying down with a migraine; so it devolved on Ethel to carry up Mrs Varley de Grey's tea – the invalid set very great store by tea, and her manifestations by door rattlings, sobs and mutters were apt to become disturbing if it did not appear. Ethel, with the not particularly dainty tray, accordingly entered the back room, this afternoon rendered dark by its outlook into a dripping uphill wood. The aunt, her visage draped in a cobweb shawl, was as usual sitting up in bed. 'Aha!' she at once cried, screwing one eye up and glittering round at Ethel with the other, 'so what's all this in the wind today?'

Ethel, as she lodged the meal on the bed, shrugged her shoulders, saying, 'I'm in a hurry.'

'No doubt you are. The question is, will you get him?'

'Oh, drink your tea!' snapped Ethel, her colour rising.

The old wretch responded by popping a lump of sugar into her cheek and sucking at it while she fixed her wink on her niece. She then observed: '*I* could tell you a thing or two!'

'We've had enough of *your* fabrications, Auntie.'

'Fabrications!' croaked Mrs Varley de Grey. 'And who's been the fabricator, I'd like to ask? Who's so nifty with the scissors and needle? Who's been going a-hunting in my clothes?'

'Oh, what a fib!' exclaimed Ethel, turning her eyes up. 'Those old musty miserable bundles of things of yours – would Elsie or I consider laying a finger on them?'

Mrs Varley de Grey replied, as she sometimes did, by heaving up and throwing the tray at Ethel. Nought, therefore, but cast-off kitchen china nowadays was ever exposed to risk; and the young woman, not trying to gather the debris up, statuesquely, thoughtfully stood with her arms folded, watching tea-steam rise from the carpet. Today, the effort seemed to have been too much for Aunt Elysia, who collapsed on her pillows, faintly blue in the face. 'Rats in the attic,' she murmured. '*I've* heard them, rats in the attic! Now where's my tea?'

'You've had it,' said Ethel, turning to leave the room. However, she paused to study a photograph in a tarnished, elaborate silver frame. 'Really quite an Adonis, poor Uncle Harry. From the first glance, you say, he never looked back?'

'My lovely tea,' said the widow, beginning to sob.

As Ethel slowly put down the photograph her eyes could be seen to calculate, her mouth hardened and a reflective cast came over her brow. Step by step, once more she approached the bed, and, as she did so, altered her tune. She suggested, in a beguiling tone, 'You said you could tell me a thing or two ...?'

Time went on; Lord Fred, though for ever promising, still

failed to come within Ethel's grasp. Ground gained one hour seemed to be lost the next – it seemed, for example, that things went better for Ethel in the afternoons, in the open air, than at the dressier evening functions. It was when she swept down on him in full plumage that Lord Fred seemed to contract. Could it be that he feared his passions? – she hardly thought so. Or did her complexion not light up well? When there was a question of dancing, he came so late that her programme already was black with other names, whereupon he would heave a gallant sigh. When they did take the floor together, he held her so far at arm's length, and with his face turned so far away, that when she wished to address him she had to shout – she told herself this must be the London style, but it piqued her, naturally. Next morning, all was as it was before, with nobody so completely assiduous as Lord Fred – but, through it all, he still never came to the point. And worse, the days of his visit were running out; he would soon be back in the heart of the London season. 'Will you ever get him, Ethel, now, do you think?' Elsie asked, with trying solicitude, and no doubt the neighbourhood wondered also.

She conjured up all her fascinations. But was something further needed, to do the trick?

It was now that she began to frequent her aunt.

In that dank little back room looking into the hill, proud Ethel humbled herself, to prise out the secret. Sessions were close and long. Elsie, in mystification outside the door, heard the dotty voice of their relative rising, falling, with, now and then, blood-curdling little knowing laughs. Mrs Varley de Grey was back in the golden days. Always, though, of a sudden it would break off, drop back into pleas, whimpers and jagged breathing. No doctor, though she constantly asked for one, had for years been allowed to visit Mrs Varley de Grey – the girls saw no reason for that expense, or for the interference which might follow. Aunt's afflic-tion, they swore, was confined to the head; all she required was quiet, and that she got. Knowing, however, how gossip spreads, they would let no servant near her for more than a minute or two, and then with one of themselves on watch at the door. They had much to bear from the foetid state of her room.

'You don't think you'll kill her, Ethel?' the out-of-it Elsie asked. 'Forever sitting on top of her, as you now do. Can it be healthy, egging her on to talk? What's this attraction, all of a sudden? – whatever's this which has sprung up between you two? She and you are becoming quite hand-in-glove.'

Elsie merely remarked this, and soon forgot: she had her own fish to fry. It was Ethel who had cause to recall the words – for, the afternoon of the very day they were spoken, Aunt Elysia whizzed off on another track, screamed for what was impossible and, upon being thwarted, went into a seizure unknown before. The worst of it was, at the outset her mind cleared – she pushed her shawl back, reared up her unkempt grey head and looked at Ethel, unblinkingly studied Ethel, with a lucid accumulation of years of hate. 'You fool of a gawk,' she said, and with such contempt! 'Coming running to me to know how to trap a man. Could *you* learn, if it was from Venus herself? Wait till I show you beauty. Bring down those trunks!'

'Oh, Auntie.'

'Bring them down, I say. I'm about to dress myself up.'

'Oh, but I cannot: they're heavy; I'm single-handed.'

'Heavy? – they came here heavy. But there've been rats in the attic. *I* saw you, swishing downstairs in my *eau-de-nil*.'

'Oh, you dreamed that!'

'Through the crack of the door. – Let me up, then. Let us go where they are, and look – we shall soon see!' Aunt Elysia threw back the bedclothes and began to get up. 'Let's take a look,' she said, 'at the rats' work.' She set out to totter towards the door.

'Oh, but you're not fit!' Ethel protested.

'And when did a doctor say so?' There was a swaying; Ethel caught her in time and, not gently, lugged her back to the bed – and Ethel's mind the whole of this time was whirling, for tonight was the night upon which all hung. Lord Fred's last local appearance was to be, like his first, at a ball: tomorrow he left for London. So it must be tonight, at this ball, or never! How was it that Ethel felt so strangely, wildly confident of the outcome? It was time to begin on her coiffure, lay out her dress. Oh, tonight she would shine as never before! She flung back the bedclothes over the helpless form, heard a clock strike, and hastily turned to go.

'I will be quits with you,' said the voice behind her.

Ethel, in a kimono, hair half down, was in her own room, in front of the open glove-drawer, when Elsie came in – home from a tennis party. Elsie acted oddly – she went at once to the drawer and buried her nose in it. 'Oh my goodness,' she cried, 'it's all too true, and it's awful!'

'What is?' Ethel carelessly asked.

'Ethel dear, would you ever face it out if I were to tell you a certain rumour I heard today at the party as to Lord Fred?'

Ethel turned from her sister, took up the heated tongs and applied more crimps to her natural curliness. She said: 'Certainly; spit it out.'

'Since childhood, he's recoiled from the breath of benzine. He wilts away when it enters the very room!'

'Who says that's so?'

'He confided it to his hostess, who is now spitefully putting it around the country.'

Ethel bit her lip and put down the tongs, while Elsie sorrowfully concluded, 'And your gloves stink, Ethel, as I'm sure do mine.' Elsie then thought it wiser to slip away.

In a minute more, however, she was back, and this time, with still more peculiar air, she demanded: 'In what state did you leave Auntie? She was sounding so very quiet that I peeped in, and _I_ don't care for the looks of her now at all!' Ethel swore, but consented to take a look. She stayed in there in the back room, with Elsie biting her thumb-nail outside the door, for what seemed an ominous length of time; when she did emerge, she looked greenish, but held her head high. The sisters' eyes met. Ethel said, stonily, 'Dozing. '

'You're certain she's _not_ . . . ? She _couldn't_ ever be – you know?'

'Dozing, I tell you.' Ethel stared Elsie out.

'If she _was_ gone,' quavered the frailer sister, 'just think of it – why, we'd never get to the ball! And a ball that everything

hangs on,' she ended, with a scared but conspiratorial glance at
Ethel.

'Reassure yourself. Didn't you hear me say?'

As she spoke Ethel, chiefly from habit, locked her late Aunt's
door on the outside. The act caused a sort of secret jingle to be
heard from inside her fist, and Elsie asked: 'What's that you've
got hold of, now?' 'Just a few little keys and trinkets she made
me keep,' replied Ethel, disclosing the small bag she had found
where she'd looked for it, under the dead one's pillow. 'Scurry
on now, Elsie, or you'll never be dressed. Care to make use of
my tongs, while they're so splendidly hot?'

Alone at last, Ethel drew in a breath, and, with a gesture of
resolution, re-tied her kimono-sash tightly over her corset. She
took the key from the bag and regarded it, murmuring, 'Provi-
dential!' then gave a glance upward, towards where the attics
were. The late spring sun had set, but an apricot afterglow, not
unlike the light cast by a Chinese lantern, crept through the
upper storey of Jasmine Lodge. The cessation of all those
rustlings, tappings, whimpers and moans from inside Mrs Varley
de Grey's room had set up an unfamiliar, somewhat unnerving
hush. Not till a whiff of singeing hair announced that Elsie was
well employed did Ethel set out on the quest which held all her
hopes. Success was imperative – she *must* have gloves. Gloves,
gloves . . .

Soundlessly, she set foot on the attic stairs.

Under the skylight she had to suppress a shriek, for a rat –
yes, of all things! – leaped at her out of an empty hatbox: and
the rodent gave her a wink before it darted away. Now Ethel
and Elsie knew for a certain fact that there never *had* been rats
in Jasmine Lodge. However, she continued to steel her nerves,
and to push her way to the one inviolate trunk.

All Mrs Varley de Grey's other Indian luggage gaped and
yawned at Ethel, void, showing its linings, on end or toppling,
forming a barricade around the object of her search. She pushed,
pitched and pulled, scowling as the dust flew into her hair. But
the last trunk, when it came into view and reach, still had something select and bridal about it: on top, the initials E. V. de G.
stared out, quite luminous in a frightening way – for indeed

how dusky the attic was! Shadows not only multiplied in the corners but seemed to finger their way up the sloping roof. Silence pierced up through the floor from that room below – and, worst, Ethel had the sensation of being watched by that pair of fixed eyes she had not stayed to close. She glanced this way, that way, backward over her shoulder. But, Lord Fred was at stake! – she knelt down and got to work with the key.

This trunk had two neat brass locks, one left, one right, along the front of the lid. Ethel, after fumbling, opened the first – then, so great was her hurry to know what might be within that she could not wait but slipped her hand in under the lifted corner. She pulled out one pricelessly lacy tip of what must be a bride-veil, and gave a quick laugh – must not this be an omen? She pulled again, but the stuff resisted, almost as though it were being grasped from inside the trunk – she let go, and either her eyes deceived her or the lace began to be drawn back slowly, in again, inch by inch. What was odder was that the spotless finger tip of a white kid glove appeared for a moment, as though exploring its way out, then withdrew.

Ethel's heart stood still – but she turned to the other lock. Was a giddy attack overcoming her? – for, as she gazed, the entire lid of the trunk seemed to bulge upward, heave and strain so that the E. V. de G. upon it rippled.

Untouched by the key in her trembling hand, the second lock tore itself open.

She recoiled, while the lid slowly rose – of its own accord.

She should have fled. But oh, how she craved what lay there exposed! – layer upon layer, wrapped in transparent paper, of elbow-length magnolia-pure white gloves, bedded on the inert folds of the veil. 'Lord Fred,' thought Ethel, 'now you're within my grasp!'

That was her last thought, nor was the grasp to be hers. Down on her knees again, breathless with lust and joy, Ethel flung herself forward on to that sea of kid, scrabbling and seizing. The glove she had seen before was now, however, readier for its purpose. At first it merely pounced after Ethel's fingers, as though making mock of their greedy course; but the hand within it was all the time filling out ... With one snowy flash through the dusk, the glove clutched Ethel's front hair, tangled itself in her black curls and dragged her head down. She began to choke among the satchets and tissue – then the glove let go, hurled her back, and made its leap at her throat.

It was a marvel that anything so dainty should be so strong. So great, so convulsive was the swell of the force that, during the strangling of Ethel, the seams of the glove split.

In any case, the glove would have been too small for her.

The shrieks of Elsie, upon the attic threshold, began only when all other sounds had died down ... The ultimate spark of the once-famous cleverness of the Miss Trevors appeared in Elsie's extrication of herself from this awkward mess – for, who was to credit how Ethel came by her end? The sisters' reputation for warmth of heart was to stand the survivor in good stead – for, could those affections nursed in Jasmine Lodge, extending so freely even to the unwell aunt, have culminated in Elsie's setting on Ethel? No. In the end, the matter was hushed up – which is to say, is still talked about even now. Ethel Trevor and Mrs Varley de Grey were interred in the same grave, as everyone understood that they would have wished. What conversation took place under the earth one does not know.

From *A Day in the Dark* by Elizabeth Bowen (Jonathan Cape Ltd, London, and Alfred A. Knopf Inc., New York).

MR FOX

Traditional English

This is a traditional English story that was old in Shakespeare's time. In 'Much Ado About Nothing' (Act I, Scene I) Benedick quotes from it: 'Like the old tale, my lord: "it is not so, nor 'twas not so, but, indeed, God forbid it should be so." '

LADY MARY was young, and Lady Mary was fair. She had two brothers, and more lovers than she could count. But of them all, the bravest and most gallant, was a Mr Fox, whom she met when she was down at her father's country house. No one knew who Mr Fox was, but he was certainly brave, and surely rich, and of all her lovers, Lady Mary cared for him alone. At last it was agreed upon between them that they should be married. Lady Mary asked Mr Fox where they should live, and he described to her his castle, and where it was; but, strange to say, did not ask her or her brothers to come and see it.

So one day, near the wedding-day, when her brothers were out, and Mr Fox was away for a day or two on business, as he said, Lady Mary set out for Mr Fox's castle. And after many searchings, she came at last to it, and a fine strong house it was, with high walls and a deep moat. And when she came up to the gateway she saw written on it:

Be bold, be bold.

But as the gate was open, she went through it, and found no one there. So she went up to the doorway, and over it she found written:

Be bold, be bold, but not too bold.

Still she went on, till she came into the hall, and went up the broad stairs till she came to a door in the gallery, over which was written:

> Be bold, be bold, but not too bold.
> Lest that your heart's blood should run cold.

But Lady Mary was a brave one, she was, and she opened the door, and what do you think she saw? Why, bodies and skeletons of beautiful young ladies all stained with blood. So Lady Mary thought it was high time to get out of that horrid place, and she closed the door, went through the gallery, and was just going down the stairs, and out of the hall, when who should she see through the window, but Mr Fox dragging a beautiful young lady along from the gateway to the door. Lady Mary rushed downstairs, and hid herself behind a cask just in time, as Mr Fox came in with the poor young lady who seemed to have fainted. Just as he got near Lady Mary, Mr Fox saw a diamond ring glittering on the finger of the young lady he was dragging, and he tried to pull it off. But it was tightly fixed, and would not come off, so Mr Fox cursed and swore, and drew his sword, raised it, and brought it down upon the hand of the poor lady. The sword cut off the hand, which jumped up into the air, and fell of all places in the world into Lady Mary's lap. Mr Fox looked about a bit, but did not think of looking behind the cask, so at last he went on dragging the young lady up the stairs into the Bloody Chamber.

As soon as she heard him pass through the gallery, Lady Mary crept out of the door, down through the gateway, and ran home as fast as she could.

Now it happened that the very next day the marriage contract of Lady Mary and Mr Fox was to be signed, and there was a splendid breakfast before that. And when Mr Fox was seated at the table opposite Lady Mary, he looked at her. 'How pale you are this morning, my dear.' 'Yes,' said she, 'I had a bad night's rest last night. I had horrible dreams.' 'Dreams go by contraries,' said Mr Fox; 'but tell us your dream, and your sweet voice will make the time pass till the happy hour comes.'

'I dreamed,' said Lady Mary, 'that I went yestermorn to your castle, and I found it in the woods, with high walls, and a deep moat, and over the gateway was written:

> Be bold, be bold.'

'But it is not so, nor it was not so,' said Mr Fox.
'And when I came to the doorway over it was written:

> Be bold, be bold, but not too bold.'

'It is not so, nor it was not so,' said Mr Fox.
'And then I went upstairs, and came to a gallery, at the end of which was a door on which was written:

> Be bold, be bold, but not too bold,
> Lest that your heart's blood should run cold.'

'It is not so, nor it was not so,' said Mr Fox.
'And then – and then I opened the door, and the room was filled with bodies and skeletons of poor dead women, all stained with their blood.'

'It is not so, nor it was not so. And God forbid it should be so,' said Mr Fox.

'I then dreamed that I rushed down the gallery, and just as I was going down the stairs, I saw you, Mr Fox, coming up to the hall door, dragging after you a poor young lady, rich and beautiful.'

'It is not so, nor it was not so. And God forbid it should be so,' said Mr Fox.

'I rushed downstairs, just in time to hide myself behind a cask, when you, Mr Fox, came in dragging the young lady by the arm. And, as you passed me, Mr Fox, I thought I saw you try to get off her diamond ring, and when you could not, Mr Fox, it seemed to me in my dreams, that you out with your sword and hacked off the poor lady's hand to get the ring.'

'It is not so, nor was it so. And God forbid it should be so,' said Mr Fox, and was going to say something else as he rose from his seat, when Lady Mary cried out:

'But it is so, and it was so. Here's hand and ring I have to show,' and pulled out the lady's hand from her dress, and pointed it straight at Mr Fox.

At once her brothers and her friends drew their swords and cut Mr Fox into a thousand pieces.

From *English Fairy Tales* collected by Joseph Jacobs (Frederick Muller Ltd, London).

CURFEW

L. M. Boston

WHILE my two brothers and I were at a preparatory school our parents were living abroad, so that we had to spend our holidays with relatives.

Our favourite uncle and aunt had bought a farmhouse on the outlying land of an old manor, of which the estate was being broken up. The big house, Abbey Manor, was being allowed to fall down in its own good time, the owner living in a small dower house in the park.

The cottage which Uncle Tom and Aunt Catherine bought had also been empty for a long time. Nettles grew up to the front door and even between the flagstones in the larder. The cottage however had been well built, with stone mullions, leaded windows and tiled floors. It had escaped the wanton smashing up that is the fate of most empty houses, perhaps because of its isolation. A profound silence brooded over it and the acres that went with it.

My Aunt had a passion for gardening, and there was much to be done before this weed-infested land should be disciplined to her intentions, but the wildness was a paradise for children.

Walks in the adjacent park were among the excitements of our visits. There was the empty Manor with its staring windows and lost melancholy garden, its weedy paths leading to locked gates. We had Sir Roger's permission to wander there, but never climbed the gate without a thrill, or chill, of expectation. One wing of the fifteenth century Manor had, with sacrilegious defiance, been built over the former Abbey graveyard. Here and there in the grounds, lying open among the rhododendrons were the empty stone coffins of forgotten Abbots, left there perhaps as being too heavy to carry away, or out of boastfulness.

They were grand things, hand-hewn from solid blocks of local stone hollowed to the austerest outline of the human body with a round resting place for the head. We passed them with great awe and even with a kind of affection, as noble things treated with contempt and now part of our private landscape.

There was also a lake, reflecting the house and the stables, which were dusty, echoing and forlorn. Uncle Tom, who liked everything ship-shape, used to sigh over all this decay, but his wife had an eye open for everything that could be moved, bought, or made use of, such as a small wrought-iron gate, a sundial, or even, in an ambitious moment, as we all stood looking up at it, the little bell tower on the stables. Its four open arches and lead dome had the beauty of extreme simplicity against the pale green sky. 'Why should it rot here?' she said. 'It would suit our yard just as well;' but the yard, surrounded by fine old barns, was Uncle's special domain and he resented intrusion. 'Rubbish,' he said, 'it's sure to be rotten. Besides I hate pretentiousness.'

On our first visit to their farmhouse Aunt Catherine had been busy making a wild garden out of an acre or two of heather and stone. It was boggy in places and we helped to make water courses for her, while she laid stepping stones and contrived rough slab bridges. There was a high mound in the middle of this patch, apparently artificial, though of some age, judging by the hawthorn tree that grew on it, and it was crowned by a large boulder. In the course of her construction Aunt Catherine needed soil to raise her beds above the level of the surrounding damp, and, resourceful woman, looking at this hillock, decided to shift the top. With what delight we responded to her invitations to see if we could roll the boulder off; but our efforts were in vain. In the end it took a team of all hands, with levers, under the personal command of Uncle in his most arbitrary mood, to dislodge it. But at last the slope took possession of it and away it rolled on a clumsy and fortuitous course and came to rest at the edge of one of our little boggy streams. 'Perfect,' said Aunt Catherine by way of thanks and dismissal.

When next we came to stay, already her heather garden was taking shape. She had perfectly preserved the wild atmosphere, and the hillock was down almost to the level of the rest.

'Look, boys,' she said, 'we struck on this yesterday.' She showed us the top of a trough or coffer of stone which her digging had half uncovered. The slab over it that had served as a lid had been prized up and now rested sideways, leaving a gaping hole through which the loose earth on top had poured in.

Aunt Catherine stopped with a gasp.

'When did you open it?' she asked Uncle.

'I haven't touched it, my dear.'

'Then who has been here, and why?'

Was it a burglar? Was it treasure? We were all agog.

Aunt Catherine laughed uneasily and said she would guess that whatever was once in was now out, unless it was just old bones, and if so she was not going to disturb them.

'Old bones?' said Robert. 'It's not the right shape for a coffin. Not like the Abbots'. There's no place for a head. Perhaps it was a criminal who had been beheaded. Or perhaps it was a case of "Double him up, double him up" like Punch's victims.'

'Or perhaps an animal Thing,' suggested John hesitantly. He was young and imaginative.

Robert had been rather gingerly shovelling off the clay that still clung to the lid. 'There are words on it,' he said.

We all got busy with penknives, trowel and sticks to clean the letters.

Libera nos quaesimus Domine ab Malo.

Uncle Tom translated it for us. 'Deliver us O Lord from the Evil One.'

'I don't like it,' said Aunt Catherine. Then she shrugged and became practical again. 'I'm short of a slab for my stepping stones,' she said. 'This will do very well. Come on, boys. All together, lift.'

The slab took its useful place face downward in one of the paths, and the coffin itself was skilfully planted with bushes of rosemary and Spanish gorse and trailing rock-roses. By the time this story really begins it had a natural and undisturbed appearance, and around the wild garden that it dominated the lapwings and wagtails made themselves at home.

It was at the beginning of the long summer holidays. Aunt Catherine having completed one plan, was now looking for something new, and the suggestion of moving the bell tower from the Manor stables was raised again. We set off with Uncle Tom one afternoon to examine it. The Manor stables surrounded three sides of a courtyard and were in atrocious condition. The once beautiful and elaborate coach house let in the rain through a hole in the roof. The loose boxes were crumbling with dry rot. Our footsteps and voices rang intrusively as we did a tour of inspection before mounting the ladder to the lofts, and we explored such of these as had floors that would bear us. Spiders and rats were all that moved there now. Uncle Tom was the first to go up the second ladder and thrust his body as far as the knees into the little cupola, while Robert and John were jostling on the lower rungs, their heads level with the opening. I was alone on a little square landing; on one side of me was the ladder, on three were doors opening into dark lofts. We had already explored them and knew them to be empty, and therefore I was very scared to hear a hoarse burst of laughter rather like a horse's cough that seemed to come from one of them. I tugged at my brothers, and they came down, including Uncle who had finished his measuring and tapping. I told them there was someone there, and we all went round again, and I am afraid I took care neither to be first nor last, in or out, of any of the rooms. But we saw nothing and I was mercilessly teased for my fear as we returned home.

At supper that night my Aunt heard all about it. The measurements were very suitable, the condition not bad – 'Though the bell's missing,' said Uncle Tom; 'You get a splendid view of our place from the roof, Catherine; I could see your Bad Man's coffin quite plainly. There's the chap that heard him too,' he added, pointing his fork at me. 'Made us all feel quite queer. I'll go and see Sir Roger tomorrow. They say he'd sell the hat off his head if he could. I like the idea of having a bit of the old house here. Anything new looks new.'

'Don't you bring anything too old over from the Manor,' said Aunt Catherine; 'leave the ghosts behind anyway.'

'It's too late to warn me about that,' he retorted. 'It was you who took the lid off the Bad Man's coffin.'

'It was open already.'

'Well, who rolled the boulder away that was supposed to keep him down?' and again he pointed at us with his fork, and we grinned, though shudders ran down our spines.

The next day Sir Roger himself happened to pass our gate. He stopped to speak to us all, even Robert, John and me, grimy and barefoot as we were.

'You are digging yourselves in very nicely here, I must say,' he said to Uncle. 'It all looks very jolly. I like the way you do it, too. Of course I have no choice but to sell what I can, but these gimcrack buildings do gall me.'

This was a good opening, and before long bargaining for the bell tower had begun. It ended in Uncle's favour, because at the last moment he brought out his trump card – there was no bell.

'But there being no bell is one of its greatest attractions,' said Sir Roger. 'There's a legend, you know. It was called the Judas bell, but where it originally came from and who betrayed what I don't know. It was the old curfew, and of course if people are out when they ought to be in, things are likely to happen to them. The old people round here say the bell had a "familiar". The last person who rang it was my great grandfather, who did it for a wager. And it is a fact that he was found dead. Rather horribly dead. After that the bell was taken down and destroyed.'

'Well, you can't expect me to buy a legend about a bell that is missing,' said Uncle Tom, and the bargain was settled at a very small figure.

Before the end of the holidays the graceful little bell tower was set up on the middle building in our stableyard. Both Uncle and Aunt were pleased. It was repainted to match its new position and looked well there.

Wet weather had set in. We had grown tired of all the games that can be played in the house. Then Robert said he would go and fish in the Manor brook and we followed with jam jars of worms. We had to cross the wild garden, which had, since Uncle's jokes, begun to stir sinister feelings in us. The lapwings cried and veered and flung themselves along the wind, the thin rain pattered in the little brown streams, and the wagtails looked sharply at us, and ran hither and thither as though disguising their real activities. We began to run, and shooed them away as if they

were unwanted thoughts, but as we paused half-way across the
stile into the park and looked back, there they all were as before,
and the curlews sounded derisive as if we had no business there.
The little stream through the park had invaded the grass at its
edge beyond the cast of Thomas's 10/6d fishing rod, and the lake
into which it flowed had swollen into damaging proportions. The
cinder road that led to the Manor farm was under water, and the
farmer was there with Sir Roger, bitterly complaining that it was
all because the outlet sluice was blocked and had never been
mended, and that the lake itself was silting up and so full of
weeds you couldn't tell where it began and where it ended. Sir
Roger was listening with a pained expression. He promised to
have it seen to as soon as the flood subsided enough to allow work
to begin. As for us, we spent the afternoon happily testing the
depth of every overflow and returned home wet to the skin.

    A week later dredging operations began on the lake. The sluice
was opened and the water sank to mud level. The weeds were cut
down, and a band of old men in waders were wheeling the smelly
fibrous mud in barrows along planks. We were there of course
to watch. Much came to light that would never have been expected. A sunken boat, a scythe blade, a weather vane, a skull,
and most surprising of all, a bell. It was of unusual shape, but
covered thickly with sharp flakes of rust. The pivot of its tongue
was rusted up solid so that it could not swing.

    'It's the old Judas bell like enough,' said one old man. 'Didn't
I hear tell that your Uncle had bought the bell tower? That's
an odd thing for anyone to buy. I'd like to hear what my old
woman would say if I came back one day and said I'd bought her
a bell tower.'

    We ran back to announce the find at home, and Uncle Tom
called for Sir Roger and took him along to look at it. Uncle had a
flair for antiques, and he thought that the bell might prove to be
incised in some pattern which might be curious or of interest.
But Sir Roger was interested in nothing but 'Sherry and whi-
pets', as we knew from Uncle's indiscreet conversation. 'Look at
the rust on it,' he said. 'I can't take any money for a thing like
that. Certainly, do what you like with it. I'm not superstitious,
but I wouldn't touch it.'

Uncle shook his head at me and said we must expect the worst.

The bell was sent away to be cleaned and repaired, but even in its absence we now had a prickly feeling of foreboding. I remember the golden September weather, the scent of southern wood and lavender, and the yellow leaves spotted with black that were beginning to fall. But for us the garden had become haunted. We no longer basked in it quite at our ease, or felt as heretofore that earth and fields, trees and sky were all our own. There were darker corners where we definitely did not go, where in a game of 'I spy', for instance, nobody thought of hiding or looking.

It was on the last morning of the holidays that the bell came back. It was delivered by van, wrapped in sacking, with its now mobile tongue thickly wedged and muffled in felt. We all hung around while Uncle unwrapped it. Seeing us so deeply interested, he made quite a ritual of it, marching off to the barn with us in procession behind him. The clapper he had kept muffled till the last. It was to be 'unveiled'. When at last he pulled the first toll the sound that it gave out was so unexpected as to be quite shocking. It was a high wide-carrying note, and though it had a certain churchiness, there was in it something wild and almost screamlike. The afternote that vibrated long after within the bell sent a creeping chill up my spine. When the last sinister tingle had faded out of the shaken air, Aunt Catherine said, 'I'm certainly not going to have *that* rung for dinner. It would take away my appetite.' Uncle seemed not disposed to dispute it. He said, 'If they rang that at curfew, they gave you fair warning.'

We were to go back to school the next day, and this was a thought that blotted out all others. It was important to get the most out of the last afternoon. Towards sunset when we were playing 'I spy', I was crouching in a deep clump of red dogwood, not far from the house, holding my panting breath and listening for the approach of Robert and John. I heard their voices drawing off in the wrong direction, and was beginning to feel I had time to straighten my stiff knees before they could possibly return, and then to hope they wouldn't be too long, when with no other warning a feeling of utter isolation and panic took me. I felt I was deserted, exposed to unknown dangers, perhaps trapped. I turned involuntarily to look behind me, and saw two long-nailed soily hands begin to part the leaves, and an evil face looked in. His hair and cheeks were clotted with earth, through which his yellow teeth showed more on one side than the other, his eye sockets were appallingly hollow, and he lifted his chin as the blind do when they seek.

I shot out of the bushes like a rabbit when the ferret looks in, and ran as hard as my legs would carry me to the house. My clamour soon brought Robert and John and Aunt Catherine, to whom I could give no better explanation than that I had seen a horrible face. She calmed me as best she could, saying it was probably a tramp coming in to pick up apples, and Uncle Tom should go round and send him off. Confidently she and Uncle exchanged that word as if it met the case perfectly – some tramps, a tramp, the tramp – as if a casual word like that could cover such lurking horror. Uncle Tom went striding off looking very fierce, but he came back having seen nobody.

Dusk had come. It was cold and the wind was rising, and we, as may be imagined, had no heart to play outside. So after tea Aunt Catherine let us light the fire, and we persuaded her and Uncle to stay with us and tell us ghost tales – the others I think out of pure love of sensation, and I because it was the only way that I could get company for my thoughts and persuade the grown-ups to talk, however insincerely, on the same subject. The session opened of course with a little lecture from Aunt Catherine about the folly of the whole thing. Then the curtains were drawn and Uncle Tom began. His personality and prestige added to the effect, for he was tall and bony and we held him in awe. He told the old stories about midnight coaches, about grinning lift-men who had been seen in a dream the night before, about grey monks who had passed people on the stairs and figures standing at midnight by one's bed; and they all to me had the same face.

The wind rose rapidly in accompaniment to his tales, and our feelings of horror were already far outstripping the merits of his invention, when a really terrible thing happened. A gust of wind tore open the casement and at the same time the bell in the tower gave a jerky ring. There was no need to tell us any more stories.

Our hearts were tight with presentiment. Its variable sound came and went with the gusts even after the window was tightly closed again. It was not like a bell rung on purpose, but a bell evilly twitching on its own.

'This is quite intolerable,' said Aunt Catherine. 'No one will sleep a wink tonight if that goes on.'

'Don't get in a fuss,' said Uncle; 'I'll go and take out the clapper. Nothing could be simpler. Now, boys, off to bed.'

Up we went perforce, keeping close together, and clustered at our bedroom window to see him do this act of bravery. He seemed to waste hours talking to Aunt in the hall while we waited upstairs and listened to that vibrating shudder from the bell, the irregularity of which made it even more fraying to the nerves. The shadows under the yard walls were peopled for me with precise terror, and so was the room at my back. The key-hole howled too, and the wind in the chimney buffeted hollowly. At last we saw Uncle Tom come out into the light from the back door, and go down the yard where we could only by straining keep him in sight. Shadows swallowed him up and we heard the barn door slam behind him. We fixed our eyes on the outline of the bell tower, and again it seemed an age before we thought we could distinguish his head, shoulders and arms waving against the sky.

'There he is,' said John, in a whisper. Uncle had seized the bell and the clanging stopped; but a moment later we heard him yell with the whole force of his great lungs, and his body disappeared down the man-hole. The bell had stopped, but the wind still blew and it was hard to tell where sounds came from. Robert thought he heard a dog-fight going on somewhere. But Uncle Tom didn't come back. Time seemed too short now. We imagined how long it would be before he would appear, then doubled it, trebled it, and began again.

At last Aunt Catherine came out and shouted for him, ran half-way down the yard and shouted again. The maid came out too, and presently the yard was full of people with lamps and flash-lights. They went into the barn after Aunt Catherine, and came staggering out carrying someone towards the house. We were seized with shame and undressed as quickly as we could, jumping into our beds. But Robert went on to the landing and called down the stairs to ask what had happened.

'Go to bed, boys, and for the Lord's sake keep quiet and keep out of the way,' said a woman neighbour. 'Your uncle has had a nasty accident.'

And then we heard the horrible mad banshee sound of the maid having hysterics in the kitchen.

JOHN BARTINE'S WATCH

A Story by a Physician

Ambrose Bierce

'THE exact time? Good God! my friend, why do you insist?
One would think – but what does it matter; it is easily bedtime –
isn't that near enough? But, here, if you must set your watch,
take mine and see for yourself.'

With that, he detached his watch – a tremendously heavy, old-
fashioned one – from the chain, and handed it to me; then
turned away, and walking across the room to a shelf of books, began an examination of their backs. His agitation and evident
distress surprised me; they appeared reasonless. Having set my
watch by his, I stepped over to where he stood and said, 'Thank
you.'

As he took his timepiece and re-attached it to the guard I observed that his hands were unsteady. With a tact upon which I
greatly prided myself, I sauntered carelessly to the sideboard and
took some brandy and water; then, begging his pardon for my
thoughtlessness, asked him to have some and went back to my
seat by the fire, leaving him to help himself, as was our custom.
He did so and presently joined me at the hearth, as tranquil as
ever.

This odd little incident occurred in my apartment, where
John Bartine was passing an evening. We had dined together at
the club, had come home in a cab and – in short, everything had
been done in the most prosaic way; and why John Bartine should
break in upon the natural and established order of things to make
himself spectacular with a display of emotion, apparently for his
own entertainment, I could nowise understand. The more I
thought of it, while his brilliant conversational gifts were com-
mending themselves to my inattention, the more curious I grew,

and of course had no difficulty in persuading myself that my curiosity was friendly solicitude. That is the disguise that curiosity usually assumes to evade resentment. So I ruined one of the finest sentences of his disregarded monologue by cutting it short without ceremony.

'John Bartine,' I said, 'you must try to forgive me if I am wrong, but with the light that I have at present I cannot concede your right to go all to pieces when asked the time o' night. I cannot admit that it is proper to experience a mysterious reluctance to look your own watch in the face and to cherish in my presence, without explanation, painful emotions which are denied to me, and which are none of my business.'

To this ridiculous speech Bartine made no immediate reply, but sat looking gravely into the fire. Fearing that I had offended I was about to apologize and beg him to think no more about the matter, when looking me calmly in the eyes he said:

'My dear fellow, the levity of your manner does not at all disguise the hideous impudence of your demand; but happily I had already decided to tell you what you wish to know, and no manifestation of your unworthiness to hear it shall alter my decision. Be good enough to give me your attention and you shall hear all about the matter.

'This watch,' he said, 'had been in my family for three generations before it fell to me. Its original owner, for whom it was made, was my great grandfather, Bramwell Olcott Bartine, a wealthy planter of Colonial Virginia, and as staunch a Tory as ever lay awake nights contriving new kinds of maledictions for the head of Mr Washington, and new methods of aiding and abetting good King George. One day this worthy gentleman had the deep misfortune to perform for his cause a service of capital importance which was not recognized as legitimate by those who suffered its disadvantages. It does not matter what it was, but among its minor consequences was my excellent ancestor's arrest one night in his own house by a party of Mr Washington's rebels. He was permitted to say farewell to his weeping family, and was then marched away into the darkness which swallowed him up for ever. Not the slenderest clue to his fate was ever found. After the war the most diligent inquiry and the offer of large rewards failed to turn up any of his captors or any fact concerning his disappearance. He had disappeared, and that was all.'

Something in Bartine's manner that was not in his words – I hardly knew what it was – prompted me to ask:

'What is your view of the matter – of the justice of it?'

'My view of it,' he flamed out, bringing his clenched hand down upon the table as if he had been in a public-house dicing with blackguards – 'my view of it is that it was a characteristic-ally dastardly assassination by that damned traitor, Washington, and his ragamuffin rebels!'

For some minutes nothing was said: Bartine was recovering his temper, and I waited. Then I said:

'Was that all?'

'No – there was something else. A few weeks after my great-grandfather's arrest his watch was found lying on the porch at the front door of his dwelling. It was wrapped in a sheet of letter paper bearing the name of Rupert Bartine, his only son, my grandfather. I am wearing that watch.'

Bartine paused. His usually restless black eyes were staring fixedly into the grate, a point of red light in each, reflected from the glowing coals. He seemed to have forgotten me. A sudden threshing of the branches of a tree outside one of the windows, and almost at the same time a rattle of rain against the glass, re-called him to a sense of his surroundings. A storm had risen, heralded by a single gust of wind, and in a few moments the steady plash of the water on the pavement was distinctly heard. I hardly know why I relate this incident; it seemed somehow to have a certain significance and relevancy which I am unable now to discern. It at least added an element of seriousness, almost solemnity. Bartine resumed:

'I have a singular feeling toward this watch – a kind of affec-tion for it; I like to have it about me, though partly from its weight, and partly for a reason I shall now explain, I seldom carry it. The reason is this: Every evening when I have it with me I feel an unaccountable desire to open and consult it, even if I can think of no reason for wishing to know the time. But if I yield to it, the moment my eyes rest upon the dial I am filled with a mysterious apprehension – a sense of imminent calamity. And

this is the more insupportable the nearer it is to eleven o'clock –
by this watch, no matter what the actual hour may be. After the
hands have registered eleven the desire to look is gone; I am
entirely indifferent. Then I can consult the thing as often as I
like, with no more emotion than you feel in looking at your own.
Naturally I have trained myself not to look at that watch in the
evening before eleven; nothing could induce me. Your insistence
this evening upset me a trifle. I felt very much as I suppose an
opium-eater might feel if his yearning for his special and particular kind of hell were reinforced by opportunity and advice.

'Now that is my story, and I have told it in the interest of your
trumpery science; but if on any evening hereafter you observe
me wearing this damnable watch, and you have the thoughtful-
ness to ask me the hour, I shall beg leave to put you to the in-
convenience of being knocked down.'

His humour did not amuse me. I could see that in relating his
delusion he was again somewhat disturbed. His concluding smile
was positively ghastly, and his eyes had resumed something more
than their old restlessness; they shifted hither and thither and
about the room with apparent aimlessness and I fancied had
taken on a wild expression, such as is sometimes observed in
cases of dementia. Perhaps this was my own imagination, but at
any rate I was now persuaded that my friend was afflicted with a
most singular and interesting monomania. Without, I trust, any
abatement of my affectionate solicitude for him as a friend, I
began to regard him as a patient, rich in possibilities of profitable
study. Why not? Had he not described his delusion in the
interest of science? Ah, poor fellow, he was doing more for
science than he knew: not only his story but himself was in
evidence.

I should cure him if I could, of course, but first I should make
a little experiment in psychology – nay, the experiment itself
might be a step in his restoration.

'That is very frank and friendly of you, Bartine,' I said cordi-
ally, 'and I'm rather proud of your confidence. It is all very odd,
certainly. Do you mind showing me the watch?'

He detached it from his waistcoat, chain and all, and passed it
to me without a word. The case was of gold, very thick and

strong, and singularly engraved. After closely examining the dial and observing that it was nearly twelve o'clock, I opened it at the back and was interested to observe an inner case of ivory, upon which was painted a miniature portrait in that exquisite and delicate manner which was in vogue during the eighteenth century.

'Why, bless my soul!' I exclaimed, feeling a sharp artistic delight – 'how under the sun did you get that done? I thought miniature painting on ivory was a lost art.'

'That,' he replied, gravely smiling, 'is not I; it is my excellent great-grandfather, the late Bramwell Olcott Bartine, Esquire, of Virginia. He was younger then than later – about my age, in fact. It is said to resemble me; do you think so?'

'Resemble you? I should say so! Barring the costume, which I supposed you to have assumed out of compliment to the art – or for *vraisemblance*, so to say – and the no moustache, that portrait is you in every feature, line, and expression.'

No more was said at that time. Bartine took a book from the table and began reading. I heard outside the incessant plash of the rain in the street. There were occasional hurried footfalls on the sidewalks; and once a slower, heavier tread seemed to cease at my door – a policeman, I thought, seeking shelter in the doorway. The boughs of the trees tapped significantly on the window panes, as if asking for admittance. I remember it all through these years and years of a wiser, graver life.

Seeing myself unobserved, I took the old-fashioned key that dangled from the chain and quickly turned back the hands of the watch a full hour; then, closing the case, I handed Bartine his property and saw him replace it on his person.

'I think you said,' I began, with assumed carelessness, 'that after eleven the sight of the dial no longer affects you. As it is now nearly twelve' – looking at my own timepiece – 'perhaps, if you don't resent my pursuit of proof, you will look at it now.'

He smiled good-humouredly, pulled out the watch again, opened it, and instantly sprang to his feet with a cry that Heaven has not had the mercy to permit me to forget! His eyes, their blackness strikingly intensified by the pallor of his face, were fixed upon the watch, which he clutched in both hands. For some time he remained in that attitude without uttering another sound; then, in a voice that I should not have recognized as his, he said:

'Damn you! It is two minutes to eleven!'

I was not unprepared for some such outbreak, and without rising replied, calmly enough:

'I beg your pardon, I must have misread your watch in setting my own by it.'

He shut the case with a sharp snap and put the watch in his pocket. He looked at me and made an attempt to smile, but his lower lip quivered and he seemed unable to close his mouth. His hands, also, were shaking, and he thrust them, clenched, into the pockets of his sack-coat. The courageous spirit was manifestly endeavouring to subdue the coward body. The effort was too great; he began to sway from side to side as from vertigo, and before I could spring from my chair to support him his knees gave way and he pitched awkwardly forward and fell upon his face. I sprang to assist him to rise; but when John Bartine rises we shall all rise.

The *post-mortem* examination disclosed nothing; every organ was normal and sound. But when the body had been prepared for burial a faint dark circle was seen to have developed around the neck; at least I was so assured by several persons who said they saw it, but of my own knowledge I cannot say if that was true.

Nor can I set limitations to the law of heredity. I do not know that in the spiritual world a sentiment or emotion may not survive the heart that held it, and seek expression in a kindred life, ages removed. Surely, if I were to guess at the fate of Bramwell Olcott Bartine, I should guess that he was hanged at eleven o'clock in the evening, and that he had been allowed several hours in which to prepare for the change.

As to John Bartine, my friend, my patient for five minutes, and – Heaven forgive me! – my victim for eternity, there is no more to say. He is buried, and his watch with him – I saw to that. May God rest his soul in Paradise, and the soul of his Virginian ancestor, if, indeed, they are two souls.

From *Can Such Things Be?* by Ambrose Bierce (Jonathan Cape Ltd, London, and Citadel Press, New York).

THE MONKEY'S PAW

W. W. Jacobs

WITHOUT, the night was cold and wet, but in the small parlour of Laburnum Villa the blinds were drawn and the fire burned brightly. Father and son were at chess; the former, who possessed ideas about the game involving radical changes, putting his king into such sharp and unnecessary perils, that it even provoked comment from the white-haired old lady knitting placidly by the fire.

'Hark at the wind,' said Mr White, who, having seen a fatal mistake after it was too late, was amiably desirous of preventing his son from seeing it.

'I'm listening,' said the latter, grimly surveying the board as he stretched out his hand. 'Check.'

'I should hardly think that he'd come tonight,' said his father, with his hand poised over the board.

'Mate,' replied the son.

'That's the worst of living so far out,' bawled Mr White, with sudden and unlooked-for violence; 'of all the beastly, slushy, out-of-the-way places to live in, this is the worst. Path's a bog, and road's a torrent. I don't know what people are thinking about. I suppose because only two houses in the road are let, they think it doesn't matter.'

'Never mind, dear,' said his wife, soothingly; 'perhaps you will win the next one.'

Mr White looked up sharply, just in time to intercept a knowing glance between mother and son. The words died away on his lips, and he hid a guilty grin in his thin grey beard.

'There he is,' said Herbert White, as the gate banged to loudly and heavy footsteps came towards the door.

The old man rose with hospitable haste, and opening the door, was heard condoling with the new arrival. The new arrival also condoled with himself, so that Mrs White said, 'Tut, Tut!' and coughed gently as her husband entered the room, followed by a tall, burly man, beady of eye and rubicund of visage.

'Sergeant-Major Morris,' he said, introducing him.

The sergeant-major shook hands, and taking the proffered seat by the fire, watched contentedly while his host got out whisky and tumblers and stood a small copper kettle on the fire.

At the third glass his eyes got brighter, and he began to talk, the little family circle regarding with eager interest this visitor from distant parts, as he squared his broad shoulders in the chair and spoke of wild scenes and doughty deeds; of wars and plagues and strange peoples.

'Twenty-one years of it,' said Mr White, nodding at his wife and son. 'When he went away he was a slip of a youth in the warehouse. Now look at him.'

'He don't look to have taken much harm,' said Mrs White politely.

'I'd like to go to India myself,' said the old man, 'just to look around a bit, you know.'

'Better where you are,' said the sergeant-major, shaking his head. He put down the empty glass, and, sighing softly, shook his head again.

'I should like to see those old temples and fakirs and jugglers,' said the old man. 'What was that you started telling me the other day about a monkey's paw or something, Morris?'

'Nothing,' said the soldier hastily. 'Leastways nothing worth hearing.'

'Monkey's paw?' said Mrs White curiously.

'Well, it's just a bit of what you might call magic, perhaps,' said the sergeant-major, offhandedly.

His three listeners leaned forward eagerly. The visitor absent-mindedly put his empty glass to his lips and then set it down again. His host filled it for him.

'To look at,' said the sergeant-major, fumbling in his pocket, 'it's just an ordinary little paw, dried to a mummy.'

He took something out of his pocket and proffered it. Mrs

White drew back with a grimace, but her son, taking it, examined it curiously.

'And what is there special about it?' inquired Mr White as he took it from his son, and having examined it, placed it upon the table.

'It had a spell put on it by an old fakir,' said the sergeant-major, 'a very holy man. He wanted to show that fate ruled people's lives, and that those who interfered with it did so to their sorrow. He put a spell on it so that three separate men could each have three wishes from it.'

His manner was so impressive that his hearers were conscious that their light laughter jarred somewhat.

'Well, why don't you have three, sir?' said Herbert White, cleverly.

The soldier regarded him in the way that middle age is wont to regard presumptuous youth. 'I have,' he said quietly, and his blotchy face whitened.

'And did you really have the three wishes granted?' asked Mrs White.

'I did,' said the sergeant-major, and his glass tapped against his strong teeth.

'And has anybody else wished?' persisted the old lady.

'The first man had his three wishes. Yes,' was the reply. 'I don't know what the first two were, but the third was for death. That's how I got the paw.'

His tones were so grave that a hush fell upon the group.

'If you've had your three wishes, it's no good to you now, then, Morris,' said the old man at last. 'What do you keep it for?'

The soldier shook his head. 'Fancy, I suppose,' he said slowly. 'I did have some idea of selling it, but I don't think I will. It has caused enough mischief already. Besides, people won't buy. They think it's a fairy tale, some of them; and those who do think anything of it want to try it first and pay me afterwards.'

'If you could have another three wishes,' said the old man, eyeing him keenly, 'would you have them?'

'I don't know,' said the other. 'I don't know.'

He took the paw, and dangling it between his forefinger and

thumb, suddenly threw it upon the fire. White, with a slight cry, stooped down and snatched it off.

'Better let it burn,' said the soldier solemnly.

'If you don't want it, Morris,' said the other, 'give it to me.'

'I won't,' said his friend doggedly. 'I threw it on the fire. If you keep it, don't blame me for what happens. Pitch it on the fire again, like a sensible man.'

The other shook his head and examined his new possession closely. 'How do you do it?' he inquired.

'Hold it up in your right hand and wish aloud,' said the sergeant-major, 'but I warn you of the consequences.'

'Sounds like *Arabian Nights*,' said Mrs White, as she rose and began to set the supper. 'Don't you think you might wish for four pairs of hands for me?'

Her husband drew the talisman from his pocket, and then all three burst into laughter as the sergeant-major, with a look of alarm on his face, caught him by the arm.

'If you must wish,' he said gruffly, 'wish for something sensible.'

Mr White dropped it back in his pocket, and placing chairs, motioned his friend to the table. In the business of supper the talisman was partly forgotten, and afterwards the three sat listening in an enthralled fashion to a second instalment of the soldier's adventures in India.

'If the tale about the monkey's paw is not more truthful than those he has been telling us,' said Herbert, as the door closed behind their guest, just in time to catch the last train, 'we shan't get much out of it.'

'Did you give him anything for it, father?' inquired Mrs White, regarding her husband closely.

'A trifle,' said he, colouring slightly. 'He didn't want it, but I made him take it. And he pressed me again to throw it away.'

'Likely,' said Herbert, with pretended horror. 'Why, we're going to be rich, and famous and happy. Wish to be an Emperor, father, to begin with; then you can't be henpecked.'

He darted round the table, pursued by the maligned Mrs White with an antimacassar.

Mr White took the paw from his pocket and eyed it dubiously.

'I don't know what to wish for, and that's a fact,' he said, slowly. 'It seems to me I've got all I want.'

'If you only cleared the house, you'd be quite happy, wouldn't you?' said Herbert, with his hand on his shoulder. 'Well, wish for two hundred pounds then; that'll just do it.'

His father, smiling shamefacedly at his own credulity, held up the talisman, as his son, with a solemn face, somewhat marred by a wink at his mother, sat down at the piano and struck a few impressive chords.

'I wish for two hundred pounds,' said the old man distinctly.

A fine crash from the piano greeted the words, interrupted by a shuddering cry from the old man. His wife and son ran towards him.

'It moved,' he cried, with a glance of disgust at the object as it lay on the floor.

'As I wished, it twisted in my hand like a snake.'

'Well, I don't see the money,' said his son, as he picked it up and placed it on the table, 'and I bet I never shall.'

'It must have been your fancy, father,' said his wife, regarding him anxiously.

He shook his head. 'Never mind, though; there's no harm done, but it gave me a shock all the same.'

They sat down by the fire again while the two men finished their pipes. Outside, the wind was higher than ever, and the old man started nervously at the sound of a door banging upstairs. A silence unusual and depressing settled upon all three, which lasted until the old couple arose to retire for the night.

'I expect you'll find the cash tied up in a big bag in the middle of your bed,' said Herbert, as he bade them good night, 'and something horrible squatting up on top of your wardrobe watching you as you pocket your ill-gotten gains.'

He sat alone in the darkness, gazing at the dying fire, and seeing faces in it. The last face was so horrible and so simian that he gazed at it in amazement. It got so vivid that, with a little uneasy laugh, he felt on the table for a glass containing a little water to throw over it. His hand grasped the monkey's paw, and with a little shiver he wiped his hand on his coat and went up to bed.

In the brightness of the wintry sun next morning as it streamed over the breakfast table, he laughed at his fears. There was an air of prosaic wholesomeness about the room which it had lacked on the previous night, and the dirty, shrivelled little paw was pitched on the sideboard with a carelessness which betokened no great belief in its virtues.

'I suppose all old soldiers are the same,' said Mrs White. 'The idea of our listening to such nonsense! How could wishes be granted in these days? And if they could, how could two hundred pounds hurt you, father?'

'Might drop on his head from the sky,' said the frivolous Herbert.

'Morris said the things happened so naturally,' said his father, 'that you might if you so wished attribute it to coincidence.'

'Well, don't break into the money before I come back,' said Herbert as he rose from the table. 'I'm afraid it'll turn you into a mean, avaricious man, and we shall have to disown you.'

His mother laughed, and following him to the door, watched him down the road; and returning to the breakfast table, was very merry at the expense of her husband's credulity. All of which did not prevent her from scurrying to the door at the postman's knock, nor prevent her from referring somewhat shortly to retired sergeant-majors of bibulous habits when she found that the post brought a tailor's bill.

'Herbert will have some more of his funny remarks, I expect, when he comes home,' she said, as they sat at dinner.

'I dare say,' said Mr White, pouring himself out some beer; 'but for all that, the thing moved in my hand; that I'll swear to.'

'You thought it did,' said the old lady soothingly.

'I say it did,' replied the other. 'There was no thought about it; I had just – What's the matter?'

His wife made no reply. She was watching the mysterious movements of a man outside, who, peering in an undecided fashion at the house, appeared to be trying to make up his mind to enter. In mental connexion with the two hundred pounds, she noticed that the stranger was well dressed, and wore a silk hat of glossy newness. Three times he paused at the gate, and then walked on again. The fourth time he stood with his hand upon it, and then with sudden resolution flung it open and walked up the path. Mrs White at the same moment placed her hands behind her, and hurriedly unfastening the strings of her apron, put that useful article of apparel beneath the cushion of her chair.

She brought the stranger, who seemed ill at ease, into the room. He gazed at her furtively, and listened in a preoccupied fashion as the old lady apologized for the appearance of the room, and her husband's coat, a garment which he usually reserved for the garden. She then waited as patiently as her sex would permit, for him to broach his business, but he was at first strangely silent.

'I – was asked to call,' he said at last, and stooped and picked a piece of cotton from his trousers. 'I come from "Maw and Meggins".'

The old lady started. 'Is anything the matter?' she asked breathlessly. 'Has anything happened to Herbert? What is it?'

Her husband interposed. 'There, there, mother,' he said hastily. 'Sit down and don't jump to conclusions. You've not brought bad news, I'm sure, sir;' and he eyed the other wistfully.

'I'm sorry –' began the visitor.

'Is he hurt?' demanded the mother wildly.

The visitor bowed in assent. 'Badly hurt,' he said quietly, 'but he is not in any pain.'

'Oh, thank God!' said the old woman, clasping her hands. 'Thank God for that! Thank –'

She broke off suddenly as the sinister meaning of the assurance dawned upon her, and she saw the awful confirmation of her fears in the other's averted face. She caught her breath, and turning to her slower-witted husband, laid her trembling old hand upon his. There was a long silence.

'He was caught in the machinery,' said the visitor at length in a low voice.

'Caught in the machinery,' repeated Mr White in a dazed fashion, 'yes.'

He sat staring blankly out at the window, and taking his wife's hand between his own, pressed it as he had been wont to do in their old courting days nearly forty years before.

'He was the only one left to us,' he said, turning gently to the visitor. 'It is hard.'

The other coughed, and rising, walked slowly to the window. 'The firm wished me to convey their sincere sympathy with you in your great loss,' he said without looking round. 'I beg that you will understand I am only their servant and merely obeying orders.'

There was no reply; the old woman's face was white, her eyes staring, and her breath inaudible; and on the husband's face was a look such as his friend the sergeant might have carried into his first action.

'I was to say that Maw and Meggins disclaim all responsibility,' continued the other. 'They admit no liability at all, but in consideration of your son's services, they wish to present you with a certain sum as compensation.'

Mr White dropped his wife's hand, and rising to his feet, gazed with a look of horror at his visitor. His dry lips shaped the words, 'How much?'

'Two hundred pounds,' was the answer.

Unconscious of his wife's shriek, the old man smiled faintly, put out his hands like a sightless man, and dropped, a senseless heap, to the floor.

In the huge new cemetery, some miles distant, the old people buried their dead, and came back to a house steeped in shadow and silence. It was all over so quickly that at first they could hardly realize it, and remained in a state of expectation as though of something else to happen – something else which was to lighten this load, too heavy for old hearts to bear.

But the days passed, and expectation gave place to resignation – the hopeless resignation of the old, sometimes miscalled apathy. Sometimes, they hardly exchanged a word, for now they had nothing to talk about, and their days were long to weariness.

It was about a week after, that the old man, waking suddenly in the night, stretched out his hand and found himself alone. The room was in darkness, and the sound of subdued weeping came from the window. He raised himself in bed and listened.

'Come back,' he said, tenderly. 'You will be cold.'

'It is colder for my son,' said the old woman, and wept afresh.

The sound of her sobs died away on his ears. The bed was warm, and his eyes heavy with sleep. He dozed fitfully and then slept until a sudden wild cry from his wife awoke him with a start.

'*The paw!*' she cried wildly. 'The monkey's paw!'

He started up in alarm. 'Where? Where is it? What's the matter?'

She came stumbling across the room towards him. 'I want it,' she said quietly. 'You've not destroyed it?'

'It's in the parlour, on the bracket,' he replied, marvelling. 'Why?'

She cried and laughed together, and bending over, kissed his cheek.

'I only just thought of it,' she said, hysterically. 'Why didn't I think of it before? Why didn't *you* think of it?'

'Think of what?' he questioned.

'The other two wishes,' she replied, rapidly. 'We've only had one.'

'Was not that enough?' he demanded fiercely.

'No,' she cried triumphantly; 'we'll have one more. Go down and get it quickly, and wish our boy alive again.'

The man sat up in bed and flung the bedclothes from his quaking limbs. 'Good God, you are mad!' he cried aghast.

'Get it,' she panted, 'get it quickly, and wish – Oh, my boy, my boy!'

Her husband struck a match and lit the candle. 'Get back to bed,' he said unsteadily. 'You don't know what you are saying.'

'We had the first wish granted,' said the old woman, feverishly; 'why not the second?'

'A coincidence,' stammered the old man.

'Go and get it and wish,' cried his wife, quivering with excitement.

The old man turned and regarded her, and his voice shook. 'He has been dead ten days, and besides he – I would not tell you else, but – I could only recognize him by his clothing. If he was too terrible for you to see then, how now?'

'Bring him back,' cried the old woman, and dragged him towards the door. 'Do you think I fear the child I have nursed?'

He went down in the darkness, and felt his way to the parlour, and then to the mantelpiece. The talisman was in its place, and a horrible fear that the unspoken wish might bring his mutilated son before him ere he could escape from the room seized upon him, and he caught his breath as he found that he had lost the direction of the door. His brow cold with sweat, he felt his way round the table, and groped along the wall until he found himself in the small passage with the unwholesome thing in his hand.

Even his wife's face seemed changed as he entered the room. It was white and expectant, and to his fears seemed to have an unnatural look upon it. He was afraid of her.

'*Wish*,' she cried in a strong voice.

'It is foolish and wicked,' he faltered.

'*Wish!*' repeated his wife.

He raised his hand. 'I wish my son alive again.'

The talisman fell to the floor, and he regarded it fearfully. Then he sank trembling into a chair as the old woman, with burning eyes, walked to the window and raised the blind.

He sat until he was chilled with the cold, glancing occasionally at the figure of the old woman peering through the window. The candle-end, which had burned below the rim of the china candlestick, was throwing pulsating shadows on the ceiling and walls, until, with a flicker larger than the rest, it expired. The old man, with an unspeakable sense of relief at the failure of the talisman, crept back to his bed, and a minute or two afterwards the old woman came silently and apathetically beside him.

Neither spoke, but lay silently listening to the ticking of the clock. A stair creaked, and a squeaky mouse scurried noisily through the wall. The darkness was oppressive, and after lying for some time, screwing up his courage, he took the box of matches, and striking one, went downstairs for a candle.

At the foot of the stairs the match went out, and he paused to strike another; and at the same moment a knock, so quiet and stealthy as to be scarcely audible, sounded on the front door.

The matches fell from his hand and spilled in the passage. He stood motionless, his breath suspended until the knock was repeated. Then he turned and fled swiftly back to his room, and closed the door behind him. A third knock sounded through the house.

'*What's that?*' cried the old woman, starting up.

'A rat,' said the old man in shaking tones, '– a rat. It passed me on the stairs.'

His wife sat up in bed listening. A loud knock resounded through the house.

'It's Herbert!' she screamed. 'It's Herbert!'

She ran to the door, but her husband was before her, and catching her by the arm, held her tightly.

'What are you going to do?' he whispered hoarsely.

'It's my boy; it's Herbert!' she cried, struggling mechanically. 'I forgot it was two miles away. What are you holding me for? Let go. I must open the door.'

'For God's sake don't let it in,' cried the old man, trembling.

'You're afraid of your own son,' she cried, struggling. 'Let me go. I'm coming, Herbert; I'm coming.'

There was another knock, and another. The old woman with a sudden wrench broke free and ran from the room. Her husband followed to the landing, and called after her appealingly as she hurried downstairs. He heard the chain rattle back and the bottom bolt drawn slowly and stiffly from the socket. Then the old woman's voice, strained and panting.

'The bolt,' she cried loudly. 'Come down. I can't reach it.'

But her husband was on his hands and knees groping wildly on the floor in search of the paw. If he could only find it before the thing outside got in. A perfect fusillade of knocks reverberated through the house, and he heard the scraping of a chair as his wife put it down in the passage against the door. He heard the creaking of the bolt as it came slowly back, and at the same moment he found the monkey's paw, and frantically breathed his third and last wish.

The knocking ceased suddenly, although the echoes of it were still in the house. He heard the chair drawn back, and the door opened. A cold wind rushed up the staircase, and a long loud wail of disappointment and misery from his wife gave him the courage to run down to her side, and then to the gate beyond. The street lamp flickering opposite shone on a quiet and deserted road.

From *The Lady of the Barge* by W. W. Jacobs (Methuen & Co. Ltd, London).

MY GRANDFATHER,
HENDRY WATTY

Sir Arthur Quiller-Couch

'TIS the nicest miss in the world that I was born grandson of my own father's father, and not of another man altogether.

Hendry Watty was the name of my grandfather that might have been; and he always maintained that to all intents and purposes he *was* my grandfather, and made me call him so – 'twas such a narrow shave. I don't mind telling you about it. 'Tis a curious tale, too.

My grandfather, Hendry Watty, bet four gallons of eggy-hot that he would row out to the Shivering Grounds, all in the dead waste of the night, and haul a trammel there. To find the Shivering Grounds by night, you get the Gull Rock in a line with Tregamenna and pull out till you open the light on St Anthony's Point; but everybody gives the place a wide berth because Archelaus Rowett's lugger foundered there one time, with six hands on board; and they say that at night you can hear the drowned men hailing their names. But my grandfather was the boldest man in Port Loe, and said he didn't care. So one Christmas Eve by daylight he and his mates went out and tilled the trammel; and then they came back and spent the forepart of the evening over the eggy-hot, down to Oliver's tiddly-wink*, to keep my grandfather's spirits up and also to show that the bet was made in earnest.

'Twas past eleven o'clock when they left Oliver's and walked down to the cove to see my grandfather off. He has told me since that he didn't feel afraid at all, but very friendly in mind, especially toward William John Dunn, who was walking on his right hand. This puzzled him at the first, for as a rule he didn't think

*Beer-house.

much of William John Dunn. But now he shook hands with him several times, and just as he was stepping into the boat he says, 'You'll take care of Mary Polly while I'm away.' Mary Polly Polsue was my grandfather's sweetheart at that time. But why my grandfather should have spoken as if he was bound on a long voyage he never could tell; he used to set it down to fate.

'I will,' said William John Dunn; and then they gave a cheer and pushed my grandfather off, and he lit his pipe and away he rowed all in the dead waste of the night. He rowed and rowed, all in the dead waste of the night; and he got the Gull Rock in a line with Tregamenna windows; and still he was rowing, when to his great surprise he heard a voice calling:

'Hendry Watty! Hendry Watty!'

I told you my grandfather was the boldest man in Port Loe. But he dropped his two oars now, and made the five signs of Penitence. For who could it be calling him out here in the dead waste and middle of the night?

'Hendry Watty! Hendry Watty! Drop me a line.'

My grandfather kept his fishing-lines in a little skivet under the stern-sheets. But not a trace of bait had he on board. If he had, he was too much a-tremble to bait a hook.

'HENDRY WATTY! HENDRY WATTY! Drop me a line, or I'll know why.'

My poor grandfather had by this time picked up his oars again, and was rowing like mad to get quit of the neighbourhood, when something or somebody gave three knocks – thump, thump, thump! – on the bottom of the boat, just as you would knock on a door.

The third thump fetched Hendry Watty upright on his legs. He had no more heart for disobeying, but having bitten his pipe-stem in half by this time – his teeth chattered so – he baited his hook with the broken bit and flung it overboard, letting the line run out in the stern-notch. Not half-way had it run before he felt a long pull on it, like the sucking of a dog-fish.

'Hendry Watty! Hendry Watty! Pull me in.'

Hendry Watty pulled in hand over fist, and in came the lead sinker over the notch, and still the line was heavy; he pulled and he pulled, and next, all out of the dead waste of the night, came two white hands, like a washerwoman's, and gripped hold of the stern-board; and on the left of these two hands, was a silver ring, sunk very deep in the flesh. If this was bad, worse was the face that followed – and if this was bad for anybody, it was worse for my grandfather who had known Archelaus Rowett before he was drowned out on the Shivering Grounds, six years before.

Archelaus Rowett climbed in over the stern, pulled the hook with the bit of pipe-stem out of his cheek, sat down in the stern-sheets, shook a small crayfish out of his whiskers, and said very coolly: 'If you should come across my wife –'

That was all that my grandfather stayed to hear. At the sound of Archelaus's voice he fetched a yell, jumped clean over the side of the boat and swam for dear life. He swam and swam, till by the bit of the moon he saw the Gull Rock close ahead. There were lashin's of rats on the Gull Rock, as he knew; but he was a good deal surprised at the way they were behaving, for they sat in a row at the water's edge and fished, with their tails let down into the sea for fishing lines; and their eyes were like garnets burning as they looked at my grandfather over their shoulders.

'Hendry Watty! Hendry Watty! You can't land here – you're disturbing the pollack.'

'Bejimbers! I wouldn't do that for the world,' says my grandfather; so off he pushes and swims for the mainland. This was a long job, and it was as much as he could do to reach Kibberick beach, where he fell on his face and hands among the stones, and there lay, taking breath.

The breath was hardly back in his body before he heard footsteps, and along the beach came a woman, and passed close by to him. He lay very quiet, and as she came near he saw 'twas Sarah Rowett, that used to be Archelaus's wife, but had married another man since. She was knitting as she went by, and did not seem to notice my grandfather; but he heard her say to herself, 'The hour is come, and the man is come.'

He had scarcely begun to wonder over this when he spied a ball of worsted yarn beside him that Sarah had dropped. 'Twas the ball she was knitting from, and a line of worsted stretched after her along the beach. Hendry Watty picked up the ball and followed the thread on tiptoe. In less than a minute he came

near enough to watch what she was doing; and what she did
was worth watching. First she gathered wreck-wood and straw,
and struck flint over touchwood and teened a fire. Then she un-
ravelled her knitting; twisted her end of the yarn between finger
and thumb – like a cobbler twisting a wax-end – and cast the
end up towards the sky. It made Hendry Watty stare when the
thread, instead of falling back to the ground, remained hanging,
just as if 'twas fastened to something up above; but it made him
stare still more when Sarah Rowett began to climb up it, and
away up till nothing could be seen of her but her ankles dangling
out of the dead waste and middle of the night.

'HENDRY WATTY! HENDRY WATTY!'

It wasn't Sarah calling, but a voice far away out to sea.

'HENDRY WATTY! HENDRY WATTY! Send me a line!'

My grandfather was wondering what to do, when Sarah speaks
down very sharp to him, out of the dark:

'Hendry Watty! Where's the rocket apparatus? Can't you
hear the poor fellow asking for a line?'

'I do,' says my grandfather, who was beginning to lose his
temper; 'and do you think, ma'am, that I carry a Boxer's rocket
in my trousers pocket?'

'I think you have a ball of worsted in your hand,' says she.
'Throw it as far as you can.'

So my grandfather threw the ball out into the dead waste and
middle of the night. He didn't see where it pitched, or how far
it went.

'Right it is,' says the woman aloft. ''Tis easy seen you're a
hurler. But what shall us do for a cradle?* Hendry Watty!
Hendry Watty!'

'Ma'am to *you*,' said my grandfather.

'If you have the common feelings of a gentleman, I'll ask you
to turn your back; I'm going to take off my stocking.'

So my grandfather stared the other way very politely; and
when he was told he might look again, he saw she had tied the
stocking to the line and was running it out like a cradle into the
dead waste of the night.

'Hendry Watty! Hendry Watty! Look out below!'

* Breeches Buoy.

Before he could answer, plump! a man's leg came tumbling past his ear and scattered the ashes right and left.

'Hendry Watty! Hendry Watty! Look out below!'

This time 'twas a great white arm and hand, with a silver ring sunk tight in the flesh of the little finger.

'Hendry Watty! Hendry Watty! Warm them limbs!'

My grandfather picked them up and was warming them before the fire, when down came tumbling a great round head and bounced twice and lay in the firelight, staring up at him. And whose head was it but Archelaus Rowett's, that he'd run away from once already that night.

'Hendry Watty! Hendry Watty! Look out below!'

This time 'twas another leg, and my grandfather was just about to lay hands on it, when the woman called down:

'Hendry Watty! Catch it quick! It's my own leg I've thrown down by mistake.'

The leg struck the ground and bounced high, and Hendry Watty made a leap after it.

And I reckon it's asleep he must have been; for what he caught was not Mrs Rowett's leg, but the jib-boom of a deep-laden brigantine that was running him down in the dark. And as he sprang for it, his boat was crushed by the brigantine's fore-foot and went down under his very boot-soles. At the same time he let out a yell, and two or three of the crew ran forward and hoisted him up to the bowsprit and in on deck, safe and sound.

But the brigantine happened to be outward bound for the River Plate; so that, with one thing and another, 'twas eleven good months before my grandfather landed again at Port Loe. And who should be the first man he sees standing above the cove but William John Dunn.

'I'm very glad to see you,' says William John Dunn.

'Thank you kindly,' answers my grandfather; 'and how's Mary Polly?'

'Why, as for that,' he says, 'she took so much looking after, that I couldn't feel I was properly keeping her under my eye till I married her, last June month.'

'You was always one to over-do things,' said my grandfather.

'But if you was alive an' well, why didn' you drop us a line?'

Now when it came to talk about 'dropping a line,' my grandfather fairly lost his temper. So he struck William John Dunn on the nose – a thing he had never been known to do before – and William John Dunn hit him back, and the neighbours had to separate them. And next day, William John Dunn took out a summons against him. Well, the case was tried before the magistrates: and my grandfather told his story from the beginning, quite straightforward, just as I've told it to you. And the magistrates decided that, taking one thing and another, he'd had a great deal of provocation, and fined him five shillings. And there the matter ended. But now you know the reason why I'm William John Dunn's grandson instead of Hendry Watty's.

From *The Wandering Heath* by Sir Arthur Quiller-Couch (J. M. Dent & Sons Ltd, London).

A SCHOOL STORY

M. R. James

Two men in a smoking room were talking of their private-school days. 'At *our* school,' said A., 'we had a ghost's footprints on the staircase. What was it like? Oh, very unconvincing. Just the shape of a shoe, with a square toe, if I remember right. The staircase was a stone one. I never heard any story about the thing. That seems odd, when you come to think of it. Why didn't somebody invent one, I wonder?'

'You never can tell with little boys. They have a mythology of their own. There's a subject for you, by the way – "The Folk-lore of the Private Schools".'

'Yes; the crop is rather scanty, though. I imagine, if you were to investigate the cycle of ghost stories, for instance, which the boys at private schools tell each other, they would all turn out to be highly-compressed versions of stories out of books.'

'Nowadays, the *Strand* and *Pearson's*, and so on, would be extensively drawn upon.'

'No doubt; they weren't born or thought of in *my* time. Let's see. I wonder if I can remember the staple ones that I was told. First, there was the house with a room in which a series of people insisted on passing a night; and each of them in the morning was found kneeling in a corner, and had just time to say, "I've seen it", and died.'

'Wasn't that the house in Berkeley Square?'

'I dare say it was. Then there was the man who heard a noise in the passage at night, opened his door and saw someone crawling towards him on all fours with his eye hanging out on his cheek. There was besides, let me think – Yes! the room where a man was found dead in bed with a horseshoe mark on his forehead, and the floor under the bed was covered with marks of horseshoes also; I don't know why. Also there was the lady who,

on locking her bedroom door in a strange house, heard a thin
voice among the bed-curtains say, "Now we're shut in for the
night." None of those had any explanation or sequel. I wonder
if they go on still, those stories.'

'Oh, likely enough – with additions from the magazines, as I
said. You never heard, did you, of a real ghost at a private school?
I thought not; nobody has that ever I came across.'

'From the way in which you said that, I gather, *you* have.'

'I really don't know; but this is what was in my mind. It happened at my private school, thirty odd years ago, and I haven't
any explanation of it.

'The school I mean was near London. It was established in a
large and fairly old house – a great white building with very
fine grounds about it; there were large cedars in the garden, as
there are in so many of the older gardens in the Thames valley,
and ancient elms in the three or four fields which we used for our
games. I think probably it was quite an attractive place, but boys
seldom allow that their schools possess any tolerable features.

'I came to the school in a September, soon after the year 1870;
and among the boys who arrived on the same day was one whom
I took to; a Highland boy, whom I will call McLeod. I needn't
spend time in describing him: the main thing is that I got to
know him very well. He was not an exceptional boy in any way
– not particularly good at books or games – but he suited me.

'The school was a large one: there must have been from 120
to 130 boys there as a rule, and so a considerable staff of masters
was required, and there were frequent changes among them.

'One term – perhaps it was my third or fourth – a new master
made his appearance. His name was Sampson. He was a tallish,
stoutish, pale, blackbearded man. I think we liked him: he had
travelled a good deal, and had stories which amused us on our
school walks, so that there was some competition among us to
get within earshot of him. I remember too – dear me, I have
hardly thought of it since then! – that he had a charm on his
watch-chain that attracted my attention one day and he let me
examine it. It was, I now suppose, a gold Byzantine coin; there
was an effigy of some absurd emperor on one side; the other side
had been worked practically smooth, and he had cut on it – rather

barbarously – his own initials G.W.S. and a date, 24th July, 1865. Yes, I can see it now. He told me he had picked it up in Constantinople; it was about the size of a florin, perhaps rather smaller.

'Well, the first odd thing that happened was this. Sampson was doing Latin grammar with us. One of his favourite methods – perhaps it is rather a good one – was to make us construct sentences out of our own heads to illustrate the rules he was trying to make us learn. Of course that is a thing which gives a silly boy a chance of being impertinent: there are lots of school stories in which that happens – or anyhow, there might be. But Sampson was too good a disciplinarian for us to think of trying that on with him. Now, on this occasion he was telling us how to express *remembering* in Latin; and he ordered us each to make a sentence bringing in the verb *memini*, "I remember". Well, most of us made up some ordinary sentence such as "I remember my father", or "He remembers his book", or something equally uninteresting: and I dare say a good many put down *memino librum meum* and so forth: but the boy I mentioned – McLeod – was evidently thinking of something more elaborate than that. The rest of us wanted to have our sentences passed, and get on to something else, so some kicked him under the desk and I, who was next to him, poked him and whispered to him to look sharp. But he didn't seem to attend. I looked at his paper and saw he had put down nothing at all. So I jogged him again harder than before and upbraided him sharply for keeping us all waiting. That did have some effect. He started and seemed to wake up, and then very quickly he scribbled about a couple of lines on his paper, and showed it up with the rest. As it was the last, or nearly the last, to come in, and as Sampson had a good deal to say to the boys who had written *"memini-scimus patri meo"* and the rest of it, it turned out that the clock struck twelve before he had got to McLeod, and McLeod had to wait afterwards to have his sentence corrected. There was nothing much going on outside when I got out, so I waited for him to come. He came very slowly when he did arrive, and I guessed there had been some sort of trouble. "Well," I said, "what did you get?" "Oh, I don't know," said McLeod, "nothing much;

but I think Sampson's rather sick with me." "Why, did you show him up some rot?" "No fear," he said. "It was all right as far as I could see; it was like this: *Memento* – that's right enough for remember, and it takes a genitive – *memento putei inter quatuor taxos.*" "What silly rot!" I said. "What made you shove that down? What does it mean?" "That's the funny part," said McLeod, "I'm not quite sure what it does mean. All I know is, it just came into my head and I corked it down. I know what I *think* it means, because just before I wrote it down I had a sort of picture of it in my head: I believe it means "Remember the well among the four – what are those dark sort of trees that have red berries on them?" "Mountain ashes, I s'pose you mean." "I never heard of them," said McLeod; "no, *i'll* tell you – yews." "Well, and what did Sampson say?" "Why, he was jolly odd about it. When he read it he got up and went to the mantelpiece and stopped quite a long time without saying anything, with his back to me. And then he said, without turning round, and rather quiet, 'What do you suppose that means?' I told him what I thought, only I couldn't remember the name of the silly tree: and then he wanted to know why I put it down, and I had to say something or other. And after that he left off talking about it, and asked me how long I'd been here, and where my people lived, and things like that: and then I came away: but he wasn't looking a bit well."

'I don't remember any more that was said by either of us about this. Next day McLeod took to his bed with a chill or something of the kind, and it was a week or more before he was in school again. And as much as a month went by without anything happening that was noticeable. Whether or not Mr Sampson was really startled, as Mcleod had thought, he did not show it. I am pretty sure, of course, now, that there was something very curious in his past history, but I'm not going to pretend that we boys were sharp enough to guess any such thing.

'There was one other incident of the same kind as the last which I told you. Several times since that day we had had to make up examples in school to illustrate different rules, but there had never been any row except when we did them wrong. At last there came a day when we were going through those dis-

mal things which people call Conditional Sentences, and we
were told to make a conditional sentence, expressing a future
consequence. We did it, right or wrong, and showed up our bits
of paper, and Sampson began looking through them. All at once
he got up, made some odd sort of noise in his throat, and rushed
out by a door that was just by his desk. We sat there for a minute
or two, and then – I suppose it was incorrect – but we went up,
I and one or two others, to look at the papers on his desk. Of
course I thought someone must have put down some nonsense
or other, and Sampson had gone off to report him. All the same,
I noticed that he hadn't taken any of the papers with him when
he ran out. Well, the top paper on the desk was written in red
ink – which no one used – and it wasn't in anyone's hand who
was in the class. They all looked at it – McLeod and all – and
took their dying oaths that it wasn't theirs. Then I thought of
counting the bits of paper. And of this, I made quite certain:
that there were seventeen bits of paper on the desk, and sixteen
boys in the form. Well, I bagged the extra paper and kept it,
and I believe I have it now. And now you will want to know
what was written on it. It was simple enough and harmless
enough I should have said.

' "*Si tu non veneris ad me, ego veniam ad te*," which means,
I suppose, "If you don't come to me, i'll come to you." '

'Could you show me the paper?' interrupted the listener.

'Yes I could: but there's another odd thing about it. That same
afternoon I took it out of my locker – I knew for certain it was
the same bit, for I made a finger-mark on it – and no single trace
of writing of any kind was there on it. I kept it, as I said, and
since that time I have tried various experiments to see whether
sympathetic ink had been used, but absolutely without result.

'So much for that. After about half an hour Sampson looked
in again; said he felt very unwell, and told us we might go. He
came rather gingerly to his desk, and gave just one look at the
uppermost paper; and I suppose he thought he must have been
dreaming; anyhow, he asked no questions.

'That day was a half-holiday, and next day, Sampson was in
school again, much as usual. That night the third and last incident in my story happened.

'We – McLeod and I – slept in a dormitory at right angles to the main building. Sampson slept in the main building on the first floor. There was a very bright full moon. At an hour which I can't tell exactly, but some time between one and two, I was woken up by somebody shaking me. It was McLeod; and a nice state of mind he seemed to be in. "Come," he said, – "come! there's a burglar getting in through Sampson's window." As soon as I could speak, I said, "Well, why not call out and wake everyone up?" "No, no," he said. "I'm not sure who it is; don't make a row; come and look." Naturally I came and looked, and naturally there was no one there. I was cross enough, and should have called McLeod plenty of names; only – I couldn't tell why – it seemed to me that there *was* something wrong – something that made me very glad I wasn't alone to face it. We were still at the window looking out, and as soon as I could, I asked him what he had heard or seen. "I didn't *hear* anything at all," he said, "but about five minutes before I woke you, I found myself looking out of this window here, and there was a man sitting or kneeling on Sampson's window-sill, and looking in, and I thought he was beckoning." "What sort of man?" McLeod wriggled. "I don't know," he said, "but I can tell you one thing – he was beastly thin; and he looked as if he was wet all over; and," he said, looking round and whispering as if he hardly liked to hear himself, "I'm not at all sure that he was alive."

'We went on talking in whispers some time longer, and eventually crept back to bed. No one else in the room woke or stirred the whole time. I believe we did sleep a bit afterwards, but we were very cheap next day.

'And next day Mr Sampson was gone; not to be found; and I believe no trace of him has ever come to light since. In thinking it over, one of the oddest things about it has seemed to me to be the fact that neither McLeod nor I ever mentioned what we had seen to any third person whatever. Of course no questions were asked on the subject, and if they had been, I am inclined to believe that we could not have made any answer; we seemed unable to speak about it.

'That is my story,' said the narrator. 'The only approach to a ghost story connected with a school that I know, but still, I think, an approach to such a thing.'

The sequel to this may perhaps be reckoned highly conventional; but a sequel there is, and so it must be produced. There had been more than one listener to the story, and, in the latter part of that same year, or of the next, one such listener was staying at a country house in Ireland.

One evening his host was turning over a drawer full of odds and ends in the smoking-room. Suddenly he put his hand upon a little box. 'Now,' he said, 'you know about old things; tell me what that is.' My friend opened the little box, and found in it a thin gold chain with an object attached to it. He glanced at the object and then took off his spectacles to examine it more narrowly. 'What's the history of this?' he asked. 'Odd enough,' was the answer. 'You know the yew thicket in the shrubbery; well, a year or two back we were cleaning out the old well that used to be in the clearing there, and what do you suppose we found?'

'Is it possible that you found a body?' said the visitor, with an odd feeling of nervousness.

'We did that; but what's more, in every sense of the word, we found two.'

'Good Heavens! Two? Was there anything to show how they got there? Was this thing found with them?'

'It was. Amongst the rags of the clothes that were on one of the bodies. A bad business, whatever the story of it may have been. One body had the arms tight around the other. They must have been there thirty years or more – long enough before we came to this place. You may judge we filled the well up fast enough. Do you make anything of what's cut on that gold coin you have there?'

'I think I can,' said my friend, holding it to the light (but he read it without much difficulty); it seems to be G.W.S., 24th July 1865.'

From *Collected Ghost Stories* by M. R. James (Edward Arnold (Publishers) Ltd, London).

THE RED CANE

E. F. Bozman

HERS was one of those timeless faces filled with the beauty of a hard-working and independent life and an unselfish disposition. Or so I thought when I caught sight of her under one of the brilliant neon lights in the street leading from the factory area to the deserted and wooded common which separates the busy industrial garden city from the open countryside.

It was half-past five on a misty December evening and cars, scooters and buses were streaming from the factories towards the residential areas of the city. I was in the district on business after many years of absence and had planned, as soon as the factories closed, to visit an old and valued friend whom I had not seen for thirty years. The shortest way to her cottage would be by one of the numerous footpaths across the common, which was a surprisingly large area, preserved more or less in its natural state and protected against building development by local legislation; its vegetation consisted of stunted woodlands, interspersed by glades, thorn bushes, stretches of tussocky grass and brambles, and in course of time the birds had selected it for themselves as a sanctuary. Apart from the birds the common was little frequented in winter, but once spring and summer came round the swimming pool there would ring with shouts and splashes, and the houses in the roads round the edge opened the gates at the ends of their gardens and released their children and dogs to the delights of freedom.

I followed the road from the factory for a few hundred yards and then turned off by the footpath I remembered. For the rest of the way, as I knew, there would be no lights except for occasional gleams through the trees and hedges from the lighted windows of houses in the distance. The pathway was not difficult to identify because, although overgrown in places, it had been artificially restored, in parts by asphalt, wherever the grass or the mud threatened seriously to take over.

To my surprise, when I had left the road behind me, I found that I was not alone in choosing this particular way, and turning round I recognized, in the gathering darkness, the timeless face I had previously glimpsed.

'A wintry evening,' I said and paused to allow the shadowy figure to catch up with me.

'Yes,' came the reply, and the figure of a small, sturdy-looking woman came alongside me; 'It's going to be a pitch-black night.'

'May I accompany you across the common? It's very lonely and it might be uncomfortable for a woman.'

'By all means, if you like. But don't worry about me. I'm used to it.'

'You can't be too careful nowadays. There are some strange people about, as you must know from the papers.'

'I've come alone this way, at all times of day and night, and no one has ever molested me – or if they had tried they've got as good as they gave. Of course, I always carry a stick.'

Despite the darkness I could see her ebony-looking cane which I realized could be a very effective weapon of defence if skilfully used.

'Well, I have no doubt you know how to look after yourself.'

'I take them by surprise, you see, before any move has been made, and I know the darkest corners so well that I can defend myself against anyone but a ghost.'

'Well,' I laughed, 'I don't believe in ghosts, but for the sake of our common humanity let us see each other as far as the road!'

Just then the figure of a man materialized from a thicket, gave one glance at my companion and seeing that she was accompanied hurried on down the path.

'There you are,' I said, 'isn't it lucky I'm with you?'

'I suppose I should be truly grateful,' she said, 'but actually he is my next-door neighbour. He moved in a year before me and his grass has only just been properly laid.'

'What?' I said.

'I have lived a long time, my friend, and I have learned to trust in God and my own resources all my life. I can tell you that, believe it or not, nine people out of ten are thoroughly good.'

'And the tenth?'

'The tenth is either a saint – or a sinner.'

'And if you happen to meet the sinner? What do you do then?'

'Christ came into the world to save that sinner. I always make a point of telling him so.'

We walked on for a few minutes in silence. At this point the narrow asphalt path wound its way across a stream. It was the quintessence of rural peace, rendered all the more striking by the dank and misty evening. Listening to the gentle tinkling of the water, so black as to be almost invisible, it was difficult to realize that there was a city nearby throbbing with life and vitality where thousands of souls, with their private ambitions and miseries, collaborated daily to produce heat and light and food and clothes and books, and to protect and preserve the waking and sleeping hours of the community.

From now on the path wound its way under the overhanging branches of low trees and saplings, dripping from the deposit of fine rain and mist. My companion had fallen silent and I turned to look at her in order to reassure myself that all was well. Her head was averted and I could only see that her movements were small and quiet.

'Don't you feel lonely,' I asked, 'coming all this way in the mornings and evenings, summer and winter?'

'Lonely? Why should I feel lonely? The place is full of my friends and I am never alone in my mind for a minute of the day or night. I never have been all my life. Just think to yourself that great gangs of young men are building an enormous double-track motorway over there on the other side of the town; and that two thousand years ago Roman soldiers were tramping the Icknield Way to build the camp on the top of the hill. Probably you know it?'

'Oh, yes. Up near the cemetery.'

'Yes, that's quite right.'

We came to a crossing footpath where she stopped.

'My way is to the left now. I expect you're going straight on to where the path joins the road.'

'Yes. How did you know?'

She ignored my question and said, 'You won't be lonely, now, or frightened in the dark, will you? You haven't far to go now.'

I laughed in astonishment. 'What on earth have I to be frightened about?'

'Well, you never know. I'll tell you what – I'll lend you my stick so that you can ward off anyone – except a ghost.'

'No! I couldn't possibly accept it!'

But she insisted. 'You can return it next time we meet. And remember this, that you need never feel lonely, for one moment. You only have to think.' She hesitated while she seemed to be probing in her mind. 'For example, think that you will never forget this little walk we have had together! Because you never will! Never. Will you?' And she gave a little laugh.

Before I could protest further she had turned to the left and disappeared in the darkness. 'Goodnight,' I called after her. There was no answer that I could hear and I turned my attention to the visit I was about to make. By now it was nearly pitch dark and I was glad of my stick to push brambles out of my way in the last hundred yards of path which curved uphill to the road. Once on the road there would be a few street-lamps, if I remembered right, and the cottage I was looking for would be a little way along on the opposite side. Yes, there it was. A light was shining through the curtains of the front window, reminding me of the oil-lamp of thirty years ago. There was the flagged path leading unsteadily between untidy beds – they would be a blaze of flowers in the spring and summer – to the front door.

And behind that door, in her sitting room where the fire always burned in a welcoming way as if it were only too anxious to boil a kettle, would be sitting the hard-headed little lady I was coming to see. She would probably be stooped over her much-loved embroidery and would be sure to remember me – I was once her lodger – even though we would both have changed. I tried to recall her appearance and the tones of her voice, the way thirty years ago she used to say, 'Don't get so worried, young man,' and I remembered that before I left the neighbourhood I had asked what she would like for a souvenir. She said that her tastes were unconventional, so much so that many of her numerous friends told her she was a witch.

'What about a nice broomstick?' I had suggested. That made her laugh and then she said that, better than anything else, she would like a red cane without a handle. So I bought her one and gave it to her and I shall never forget the smile of beauty on her timeless face ...

What did I say? Timeless face? A shiver passed over me. Was it a shiver of fear, or loneliness?

I grasped my stick and rapped on the front door with it.

The door was opened by a stranger.

'Is Kate at home?' I asked, then faltered at the expression on his face. 'I have come down specially to see her,' I went on hurriedly, 'from the other side of London ...' My voice trailed away to nothingness.

'Haven't you heard?' he said, in a matter of fact voice. 'She died over a year ago and we bought this cottage.'

The opening of the door had released a pool of light on the path and as I turned to go I caught sight of the stick I was carrying in my hand. It was red.

'God rest her soul,' I said.

A DIAGNOSIS OF DEATH

Ambrose Bierce

'I AM not so superstitious as some of you physicians – men of science, as you are pleased to be called,' said Hawver, replying to an accusation that had not been made. 'Some of you – only a few, I confess – believe in the immortality of the soul, and in apparitions which you have not the honesty to call ghosts. I go no further than a conviction that the living are sometimes seen where they are not, but have been – where they have lived so long, perhaps so intensely, as to have left their impression on everything about them. I know, indeed, that one's environment may be so affected by one's personality as to yield, long afterward, an image of one's self to the eyes of another. Doubtless the impressing personality has to be the right kind of personality as the perceiving eyes have to be the right kind of eyes – mine, for example.'

'Yes, the right kind of eyes, conveying sensations to the wrong kind of brain,' said Dr Frayley, smiling.

'Thank you; one likes to have an expectation gratified; that is about the reply that I supposed you would have the civility to make.'

'Pardon me. But you say that you know. That is a good deal to say, don't you think? Perhaps you will not mind the trouble of saying how you learned.'

'You will call it an hallucination,' Hawver said, 'but that does not matter.' And he told the story.

'Last summer I went, as you know, to pass the hot weather term in the town of Meridian. The relative at whose house I had intended to stay was ill, so I sought other quarters. After some difficulty I succeeded in renting a vacant dwelling that had been occupied by an eccentric doctor of the name of Mannering, who had gone away years before, no one knew where, not even his agent. He had built the house himself and had lived in it with an old servant for about ten years. His practice, never very extensive, had after a few years been given up entirely. Not only so, but he had withdrawn himself almost altogether from social life and become a recluse. I was told by the village doctor, about the only person with whom he held any relations, that during his retirement he had devoted himself to a single line of study, the result of which he had expounded in a book that did not commend itself to the approval of his professional brethren, who, indeed, considered him not entirely sane. I have not seen the book and cannot now recall the title of it, but I am told that it expounded a rather startling theory. He held that it was possible in the case of many a person in good health to forecast his death with precision, several months in advance of the event. The limit, I think, was eighteen months. There were local tales of his having exerted powers of prognosis, or perhaps you would say diagnosis; and it was said that in every instance the person whose friends he had warned had died suddenly at the appointed time, and from no assignable cause. All this, however, had nothing to do with what I have to tell; I thought it might amuse a physician.

'The house was furnished, just as he had lived in it. It was a rather gloomy dwelling for one who was neither a recluse nor a student, and I think it gave something of its character to me – perhaps some of its former occupant's character; for always I felt in it a certain melancholy that was not in my natural disposition, nor, I think, due to loneliness. I had no servants that slept in the house, but I have always been, as you know, rather fond of my own society, being much addicted to reading, though little to study. Whatever was the cause, the effect was dejection and a sense of impending evil; this was especially so in Dr Mannering's study, although that room was the lightest and most airy in the house. The doctor's life-size portrait in oil hung in that room, and seemed completely to dominate it. There was nothing unusual in the picture; the man was evidently rather good-looking, about fifty years old, with iron-grey hair, a smooth-shaven face and dark, serious eyes. Something in the picture always drew and held my attention. The man's appearance became familiar to me, and rather "haunted" me.

'One evening I was passing through this room to my bedroom, with a lamp – there is no gas in Meridan. I stopped as usual before the portrait, which seemed in the lamplight to have a new expression, not easily named, but distinctly uncanny. It interested but did not disturb me. I moved the lamp from one side to the other and observed the effects of the altered light. While so engaged I felt an impulse to turn round. As I did so I saw a man moving across the room directly towards me! As soon as he came near enough for the lamplight to illuminate the face I saw that it was Dr Mannering himself; it was as if the portrait were walking!

'"I beg your pardon," I said, somewhat coldly, "but if you knocked I did not hear."

'He passed me, within an arm's length, lifted his right forefinger, as in warning, and without a word went on out of the room, though I observed his exit no more than I had observed his entrance.

'Of course, I need not tell you that this was what you will call an hallucination and I call an apparition. That room had only two doors, of which one was locked; the other led into a bedroom, from which there was no exit. My feeling on realizing this is not an important part of the incident.

'Doubtless this seems to you a very commonplace "ghost story" – one constructed on the regular lines laid down by the old masters of the art. If that were so I should not have related it, even if it were true. The man was not dead; I met him today in Union Street. He passed me in a crowd.'

Hawver had finished his story and both men were silent. Dr Frayley absently drummed on the table with his fingers.

'Did he say anything today?' he asked – 'anything from which you inferred that he was not dead?'

Hawver stared and did not reply.

'Perhaps,' continued Frayley, 'he made a sign, a gesture – lifted a finger, as in warning. It's a trick he had – a habit when saying something serious – announcing the result of a diagnosis, for example.'

'Yes, he did – just as his apparition had done. But, good God! did you ever know him?'

Hawver was apparently growing nervous.

'I knew him. I have read his book, as will every physician some day. It is one of the most striking and important of the century's contributions to medical science. Yes, I knew him; I attended him in an illness three years ago. He died.'

Hawver sprang from his chair, manifestly disturbed. He strode forward and back across the room; then approached his friend, and in a voice not altogether steady, said: 'Doctor, have you anything to say to me – as a physician?'

'No, Hawver; you are the healthiest man I ever knew. As a friend I advise you to go to your room. You play the violin like an angel. Play it; play something light and lively. Get this cursed bad business off your mind.'

The next day Hawver was found dead in his room, the violin at his neck, the bow upon the strings, his music open before him at Chopin's funeral march.

From *Can Such Things Be?* by Ambrose Bierce (Jonathan Cape Ltd, London, and Citadel Press, New York).

BAD COMPANY

Walter de la Mare

It is very seldom that one encounters what would appear to be sheer unadulterated evil in a human face; an evil, I mean, active, deliberate, deadly, dangerous. Folly, heedlessness, vanity, pride, craft, meanness, stupidity – yes. But even Iagos in this world are few, and devilry is as rare as witchcraft.

One winter's evening some little time ago, bound on a visit to a friend in London, I found myself on the platform of one of its many subterranean railway stations. It is an ordeal that one may undergo as seldom as one can. The glare and glitter, the noise, the very air one breathes affect nerves and spirits. One expects vaguely strange meetings in such surroundings. On this occasion, the expectation was justified. The mind is at times more attentive than the eye. Already tired, and troubled with personal cares and problems, which a little wisdom and enterprise should have refused to entertain, I had seated myself on one of the low, wooden benches to the left of the entrance to the platform, when, for no conscious reason, I was prompted to turn my head in the direction of a fellow traveller, seated across the gangway on the fellow to my bench some few yards away.

What was wrong with him? He was enveloped in a loose cape or cloak, sombre and motionless. He appeared to be wholly unaware of my abrupt scrutiny. And yet, I doubt it; for the next moment, although the door of the nearest coach gaped immediately opposite him, he had shuffled into the compartment I had entered myself, and now in its corner, confronted me, all but knee to knee. I could have touched him with my hand. We had, too, come at once into an even more intimate contact than that of touch. Our eyes – his own fixed in a dwelling and lethargic stare – had instantly met, and no less rapidly had uncharitably recoiled, not only in misgiving, but in something little short of disgust. The effect resembled that of an acid on milk, and for the time being cast my thoughts into confusion. Yet that one glance had taken him in.

He was old – over seventy. A wide-brimmed rusty and dusty black hat concealed his head – a head fringed with wisps of hair, lank and paper-grey. His loose, jaded cheeks were of the colour of putty; the thin lips above the wide unshaven and dimpled chin showing scarcely a trace of red. The cloak suspended from his shoulders mantled him to his shins. One knuckled, cadaverous, mittened hand clasped a thick ash stick, its handle black and polished with long usage. The only sign of life in his countenance was secreted in his eyes – fixed on mine – hazed and dully glistening, as a snail in winter is fixed to a wall. There was a dull deliberate challenge in them, and as I fancied, something more than that. They suggested that he had been in wait for me; that for him it was almost 'well met!'

For minutes together I endeavoured to accept their challenge, to make sure. Yet I realized, fascinated the while, that he was well aware of the futility of this attempt, as a snake is of the restless, fated bird in the branches above its head.

Such a statement, I am aware, must appear wildly exaggerated, but I can only record my impression. It was already latish – much later than I had intended. The passengers came and went, and, whether intentionally or not, none consented to occupy the seat vacant beside him. I fixed my eyes on an advertisement – that of a Friendly Society I remember! – immediately above his head, with the intention of watching him in the field of an eye that I could not persuade to meet his own in full focus again.

He had instantly detected this ingenious device. By a fraction of an inch he had shifted his grasp upon his stick. So intolerable, at length, became the physical – psychical – effect of his presence on me that I determined to leave the train at the next station, and there to await the next. And at this precise moment, I was conscious that he had not only withdrawn his eyes, but closed them.

I was not so easily to free myself of his company. A glance over my shoulder as, after leaving the train, I turned towards the

lift, showed him hastily groping his way out of the carriage. The
metal gate clanged. The lift slid upwards and, such is the con-
trariness of human nature, a faint disappointment followed. One
may, for example, be appalled and yet engrossed in reading an
account of some act of infamous cruelty.

Concealing myself as best I could at the book-stall, I awaited
the next lift-load. Its few passengers having dispersed, he himself followed. In spite of age and infirmity, he had, then, ascended
alone the spiral staircase. Glancing, it appeared, neither to
right nor left, he passed rapidly through the barrier. And yet –
had he not seen me?

The ticket collector raised his head, opened his mouth,
watched his retreating figure, but made no attempt to retrieve
his. It was dark now – the dark of London. In my absence under-
ground, minute frozen pellets of snow had fallen, whitening the
streets and lulling the sound of the traffic. On emerging into the
street, he turned in the direction of the next station – my own.
Yet again – had he, or had he not, been aware that he was being
watched? However that might be, my journey lay his way, and
that way my feet directed me; although I was already later than
I had intended. I followed him, led on, no doubt, in part – merely
by the effect he had had on me. Some twenty or thirty yards
ahead, his dark shapelessness showed – distinct against the
whitening pavement.

The waters of the Thames, I was aware, lay on my left. A
muffled blast from the siren of a tug announced its presence.
Keeping my distance, I followed him on. One lamp-post – two
– three. At that, he seemed to pause for a moment, as if to listen,
momentarily glanced back (as I fancied) and vanished.

When I came up with it, I found that this third lamp-post
vaguely illuminated the mouth of a narrow, lightless alley between highish walls. It led me, after a while, into another alley,
yet dingier. The wall on the left of this was evidently that of a
large garden; on the right came a row of nondescript houses,
looming up in their neglect against a starless sky.

The first of these houses *appeared* to be occupied. The next
two were vacant. Dingy curtains, soot-grey against their snowy
window-sills, hung over the next. A litter of paper and refuse –

abandoned by the last long gust of wind that must have come whistling round the nearer angle of the house – lay under the broken flight of steps to a mid-Victorian porch. The small snow clinging to the bricks and to the worn and weathered cement of the wall only added to its gaunt lifelessness.

In the faint hope of other company coming my way, and vowing that I would follow no further than to the outlet of yet another pitch-black and uninviting alley or court – which might indeed prove a dead end – I turned into it. It was then that I observed, in the rays of the lamp over my head, that in spite of the fineness of the snow and the brief time that had elapsed, there seemed to be no trace on its surface of recent footsteps.

A faintly thudding echo accompanied me on my way. I have found it very useful – in the country – always to carry a small electric torch in my greatcoat pocket; but for the time being I refrained from using it. This alley proved not to be blind. Beyond a patch of waste ground, a nebulous, leaden-grey vacancy marked a loop here of the Thames – I decided to go no further; and then perceived a garden gate in the wall to my right. It was ajar, but could not long have been so because no more than an instant's flash of my torch showed marks in the snow of its recent shifting. And yet there was little wind. On the other hand, here was the open river, just a breath of a breeze across its surface might account for this. The cracked and blistered paint was shimmering with a thin coat of rime – of hoar-frost, and as if a finger had but just now scrawled it there, a clumsy arrow showed, its 'V' pointing inward. A tramp, an errand-boy, mere accident might have accounted for this. It may indeed have been a mark made some time before on the paint.

I paused in an absurd debate with myself, chiefly I think because I felt some little alarm at the thought of what might follow; yet led on also by the conviction that I had been intended, decoyed to follow. I pushed the gate a little wider open, peered in, and made my way up a woody path beneath ragged unpruned and leafless fruit trees towards the house. The snow's own light revealed a ramshackle flight of steps up to a poor, frenchified sort of canopy above french windows, one-half of their glazed doors ajar. I ascended, and peered into the intense gloom beyond it. And thus and then prepared to retrace my steps as quickly as possible, I called (in tones as near those of a London policeman as I could manage): 'Hello there! Is anything wrong? Is anyone wanted?' After all, I could at least explain to my fellow-passenger if he appeared that I found both his gate and his window open; and the house was hardly pleasantly situated.

No answer was returned to me. In doubt and disquietude, but with a conviction that all was not well, I flashed my torch over the walls and furniture of the room and its heavily framed pictures. How could anything be 'well' – with unseen company such as this besieging one's senses! Ease and pleasant companionship, the room may once have been capable of giving; in its dirt, cold and neglect, it showed nothing of that now. I crossed it, paused again in the passage beyond it, and listened. I then entered the room beyond that. Venetian blinds, many of the slats of which had outworn their webbing, and heavy, crimson chenille side-curtains concealed its windows.

The ashes of a fire showed beyond rusty bars of the grate under a black marble mantelpiece. An oil lamp on the table, with a green shade, exuded a stink of paraffin; beyond was a table littered with books and papers, and an overturned chair. There I could see the bent-up old legs, perceptibly lean beneath the trousers, of the occupant of the room. In no doubt of whose remains these were, I drew near, and with bared teeth and icy, trembling fingers, drew back the fold of the cloak that lay over the face. Death has a strange sorcery. A shuddering revulsion of feeling took possession of me. This cold, once genteel, hideous, malignant room – and this!

The skin of the blue loose cheek was drawn tightly over the bone; the mouth lay a little open, showing the dislodged false teeth beneath; and the dull unspeculative eyes stared out from beneath lowered lids towards the black mouth of the chimney above the fireplace. Vileness and iniquity had left their marks on the lifeless features, and yet it was rather with compassion than with horror and disgust that I stood regarding them. What desolate solitude, what misery must this old man, abandoned to himself, have experienced during the last years of his life; encountering nothing but enmity and the apprehension of his fellow creatures. I am not intending to excuse or even commiserate what I cannot understand, but the almost complete absence of any goodness in the human spirit cannot but condemn the heart to an appalling isolation. Had he been murdered or, had he come to a violent but natural end? In either case, horror and terror must have supervened.

That I had been enticed, deliberately led on, to this discovery I hadn't the least doubt, extravagant though this, too, may seem. Why? What for?

I could not bring myself to attempt to light the lamp. Besides, in that last vigil, it must have burnt itself out. My torch revealed a stub of candle on the mantelpiece. I lit that. He seemed to have been engaged in writing when the enemy of us all had approached him in silence and had struck him down.

A long and unsealed envelope lay on the table. I drew out the contents – a letter and a Will, which had been witnessed some few weeks before, apparently by a tradesman's boy and, possibly, by some derelict charwoman, Eliza Hinks. I knew enough about such things to be sure that the Will was valid and complete. This old man had been evidently more than fairly rich in this world's goods, and reluctant to surrender them. The letter was addressed to his two sisters: 'To my two Sisters, Amelia and Maude.' Standing there in the cold and the silence, and utterly alone – for, if any occupant of the other world had decoyed me there, there was not the faintest hint in consciousness that he or his influence was any longer present with me – I read the vilest letter that has ever come my way. Even in print. It stated that he knew the circumstances of these two remaining relatives – that he was well aware of their poverty and physical conditions. One of them, it seemed to me, was afflicted with cancer. He then proceeded to explain that, although they should by the intention of their mother have had a due share in her property and in the money she had left, it rejoiced him to think that his withholding of this knowledge must continually have added to their wretchedness. Why he so hated them was only vaguely suggested.

The Will he had enclosed with the letter left all that he died possessed of to – of all human establishments that need it least

– the authorities of Scotland Yard. It was to be devoted, it ran, to the detection of such evil doers as are ignorant or imbecile enough to leave their misdemeanours and crimes detectable.

It is said that confession is good for the soul. Well then, as publicly as possible, I take this opportunity of announcing that, there and then, I made a little heap of envelope, letter and Will on the hearth and put a match to them. When every vestige of the paper had been consumed, I stamped the ashes down. I had touched nothing else. I would leave the vile, jaded, forsaken house to reveal its own secret; and I might ensure that would not long be delayed.

What continues to perplex me is that so far as I can see no other agency but that of this evil old recluse himself had led me to my discovery. Why? Can it have been with this very intention? I stooped down and peeped and peered narrowly in under the lowered lids in the light of my torch, but not the feeblest flicker, remotest signal – or faintest syllabling echo of any message rewarded me. Dead fish are less unseemly.

And yet. Well – we are all of us, I suppose, at any extreme *capable* of remorse and not utterly shut against repentance. Is it possible that this priceless blessing is not denied us even when all that's earthly else appear to have come to an end?

From *A Beginning and Other Stories* by Walter de la Mare (Faber & Faber Ltd, London).

PROOF

Henry Cecil

THE pompous self-satisfied little lawyer from London had been
holding forth the whole evening and I had tried in vain to deflate
him. I had an instinctive dislike of lawyers, and this one was a
particularly odious specimen. I disliked him all the more because everyone else seemed interested in what he had to say and
he was allowed virtually to monopolize the conversation.

We had been sitting in the bar of the small Lakeland hotel
where I had been spending a much-needed holiday from going
up and down the country trying to sell the publications of a
new physical research society. As my earnings were entirely de-
pendent on what I sold, I had a hard time of it to make a living,
trying to persuade very matter-of-fact earthy people to buy our
books on psychic phenomena. How I wished that some manifestation would present itself to the busy little lawyer and reduce
his self-esteem, but nothing happened.

On and on he went and it was a great relief to me when two
strangers suddenly came in and distracted everyone's attention
from him. They were very ordinary-looking people, but they
entered with some noise and, as their faces were unknown to any
of us, their entrance automatically stopped the conversation.
They walked straight up to the bar, ordered a pint of beer
each and drank it without a word. That done, they repeated
the dose and only then did they seem to relax. Finally, one said
to the other:

'That was a complete and utter waste of time.'

'Absolutely.'

'D'you know,' said the first, addressing us generally, 'we've
been all the way to the top of Grimstone Crag, and we didn't
see a thing.'

They could not have been ordinary climbers, as no climber would consider any climb a waste of time, view or no view. Accordingly, none of us was much impressed and I was afraid that the little lawyer would soon be holding forth again. However, after the second stranger had said: 'Terrible waste of time. Hours of solid climbing and nothing to show for it except a thirst,' a small man at the end of the bar, whom I had not previously noticed, said:

'You don't know what a waste of time is.'

Everyone turned towards the speaker.

'Waste of time,' he repeated. 'Let me tell you of a waste of time which will make you feel that every moment of your climb was well spent.'

Without waiting for an invitation to proceed, he went on:

'It was a good many years ago and it happened in these parts. A detective was trailing a badly-wanted criminal. He had almost caught up with him when the fellow went off into the mountains at night. It was moonlight and the detective, who was dead keen, went after him. By luck he sighted him against the sky and, after a scrambling climb, at last he got within hailing distance and called on the man to surrender. As he did so, the detective slipped and eventually found himself, by the mercy of God, with a sprained or broken ankle on a slightly projecting ledge. Below, a drop of hundreds of feet; above, almost sheer. He regretted his hasty pursuit and was wondering whether and when he would be rescued when he heard the criminal hailing him.

' "Hallo, there," said the criminal, "I'll go and get a rope."

'The detective said nothing for a moment and then he shouted, "Are you William Turner?"

' "Certainly."

' "I have a warrant for your arrest for the murder of Sidney Blunt."

' "Well, what are you going to do about it?" asked Turner.

' "You're under arrest now," said the detective.

' "Doesn't feel like it," said Turner.

' "Now, look here," said the detective, "I naturally want to get out of here but I can't let you haul me out without telling

you that I shall arrest you as soon as you do." It will be seen that
the detective had a peculiarly high standard of morals.

' "Oh, shut up," said the criminal, whose morals were – except
for the little matter of the murder – equally high. "I'm going for
a rope," and he went away.

'Hours later he returned, when the detective had almost given
him up. It had come on to rain during the night and rained incessantly next day, and no one had come into his sight since Turner left.

' "You still alive?" shouted Turner. "I don't want to waste
my time if you're not."

' "Yes," shouted the detective.

' "I'm afraid I'm by myself," said Turner, "but you'll understand that, in the circumstances." The detective did understand,
but he began to wonder how he could be rescued by one man
alone – even with a rope.

' "You'll have to wait a bit," said Turner, and began to make
the descent.

'I won't describe the difficulties to experts like you gentlemen,' said the speaker, 'but you may take it that even you would
have found it a tough proposition. As it was, neither Turner
nor the detective were real climbers and it was remarkable
that Turner was able to reach the detective at all. However, after
some time, he did so and threw one end of the rope to him. Now,
whether the detective's ankle was broken or sprained doesn't very
much matter. You can perhaps visualize the appalling nature of
their attempt to climb to safety. It required every ounce of
strength and nerve each of them possessed. However, at long –
very long – last their almost superhuman efforts (very different,
I may say, from those needed for the little stroll you two gentlemen have just taken) were rewarded and they got to safety and
stood looking at each other. The detective almost fainted as a
result of the pain and exertion, but he had enough strength to
say:

' "Thank you. I'm sorry . . ." and, with the last words, to aim
a blow at Turner's jaw with the idea of knocking him out. He
had, of course, realized that, unless he could do this, Turner
would make good his escape. He had warned him that he would

arrest him and, like a good detective, he felt bound to do so if he could. Unfortunately he had wholly insufficient strength to carry out his purpose and, as Turner avoided the blow, the detective lurched sideways and fell over the edge. As he was still roped to Turner, the latter was carried after him and they crashed to death hundreds of feet below. And you two gentlemen talk of a waste of time.'

'Very interesting,' piped up the lawyer and, once again, attention was focused on him. 'But d'you suggest that story is true?'

'Absolutely,' said the small man gravely.

'Now, gentlemen,' said the lawyer, 'I think I can demonstrate to you conclusively that our friend here has been pulling your legs. The story can't be true.' He paused and took the middle of the floor. 'Now, sir,' he went on, 'did I rightly understand you to infer that there were no witnesses of this accident?'

'Quite,' said the small man.

'Did both men die instaneously?'

'Quite.'

'Then,' said the lawyer, 'as no one saw them die and as they could have told their story to no one, you couldn't possibly know that it happened as you have told us.'

He paused and gazed in triumph round his audience.

'Unless, of course,' he added facetiously, 'you chance to be the ghost of one of the men.'

'Quite,' said the small man and vanished.

From *Portrait of a Judge and Other Stories* by Henry Cecil (Michael Joseph Ltd, London, and Harper & Row, Inc., New York).

THE AMULET

Thomas Raddall

THE REVEREND PHILIP MUIR had chosen a pleasant spot
for his retirement. The old colonial farmhouse stood on a
green bluff by the river. Its clapboards were painted white, its
doors and shutters green, its roof a cheerful red. It had been built
in early times by an aesthete among pioneers who turned his
back on the wandering dirt road and faced his abode towards
the river for the view, the broad shining stream, the island
tufted with swamp maples and fringed with reeds, the rolling
pine woods on the other side. It was a place for meditation.

The young licentiate from River Gap, a mile or two down
river, liked to walk there on sunny afternoons to discuss theology
and its place in the lives of his fishermen. His name was Carson
and he was city-bred, an earnest young man rather flabbergasted
to find himself in a community that measured the world by a
literal interpretation of the scriptures – and demanded that its
minister do the same.

'I've given my views on Jonah and the whale, the Creation,
the Flood,' he said whimsically, 'and yesterday a patriarch fixed
me with a bright blue eye and demanded to know how I stood
on Methuselah.'

'What did you say?' asked the Reverend Philip.

'Oh, the usual things. Giants on the earth in those days, and
all that. It seemed dangerous to suggest that the scriptures, being
human works, were subject to human misinterpretations. They
regard the Bible as the absolute word of God.'

'Then you don't believe, yourself, that man could live for
centuries?'

'Frankly, no.'

The Reverend Philip smiled.

'Do you believe in metempsychosis?'

'The transmigration of souls? Of course not. That's purely pagan.'

The little grey man leaned back in the deep verandah chair and closed his eyes.

'I'm going to tell you something that may shake your ideas. It's not something I read or heard. It's something I saw with my own eyes.

'Just after the first German war I had a church in Alding, fifteen miles up the river. There's a Micmac Indian community in the outskirts, a few little huts, half a dozen families, the usual thing. They weren't my parishioners – they were Roman Catholics as a matter of fact, although my good friend Father Egan could never get them near his church except to bury them. Now and again you find groups like that, professing Christianity as a sort of fire insurance but secretly confirmed in the vague nature worship of their ancestors.

'Sometimes I went fishing with an Indian named Paul Luksi, a big fine-looking man with a broad dark face and sombre black eyes and the light husky voice that always makes you wonder how they managed a war-whoop. I should say Paul was forty at the time, his wife perhaps thirty-five – Indians are hard to judge after thirty – and they had a son and daughter grown up and gone away. There was another member of the household, and the first time I was invited inside the little two-room shack I got a shock.

'I suppose I'd been there a full minute before I looked in a corner and met the eyes of an extraordinary creature sitting on the floor. By the dress, it was a woman, a little old squaw with almost no hair, a few straggling wisps, and a face fallen in upon itself like a brown withered apple, a living skull.

'I can't describe the skin of her face. It sagged against the bones in a confusion of lifeless wrinkles. Her lips were thin lines of violet, tucked back into the toothless jaws. Her eyes were black and so glazed with age that in some lights they looked blue, a horrible unearthly blue, and they were set very deep in those wrinkled sockets. She was like an unwrapped mummy.

'I spoke to her but beyond a flicker of the eyes she gave no sign of having heard. Her dress was of heavy black cloth in voluminous folds, the sort women wore everywhere forty or fifty years ago. It was patched in many places. Her one ornament was a curious amulet of putty-coloured stone. I'd no chance to examine it closely but I saw it was a crude representation of a turtle and that it had been broken and a lower portion detached. It hung from her skinny neck by a thong.

'I saw her a number of times after that, usually squatting in the corner or crawling like some incredible beast about the floor. I decided she was semi-paralytic, but one day I saw her splitting wood in the door-yard, standing up and swinging the axe vigorously, an amazing sight ... as if you saw me, for instance, get up at this moment and turn handsprings the length of the verandah.

'Once or twice I heard her speak, a strange mewing that Paul and his wife seemed to understand quite readily. I could never get them to say what relation she was to them. They spoke of her reluctantly and in a queer disinterested way, as if she were a keepsake passed down to them through so many generations that her origin had been forgotten. They held her in great respect, though. I fancied she was a great-grandmother on one side or the other, and the air of mystery they hung about her was just one of those inexplicable Indian whims.

'One day she disappeared. Completely. The Indians had spent the day in Alding, dipping alewives out of the brook that flowed past my church, and when they returned to their shacks in the evening with their dip-nets and their sacks of fish the old crone was missing. Paul was in a fearful state. None of the traditional Indian calm. He and his wife were weeping loudly on their doorstep when Bailey, the Alding constable – we hadn't the Mounted Police in Nova Scotia then – came to organize a search party.

'They found nothing except that someone had stolen Paul's canoe from the river bank. For three days they hunted the woods and dragged the river without success. On the fourth day the old squaw was found at Anse Blanche, a small uninhabited inlet down the coast, twenty miles by river and sea from Alding. A fisherman discovered her while hunting for sapling oak to make bows for his lobster traps. The missing canoe was drawn up on the banks of a small brook flowing into Anse Blanche. The squaw was dead.

'I came down from Alding with Father Egan and the constable and one or two others, and we went to Anse Blanche in a motor boat from River Gap. The place was five miles along the coast from the mouth of the river. The body was lying curled up on a low mound in the bush about a hundred yards from the shore. There was a similar mound a few steps away. The small stream flowed between. We searched the spot thoroughly, probing amongst the ferns with sticks, and somebody turned up a bit of turf at the side of the mound, and revealed a mass of crumbled clam shells.

'We widened the hole a bit and found that the shells went down a foot or more, with little pockets of decayed bird and fish and animal bones. An old camp site, evidently. Among the shells was a piece of crude pottery such as I'd seen in the Micmac section of the Halifax museum, thick drab-coloured stuff made of clay and tempered with fragments of shell, and decorated with marks like basketwork, and fired at low temperatures. That clinched the matter. That poor old thing had gone back to some long-remembered scene of her youth. It was spring, the season of the ancient migration to the coast, and somewhere in the back of that senile skull there had flickered a memory, an instinct, an animal stirring that made her go down to the canoes and start for the sea. The river carried her fifteen miles to the tide, but she must have paddled the whole five miles along the coast to that lonely spot.

'We took that little rigid wisp back to Alding, and the inquest was short. Death was due to natural causes ... in fact young Doctor Ridgeway said she'd lived a long time in defiance of all natural causes. He told the coroner, "She's like something out of a tomb in Egypt." We all smiled of course. Ridgeway was given to picturesque phrases. Nothing was gained from the testimony of the Indians. They were ill at ease in the midst of this solemnity and when questioned they blurted out a few absurd statements and relapsed into a glum silence that nothing could shake. They had some sort of tradition about an annual migration to the sea

shore, but nothing in their own time or the time of their fathers
and grandfathers.

'The Micmacs gave up their seasonal movements when civilization compelled them to squat on any land they wished to keep.
Of seventeen Indian adults in Alding only three had ever seen
the sea, just fifteen miles away.

'There was some difficulty over the old woman's name. At
first Paul insisted he didn't know her name. That seemed absurd.
Braxton, the Alding coroner, a fussy little man full of his momentary importance, snapped, "Come now, Paul! Answer the
questions properly or there will be trouble. You'll be liable for
contempt if you keep this up. Who did she belong to, you or your
wife?"

'Now the modern Micmac speaks English quite well, but
within the family he sticks to his own tongue; it's the language
of the household, the peg he hangs his private life on; he thinks
in it even when he's talking English. I could see him struggling
with a phrase that would not flow in English. At last he blurted
out, "Sa-ak-a-wach-kik!"

'Braxton *was* annoyed. "How many times, Paul, must I tell you
to speak English at this inquest? You know English. You must
speak English. Let's have no more of this nonsense. Come now,
her name was Luksi, wasn't it?"

'Paul's face settled in that frozen look an Indian puts on when
he doesn't want to talk. "Yes," he said sullenly.

' "And her Christian name?"

' "No Christian name."

' "Nonsense! She *must* have a Christian name."

'Paul shrugged, and grunted, "Molly."

'Braxton told the clerk to write it down, and I remember he
turned to us quite pleased with himself and delivered a little
homily on the virtue of perseverance in dealing with cases of this
kind. As if he or anyone else in MacDougal's mortuary had ever
seen a case of this kind! It seemed to me that Paul said "Molly"
just as you or I would have said Tom, Dick, or Harry if somebody demanded – in plain English and no quibbling – the Christian name of the Piltdown Man. Molly's a very common name
amongst Micmac women.

'So Father Egan conducted the funeral of "Molly Luksi" and consigned her to a Christian grave in the churchyard of Saint Gregory's, a lovely little church that you must see if you want to appreciate all that is simple and beautiful in wooden architecture. Most of the Indians were there, standing well back, as if the old lady might jump out of the coffin any minute, and crossing themselves vigorously.

'After the service Father Egan presented me with the little stone necklet. "Here," he said. "You're interested in these things. I wouldn't bury the woman with that pagan symbol about her neck; I made the undertaker take it off." It wasn't much of a trinket; just a crude little turtle cut out of some fairly hard stone and polished a bit. On the top the stone went upwards in a V-shape like the tip of a Maltese cross, and there was a hole bored for the thong. The lower side of the turtle extended in the same fashion, but what might have been another V was broken off. I looked at the thing and threw it in a drawer.

'A year or two later an archaeologist came to see me. I'd never seen one before. I'd pictured them as a breed apart, thin men with sun helmets and grey torpedo beards, and associated always with the pyramids and Mongol ponies and mysterious ruins in the Central American jungle. Beckles didn't fit the picture. A thick-set powerful man with a bald sloping brow, a humorous mouth and a nose like a potato. Said he was making a study of the prehistoric Micmacs, one of the least-known tribes in North America, and he understood I knew of a kitchen midden somewhere in this vicinity. Middens are fairly common in some parts of Nova Scotia but they've been ruined by souvenir hunters. Beckles wanted one absolutely untouched.

'He explained to me, "These prehistoric Micmacs went inland in winter and lived in communities for mutual warmth and protection. By doing so they avoided the bitter coastal storms and got the best of the caribou hunting. But it must have been a miserable existence in those bark huts in the cold, and the fortunes of hunting meant famine more often than feast. So in spring they were very glad to go down the rivers in canoes as soon as the ice was out. They scattered in small groups along the coast, setting up a few wigwams wherever there was a clam-flat, a trickle of fresh water, and a chance to fish. There were sea fish of all kinds, especially alewives and salmon and shad crowding into the rivers to spawn. There were seals and probably walrus. Wild fowl were in multitude, migrating from the south. And in the woods there was always a chance of meeting anything from a squirrel to a bull moose. For the Micmacs summer was the good time, the warm time, the easy time. When all else failed, the squaw could go out on the clam flat at low tide and dig up a dinner with a stick. These coastal middens contain all we'll ever know of Micmac life at its best."

'I told him, "Well, I could show you such a midden but it's not the thing you want. I mean it's been occupied within the life-time of a squaw I knew." He looked surprised at that, for he thought – what we all thought – that the Micmacs had given up their coastal camps at least a century before. I told him the story of Molly Luksi and he was impressed but, he said, "Say she was a hundred years old; that puts the mound well into historic times, of course. It's relatively modern when you remember that European influence in Nova Scotia began before the Spanish Armada. I'd like to have a dig at it, though. The mound may go back to antiquity, in which case we'd be able to trace the culture right into modern times. That would be simply marvellous."

'Off he went, and came back in a week's time with a small party – his son, Bob, a student at McGill; Doctor Daly, who was osteologist at the Werning Museum of Natural History; and a cook-handyman. They had two cars piled with tents and equipment and groceries and baggage.

'I went out with them in a small fishing schooner from River Gap. The coast is a saw-edge of narrow bays and coves, and those that run far back into the land are almost dry at low tide. Anse Blanche is like that. The ebb-tide leaves a long shining basin of sand speckled with fragments of clam shell. You have to come and go at high tide. It's a desolate place. The surrounding ridges were burned to the granite rock by a bad forest fire about 1919; the woods were very dry that year and the soil burned like peat; then the rains came and washed all the residue into the lower levels. At Anse Blanche now the bald rocks occupy most of the landscape, with thickets of wire birch and scrub maple in the hollows. It's a miracle how that old Indian woman recognized the place at all, for when she was young the whole place was covered in virgin timber.

'Those bygone Indians had chosen the site with care, well back from the shore and around a bend in the little stream, so that nothing was visible from the sea. The brook is now a miserable trickle seeping down from the barren ridges, but it must have been a good trout stream in the days of the green forest. I waited over between tides and watched the party set up their tents. They pitched them by the shore for the benefit of the sea breeze, for it was hot in Anse Blanche, especially with the tide out and the sun beating on the flats. They did some exploring but found no more than the two low mounds beside the brook.

' "Two wigwams," Daly said. "Generation after generation, gradually building up those middens. What happened to their natural increase, I wonder? Disease? War? The perils of a hunting life? Or did they rule that the place could support two wigwams and no more? It almost suggests a system of seasonal land tenure." The mounds were about four feet above the general level of the foot of the ridge, and spread in irregular circles perhaps forty feet across, rising gradually to the flat wigwam site at the top. You could picture those ancient savages roasting meat over the fire, or baking clams in a wrapping of seaweed, or boiling fish in their brittle pots, and tossing the shells and bones right and left.

'There was now a stout growth of ferns and wire birch, nourished in the rich humus of the heaps and the lime in the shells. Where we'd turned up the turf in 1920 the exposed clam shells, washed clean by the rains, were shining white, marking the spot where we'd found the old squaw like the X in a news photograph. Beckles and the others were enthusiastic. I went away promising to visit them soon; but church affairs came in a swarm, as they always do, and it was three weeks before I returned to Anse Blanche. Just before I left the parsonage I slipped the little pagan necklace into my pocket. It might be of some value to Beckles. It was wasted in my drawer.

'I found the whole party taking advantage of the tide, enjoying a swim. They must have lived in their bathing trunks, for they were wonderfully sunburned and, as I told them, a fine looking lot of savages. They all came splattering out of the water and dragged me off to see their operations. They'd worn a path through the bush to the mounds, probably on the site of the original Indian track. The first mound – the mound of the dead squaw – had been sifted and shovelled aside, a great heap of broken shells and black dust. At the bottom they'd found two inches of black humus containing a few scraps of charcoal, and then the hard yellow subsoil.

'The second mound had been cleared of the flourishing birches and a working fence dug at one side. The whole thing was marked off in small squares by stakes driven right down through the mound, and the stakes were lettered and numbered so that every find could be recorded in its exact position. The working face was a story in itself, a close-knit mass of clam shells with pockets of bird, fish, and animal bones; occasional layers of grey ash; and the whole sifted through with black dust. They showed me how they took off layer after layer with trowels, sifting everything. It was marvellous, you know. So painstaking. I could understand Beckles's scorn of "pick-and-shovel amateurs".

'And with great pride they showed me what young Bob called the loot. The site had proved rich. There were arrowheads in all stages of manufacture, of chipped quartz and flint, of bone, and two made very simply and effectively from sharks' teeth. Several harpoon points of bone and walrus ivory – made with a toggle, mind you, and a hole bored for the line, just like the lily-irons our fishermen use today for swordfish. Knives and cutting tools made of split beaver teeth and the teeth of porcupine and woodchuck, fitted in wooden handles originally, no doubt, and the wood gone to dust long since. Bear teeth and wolf teeth bored to hang as pendants or part of a necklace; bone awls and needles of all sizes; a few celts of hard stone, battered from use; a lot of fan-shaped tools of chipped quartz, probably used by the squaw for scraping skins; and several hundred shards of pottery, all decorated with milled impressions like basket-work, some pieces containing the hole for the pot-bail, and two bearing the clear imprint of the potter's finger nails. And there were two large packing cases full of bones and teeth, representing, Daly said, everything from eider duck to moose. It was enormously interesting. I could have stayed for hours just picking the things over and trying to imagine them in use.

'Beckles said, "I'm afraid you'll have to put the old squaw's visit down to sheer coincidence. Everything here is prehistoric. The Micmacs stopped making pottery and stone arrowheads soon after the Europeans came with metal to trade. And we haven't found so much as a nail."

' "Coincidence?" I said. "That's not possible. Look here, that woman came fifteen miles down the river and then paddled five miles along the shore, passing a number of inlets exactly like this, until she came to Anse Blanche, to this little stream. After all that exertion she had to struggle through a hundred yards of thicket to reach the mound. No, no! It's impossible that it was a chance. She knew exactly where she was going and she spent her last breath getting here."

'Beckles looked at Daly and they smiled broadly.

' "The last wolf recorded in Nova Scotia," Beckles said, "was killed in the late 1790s, more than a hundred and twenty years ago. We've found bones and teeth of the wolf all through this mound, a whole jawbone within two inches of the top – in other words, towards the end of the life of this camp."

' "But that's not proof enough," I protested. "After all, the woman may have been well over a hundred when she died in 1920. Centenarians aren't rare."

' "Right," agreed Daly. "We also found bones of an extinct native dog. But let that go. Here's something that shoots your theory to pieces. We found bones of the white-tailed deer – *odocoileus virginianus* – all through the mound. Need I tell you that the deer was extinct in Nova Scotia when the Europeans came? It was reintroduced by sportsmen in 1888, and the deer now in this province are sprung from that stock. Now surely, Mr Muir, you'll admit these mounds are prehistoric."

' "Besides," Beckles said, "we found the charred stump of an oak, killed obviously in the fire of 1910. Its roots were all through Mound Two. We counted 120 rings on that stump, which takes you back to 1790 at the very least. And remember, please, it would take years after the camp was abandoned before enough forest humus gathered on the heap to support tree growth. Why, the proofs are overwhelming!"

'Well, they were. The old squaw's choice of a place to die was simply a curious accident. It couldn't possibly have meant anything in her lifetime. I put my hand in my pocket absently and my fingers encountered the little stone amulet. I'd forgotten the thing. It had never seemed more than a worthless bit of Indian trumpery, crude in design and workmanship, not even intact. I passed it over to Beckles diffidently and said something about it, about the squaw wearing it around her neck – I don't remember now – but I remember how they all gasped. They stared at the thing as if it were poisonous. I felt abashed. Then with a most unscientific violence they rummaged in their "unclassified" boxes and – you've guessed, haven't you? – brought out the missing fragment.

'The ragged edges fitted perfectly. The part they'd found was in the shape of a beaver, the same queer putty-coloured stone, the same sort of design and workmanship, and they'd found it – they searched their records feverishly – thirteen inches below the surface of Mound One. "In an undisturbed stratum of fish and bird bones, with some humus and shell, and in proximity to a nugget of hematite showing no signs of grinding, possibly used in the making of war paint."

'There it was. The incontrovertible fact. I was just as stupefied as they were. I even went so far as to question Daly's identification of the deer bones, which to the osteologist of a famous natural history museum must have seemed downright heresy. He was polite, as well as positive, and pointed out that *odocoileus virginianus* had been identified in other Nova Scotia middens by authorities beyond question.

'I stayed that night with them and we talked into the small hours, trying to make some sense of it. They cross-examined me severely about the old squaw and all the circumstances that led up to the finding of the body. They'd ask me suddenly, without warning, in the midst of something else, when I saw the amulet on the old squaw's neck. Things like that, brusquely – like policemen, you know. Well, I didn't blame them. When you tread on the corns of science you can't expect science to be polite about it.

'We sat over a folding canvas table in the larger of the tents, in the violet glare of a patent gasolene lamp, staring at those inscrutable pieces of stone and at each other. And before we stumbled off to bed I could see their minds uniting in a single accusation. They didn't make it aloud, of course, out of respect for the cloth, I suppose. But they went away ten days later firmly convinced that I'd found the gorget – Beckles's word – when we scratched the heap in 1920, and that for some senile reason I was giving their legs a terrific pull.

'At any rate, when Beckles sent me a copy of his report – an inch thick, illustrated with photographs and a map, a brilliant piece of work – I couldn't find the stone beaver fragment anywhere in the list of "artifacts". A pity, you know. Finds like that are rare. Any sort of sculpture was rare amongst the Micmacs, and such an amulet would be worn only by a person of importance, a chief perhaps, or more likely a medicine man.'

Young Carson stirred in his chair. 'What do you make of it, yourself?'

'To my mind,' the Reverend Philip said, 'the old squaw knew exactly where she was going. The place was familiar to her by actual association. The significance of the broken amulet, of course, we shall never know. That goes back to a remote age when the Micmacs took birds and beasts and fish for their totems and believed that man could transfer his life-spirit into the body of his totem-beast at will. Why were the Beaver and the Turtle joined in stone, in a single imperishable totem, and then broken asunder? A tribal alliance perhaps, ended by a symbolic sundering and war. The Micmacs and the other Algonkian tribes never had that instinct for confederacy which made the Iroquois the Romans of their world.'

'But the woman!' Carson said impatiently.

'Ah, the woman, to be sure. You've got a choice of two things. You've got to believe in the transmigration of souls and say that "Molly Luksi" was the essence – I don't know what else to call it – of an Indian who lived on that shell-mound, and that the broken amulet had passed from hand to hand in a direct line of descent, following exactly the descent of the spirit. In that you'd be voicing the tenets of ancient savages, which as a minister of the Christian faith you must reject. Or you've got to believe – you have no other choice – that old age, or rather senility, is pathological and preventable, and assume that now and again an individual may escape the various toxins that give rise to it and live to a tremendous age.

'The distinction between senescence and senility may be as wide as the sea, as wide as the division of medical opinion on the subject. Of course I'm well aware that Indians – like some white people – have a tendency to exaggerate their age after passing four-score. At ninety they're calling it a hundred, and at a hundred they may say anything, depending on the credulity of the listener.

'But the woman Father Egan buried as Molly Luksi had no age. None of the Indians at the inquest would hazard a guess. One after another they said she had "always been there", and would say no more. And there was the strange word Paul used.

'Afterwards, after that amazing discovery of the missing fragment, the word came back to me with the force of a blow. For *Sa-ak-a-wach-kik* means literally "The Folk of Old", or getting to the root of it, "The Primitives".

'Of course Paul and the others stood in great awe of the coroner. They thought they were being held responsible for the old lady's escapade. There was a tendency – very natural if you know Indians – to dissociate themselves from her as much as possible.'

The young licentiate sat up very straight. 'Do you know what you're suggesting? You're suggesting that this Micmac woman lived well over three thousand years ago, before Demonts and Champlain came to Nova Scotia!'

The older clergyman nodded absently. 'Exactly. That old woman might have told us all we want to know about the Micmacs. Where did they come from and why? What people did they find here? Was it the Eskimo? If not, what's the explanation of those typical Eskimo harpoon points in the same heap with Micmac pottery?

'What happened to the white-tailed deer? What's the meaning of the picture-carving on the rocks at Kejumkujik? Of the curious milled pottery decoration, always the same? What was the use of those stone tools we call "gouges", of the slim and brittle slate blades we call "bayonets", and why do we find them in the sites of winter camps and never in the shell-mounds on the coast? How did they make those arrowheads of the hardest quartz, without steel tools and a jeweller's vice? A thousand things. All lost now.'

'It's incredible!' young Carson cried. 'Incredible!'

'So,' murmured the Reverend Philip, 'is Methuselah.'

THE HAIR

A. J. Alan

I'M going to give you an account of certain occurrences. I shan't attempt to explain them because they're quite beyond me. When you've heard all the facts, some of you may be able to offer suggestions. You must forgive me for going into a certain amount of detail. When you don't understand what you're talking about it's so difficult to know what to leave out.

This business began in the dark ages, before there was any broadcasting. In fact, in 1921.

I'd been staying the week-end with a friend of mine who lives about fifteen miles out of Bristol.

There was another man stopping there, too, who lived at Dawlish. Well, on the Monday morning our host drove us into Bristol in time for the Dawlish man to catch his train, which left a good deal earlier than the London one. Of course, if old Einstein had done his job properly, we could both have gone by the same train. As it was, I had over half an hour to wait. Talking of Einstein, wouldn't it be almost worth while dying young so as to hear what Euclid says to him when they meet – wherever it is?

There was a funny little old sort of curiosity shop in one of the streets I went down, and I stopped to look in the window. Right at the back, on a shelf, was a round brass box, not unlike a powder box in shape, and it rather took my fancy. I don't know why – perhaps it was because I'd never seen anything quite like it before. That must be why some women buy some hats.

Anyway, the shop window was so dirty that you could hardly see through it, so I went inside to have a closer look. An incredibly old man came out of the back regions and told me all he knew about the box, which wasn't very much. It was fairly heavy, made of brass, round, four inches high, and about three inches in diameter. There was something inside it, which we could hear when we shook it, but no one had ever been able to get the lid off. He'd bought it from a sailor some years before, but couldn't say in the least what part of the world it came from.

'What about fifteen bob?'

I offered him ten, and he took it very quickly, and then I had to sprint back to the station to catch my train. When I got home I took the box up into my workshop and had a proper look at it. It was extremely primitive as regards work, and had evidently been made by hand, and not on a lathe. Also, there had been something engraved on the lid, but it had been taken off with a file. Next job was to get the lid off without doing any damage to it. It was a good deal more than hand-tight, and no ordinary methods were any good. I stood it lid downwards for a week in a dish of glycerine as a start, and then made two brass collars, one for the box and one for the lid. At the end of the week I bolted the collars on, fixed the box in the vice and tried tapping the lid round with a hammer – but it wouldn't start. Then I tried it the other way, and it went at once. That explained why no one had ever been able to unscrew it – it had a left-hand thread on it. Rather a dirty trick – especially to go and do it all those years before.

Well, here it was, unscrewing very sweetly, and I began to feel quite like Howard Carter, wondering what I was going to find. It might go off bang, or jump out and hit me in the face. However, nothing exciting happened when the lid came off. In fact, the box only seemed to be half-full of dust, but at the bottom was a curled-up plait of hair. When straightened out, it was about nine inches long and nearly as thick as a pencil. I unplaited a short length, and found it consisted of some hundreds of very fine hairs, but in such a filthy state (I shoved them under the microscope) that there was nothing much to be seen. So I thought I'd clean them. You may as well know the process – first of all a bath of dilute hydrochloric acid to get the grease off, then a solution of washing soda to remove the acid. Then a washing in distilled water, then a bath of alcohol to get rid of any traces of water, and a final rinsing in ether to top off with.

Just as I took it out of the ether they called me down to the telephone, so I shoved it down on the first clean thing which came handy, namely, a piece of white cardboard, and went downstairs. When I examined the plait later on, the only thing of interest that came to light was the fact that the hairs had all apparently belonged to several different women. The colours ranged from jet-black, through brown, red, and gold, right up to pure white. None of the hair was dyed which proved how very old it was. I showed it to one or two people, but they didn't seem very enthusiastic, so I put it, and its box, in a little corner cupboard we have, and forgot all about it.

Then the first strange coincidence happened.

About ten days later a pal of mine called Matthews came into the club with a bandage across his forehead. People naturally asked him what was the matter, and he said he didn't know, and what's more his doctor didn't know. He'd suddenly flopped down on his drawing-room floor, in the middle of tea, and lain like a log. His wife was in a fearful stew, of course, and telephoned for the doctor. However, Matthews came round at the end of about five minutes, and sat up and asked what had hit him. When the doctor blew in a few minutes later he was pretty well all right again except for a good deal of pain in his forehead. The doctor couldn't find anything the matter except a red mark which was beginning to show on the skin just where the pain was.

Well, this mark got clearer and clearer, until it looked just like a blow from a stick. Next day it was about the same, except that a big bruise had come up all round the mark. After that it got gradually better. Matthews took the bandage off and showed it me at the club, and there was nothing much more than a bruise with a curved red line down the middle of it, like the track of a red-hot worm.

They'd decided that he'd had an attack of giddiness and must somehow have bumped his head in falling. And that was that.

About a month later, my wife said to me: 'We really must tidy your workshop!' And I said: 'Must we?' And she said: 'Yes, it's a disgrace.' So up we went.

Tidying my workshop consists of putting the tools back in their racks, and of my wife wanting to throw away things she finds on the floor, and me saying: 'Oh, no, I could use that for so and so.'

The first thing we came across was the piece of white cardboard I'd used to put the plait of hair on while I'd run down to the telephone that day.

When we came to look at the other side we found it was a flashlight photograph of a dinner I'd been at. You know what happens. Just before the speeches a lot of blighters come in with a camera and some poles with tin trays on the top, and someone says: 'Will the chairman please stand?' and he's helped to his feet. Then there's a blinding flash and the room's full of smoke, and the blighters go out again. Later on a man comes round with proofs, and if you are very weak – or near the chairman – you order one print.

Well, this dinner had been the worshipful company of skate-fasteners or something, and I'd gone as the guest of the same bloke Matthews I've already been telling you about, and we'd sat 'side by each', as the saying is. My wife was looking at the photograph and she said: 'What's that mark on Mr Matthews's forehead?' And I looked – and there, sure enough, was the exact mark that he'd come into the club with a month before. The curious part being, of course, that the photograph had been taken at least six months before he'd had the funny attack which caused the mark. Now, then – on the back of the photograph, when we examined it, was a faint brown line. This was evidently left by the plait of hair when I'd pinned it out to dry, and it had soaked through and caused the mark on Matthews's face. I checked it by shoving a needle right through the cardboard. Of course, this looked like a very strange coincidence, on the face of it. I don't know what your experience of coincidences is – but mine is that they usually aren't. Anyway, I took the trouble to trace out the times, and I finally established, beyond a shadow of doubt, that I had pinned the hair out on the photograph between four and a quarter-past on a particular day, and that Matthews had had his funny attack on the same day at about a quarter-past four. That was something *like* a coincidence. Next, the idea came

to me to try it again. Not on poor old Matthews, obviously –
he'd already had some – and, besides, he was a friend of mine.
I know perfectly well that we are told to be kind to our enemies,
and so on – in fact, I do quite a lot of that – but when it comes to
trying an experiment of this kind – even if the chances are a
million to one against it being a success, I mean having any result – one naturally chooses an enemy rather than a friend. So I
looked round for a suitable – victim – someone who wouldn't be
missed much in case there happened to be another coincidence.
The individual on whom my choice fell was the nurse next door.

We can see into their garden from our bathroom window – and
we'd often noticed the rotten way she treated the child she had
charge of when she thought no one was looking. Nothing one
could definitely complain about – you know what a thankless job
it is to butt into your neighbour's affairs – but she was system-
atically unkind, and we hated the sight of her. Another thing –
when she first came she used to lean over the garden wall and
sneak our roses – at least, she didn't even do that – she used to
pull them off their stalks and let them drop – I soon stopped that.
I fitted up some little arrangements of fish-hooks round some of
the most accessible roses and anchored them to the ground with
wires. There was hell-and-tommy the next morning, and she had
her hand done up in bandages for a week.

Altogether she was just the person for my experiment. The
first thing was to get a photograph of her, so the next sunny
morning, when she was in the garden, I made a noise like an
aeroplane out of the bathroom window to make her look up, and
got her nicely. As soon as the first print was dry, about eleven
o'clock the same night, I fastened the plait of hair across the forehead with two pins – feeling extremely foolish, as one would, of
course, doing an idiotic thing like that – and put it away in a
drawer in my workshop. The evening of the next day, when I got
home, my wife met me and said: 'What do you think – the nurse
next door was found dead in bed this morning.' And she went on
to say that the people were quite upset about it, and there was
going to be an inquest, and all the rest of it. I tell you, you could
have knocked me down with a brick. I said: 'No, not really;
what did she die of?' You must understand that my lady wife

didn't know anything about the experiment. She'd never have let me try it. She's rather superstitious – in spite of living with me. As soon as I could I sneaked up to the workshop drawer and got out the photograph, and – I know you won't believe me, but it doesn't make any difference – when I unpinned the plait of hair and took it off there was a clearly-marked brown stain right across the nurse's forehead. I tell you, that *did* make me sit up, if you like – because that made twice – first Matthews and now – now.

It was rather disturbing, and I know it sounds silly, but I couldn't help feeling to blame in some vague way.

Well, the next thing was the inquest – I attended that, naturally, to know what the poor unfortunate woman had died of. Of course, they brought it in as 'death from natural causes', namely, several burst blood-vessels in the brain; but what puzzled the doctors was what had caused the 'natural causes' – also, she had the same sort of mark on her forehead as Matthews had had. They had gone very thoroughly into the theory that she might have been exposed to X-rays – it *did* look a bit like that – but it was more or less proved that she couldn't have been, so they frankly gave it up. Of course, it was all very interesting and entertaining, and I quite enjoyed it, as far as one can enjoy an inquest, but they hadn't cleared up the vexed question – did she fall or was she pu— well, had she snuffed it on account of the plait of hair, or had she not? Obviously the matter couldn't be allowed to rest there – it was much too thrilling. So I looked about for someone else to try it on, and decided that a man who lived in the house opposite would do beautifully. He wasn't as bad as the nurse because he wasn't cruel – at least, not intentionally – he played the fiddle – so I decided not to kill him more than I could help.

The photograph was rather a bother because he didn't go out much. You've no idea how difficult it is to get a decent full-face photograph of a man who knows you by sight without him knowing. However, I managed to get one after a fortnight or so. It was rather small and I had to enlarge it, but it wasn't bad considering. He used to spend most of his evenings up in a top room practising, double-stopping and what-not – so after din-

ner I went up to my workshop window, which overlooks his,
and waited for him to begin. Then, when he'd really warmed up
to his job, I just touched the plait across the photograph – not
hard, but – well, like you do when you are testing a bit of twin
flex to find out which wire is which, you touch the ends across
an accumulator or an H.T. battery. Quite indefensible in theory,
but invariably done in practice. (Personally, I always use the
electric light mains – the required information is so instantly
forthcoming.) Well, that's how I touched the photograph with
the plait. The first time I did it my bloke played a wrong note.
That was nothing, of course, so I did it again more slowly. This
time there was no doubt about it. He hastily put down his fiddle
and hung out of the window, gasping like a fish for about five
minutes. I tell you, I was so surprised that I felt like doing the
same.

However, I pulled myself together, and wondered whether
one ought to burn the da – er – plait or not. But there seemed
too many possibilities in it for that – so I decided to learn how
to use it instead. It would take too long to tell you about my
experiments. They lasted for several months, and I reduced the
thing to such an exact science that I could do anything from giving a gnat a headache to killing a man. All this, mind you, at the
cost of one man, one woman, lots of wood-lice, and a conscientious objector. You must admit that that's pretty moderate, considering what fun one could have had with a discovery of that
kind.

Well, it seemed to me that, now the control of my absent
treatment had been brought to such a degree of accuracy, it
would be rather a pity not to employ it in some practical way.
In other words, to make a fortune quickly without undue loss
of life.

One could, of course, work steadily through the people one
disliked, but it wouldn't bring in anything for some time.

I mean, even if you insure them first you've got to wait a year
before they die, or the company won't pay, and in any case it
begins to look fishy after you've done it a few times. Then I had
my great idea: why shouldn't my process be applied to horse-
racing? All one had to do was to pick some outsider in a race –

back it for all you were worth at about 100 to 1, and then see that it didn't get beaten.

The actual operation would be quite simple. One would only have to have a piece of cardboard with photographs of all the runners stuck on it – except the one that was to win, of course – and then take up a position giving a good view of the race.

I wasn't proposing to hurt any of the horses in the least. They were only going to get the lightest of touches, just enough to give them a tired feeling, soon after the start. Then, if my horse didn't seem to have the race well in hand near the finish, I could give one more light treatment to any horse which still looked dangerous.

It stood to reason that great care would have to be taken not to upset the running too much. For instance, if all the horses except one fell down, or even stopped and began to graze there would be a chance of the race being declared void.

So I had two or three rehearsals. They worked perfectly. The last one hardly was a rehearsal because I had a tenner on at 33 to 1, just for luck – and, of course, it came off.

However, it wasn't as lucky as it sounds. Just outside the entrance to the grand-stand there was rather a squash and, as I came away I got surrounded by four of five men who seemed to be pushing me about a bit, but it didn't strike me what the game was until one of them got his hand into the breast-pocket of my coat.

Then I naturally made a grab at him and got him just above the elbow with both hands, and drove his hand still further into my pocket. That naturally pushed the pocket, with his hand inside it, under my right arm, and I squeezed it against my ribs for all I was worth.

Now, there was nothing in that pocket but the test tube with the plait of hair in it, and the moment I started squeezing it went with a crunch. I'm a bit hazy about the next minute because my light-fingered friend tried to get free, and two of his pals helped him by bashing me over the head. They were quite rough. In fact, they entered so heartily into the spirit of the thing that they went on doing it until the police came up and collared them.

You should have seen that hand when it did come out of my pocket. Cut to pieces, and bits of broken glass sticking out all over it – like a crimson tipsy cake. He was so bad that we made a call at a doctor's on the way to the police-station for him to have a small artery tied up. There was a cut on the back of my head that wanted a bit of attention, too. Quite a nice chap, the doctor, but he was my undoing. He was, without doubt, the baldest doctor I've ever seen, though I once saw a balder alderman.

When he'd painted me with iodine, I retrieved the rest of the broken glass and the hair from the bottom of my pocket and asked him if he could give me an empty bottle to put it in. He said: 'Certainly,' and produced one, and we corked the hair up in it. When I got home, eventually, I looked in the bottle, but apart from a little muddy substance at the bottom it was empty – the plait of hair had melted away. Then I looked at the label on the bottle, and found the name of a much advertised hair-restorer.

From *The Best of A. J. Alan*, selected by Kenelm Foss (Richards Press, London).

THE RETURN OF THE NATIVE

William Croft Dickinson

ABOUT a year after the end of World War II, when I was still an officer in the American Intelligence, and stationed in London, I decided to seize the opportunity of visiting Scotland and seeing, for the first time, the land of my folk. I had little difficulty in obtaining a fortnight's leave and, after spending a week-end in Edinburgh, I hired a small car to drive to Arisaig and Morar – the district from which I knew my forbears had emigrated some two hundred years ago.

Setting off from Edinburgh on the Monday morning, I made that marvellous drive through Callander, Lochearnhead, and Tyndrum, and on through Glencoe to Ballachulish, where I put up for the night. Passing through Balquhidder country on my way from Callander to Tyndrum, I had recalled the story of assembled Macgregors swearing their oaths on the severed head of a royal forester; and, as I had passed through Glencoe, I had recalled the tragedy of sleeping MacDonalds who were massacred by those to whom they had given food and shelter. Yet that night, in the inn at Ballachulish, as I brooded over the stories of the past, I little thought that I myself was soon to be touched by the past – touched too closely for my liking – and simply because I, too, was a MacDonald, though a MacDonald of a different sept from the MacIans of Glencoe.

The Tuesday morning broke fine and clear. Leaving Ballachulish, I crossed by the ferry and took the lovely road by the shores of Loch Linnhe and Loch Eil, and on to Glenfinnan, where Prince Charlie's standard was raised, and where I thought the monument a poor thing to commemorate so stirring an event. From Glenfinnan the scenery became more wonderful still, as the narrow road, still 'unimproved', twisted and turned on its ledge between the hills and the sea: and I remembered I was on 'The Road to the Isles'.

It may be that my head was too full of the tales of the Young Chevalier, or it may be that my eyes strayed too often to the beauty of land and sea: I do not know. But, almost too late, I caught sight of an enormous boulder crashing down the hillside and almost on top of my car. Braking hard, and wrenching the wheel violently to the right, I lost control of the car and ran into the bank of the hill, while the boulder, missing the front of the car by inches, thundered across the road and bounded over the opposite verge.

Slightly shaken, I got out to see what damage I had done, and, as I did so, I was astonished to see an old woman standing on the other side of the road just where the boulder had crashed across. For a moment I wondered how she had escaped; then, something in her appearance made me look at her more closely. I was startled to see that her dark and deep-set eyes were glaring at me with a look of intense hate. I saw, too, that water was dripping from her clothes and that her grey hair was hanging round her shoulders, dank and wet. And, looking at her, I experienced a strange sense of danger, or it might even have been fear, which it is wholly impossible to describe.

So we stood, facing one another, and myself in a kind of trance, until, suddenly the woman turned away and, apparently stepping down from the road, disappeared over the edge. Recovering my wits, I ran across the road, only to pull myself up with a jerk. On that side of the road, and guarded only by a single strand of wire, there was a sheer drop of a hundred feet or more to the rocks on the loch-side below. Had I wrenched my wheel the other way, or had that boulder crashed into my small car, broadside on, nothing could have saved me.

I made myself look again at that sheer drop. What had happened to the old woman? There was no sign of her anywhere. Not even a ghastly huddle of body and clothes on the rocks below. Yet I had seen her clearly enough; and she had stepped down from the road at this very spot. And why had she glared at me with such bitter hate? Surely I had not fallen asleep at the wheel and dreamed the whole thing – a boulder crashing down and a malevolent old hag with dripping clothes?

I walked slowly back to the car, trying to puzzle things out. Fortunately the car was not badly damaged: a buckled wing and little more. But it was firmly wedged in the bank and would not move. I sat down beside it and waited for help. And help soon came in the shape of a delivery van; its driver fortunately had a length of rope; and within a few minutes he had hauled me clear.

'You were lucky in your skid,' he said, cheerfully. 'Had you skidded the other way you'd have finished driving for good. And it would have been pretty difficult to recover your remains for the funeral. However, all's well now. And that front wheel seems all right, too. But it's queer the way you managed to skid on a dry surface like this.'

'I didn't skid,' I replied, slowly. 'I was trying to avoid a boulder that was rolling down the hillside on to the road.'

'Boulder!' he answered, looking me hard in the eye. 'It's the first time I've heard of a boulder rolling down on to this road. And I've driven over it six days a week for the last twelve years or so.' Then, still looking me straight in the eye, he wavered a little and condescended to add: 'However, strange things do happen. But I'd like to know where that boulder came from. So long.'

He waved a friendly hand, got into his van, and drove off, leaving me alone with uncomfortable thoughts. I was positive I had not fallen asleep. I was equally positive that a large boulder had missed my car by inches. And what of that old woman with her dank hair and dripping clothes, who might almost have risen from the waters of the loch below, and who, after glaring at me with burning hate, had apparently been swallowed up in the waters again? If not, where had she gone? And who was she, anyway? How did she fit in? 'Well,' I said to myself, resignedly, 'strange things certainly do happen. But I'd be glad of an explanation, if anyone could give it.'

I stepped into my car, started the engine, and drove on again. Possibly I was more shaken than I had at first realized, and possibly I was worried with my thoughts; certainly I now crawled along the road, through Arisaig, and on to Morar. I remember that when at last I pulled into the drive of my hotel I felt as though a great burden had suddenly been lifted from my back.

Morar is a lovely spot, with its stretch of silver sand and with the islands of Rum, Eigg and Muck standing like sentinels in the sea. Inland, I found delightful walks, especially one by the side of the loch. In a couple of days the old woman of my adventure on the road from Glenfinnan had become a puzzling memory, and nothing more.

I had reached Morar on the Tuesday evening. Wednesday and Thursday I spent in lazily wandering about, or in lying in the heather and feeling how good, for a time, was a life of ease. On Friday, much against my inclination, I caught up with some long-delayed mail from home and then, in the early evening, took a short walk that led to the falls, where the waters of the loch, at that time still unharnessed for electric power, poured through a gorge before finding their way to the sea.

I had scrambled down a steep and narrow path that led to the foot of the falls, and had taken my stance on a boulder there, when a noise, rising above the thunder of the falls, made me turn round. I was only half-interested, and I turned round casually, but, to my horror, I saw a large rock hurtling down the narrow path on which I stood. How I managed to make the right decision in a split second of time, I shall never know. I flung myself down behind the boulder on which I was standing. The rock struck it with a mighty crack, bounced harmlessly over my head, and plunged into the whirlpool at the bottom of the falls.

Dazed and trembling, I carefully picked myself up. Then pain made itself felt, and I discovered that I had injured my left knee by throwing myself down to the ground. Would I be able to climb back again to the top of the path? I looked up at that steep and broken slope, and my heart suddenly jumped into my throat. An old woman with dank grey hair, and with clothes that were dripping wet, was glaring at me from above; glaring at me with intense hate, as three days before she had glared at me on the road from Glenfinnan. And again, though this time far more pronounced, I felt the same strange fear, and, with it, a weakness that seemed to affect every part of me.

I gripped the boulder beside me with both hands, frightened lest I should fall backwards into the whirlpool below. Gradually the weakness passed. Then, summoning the little courage that was left in me, I began a slow and painful crawl on hands and knees, taking advantage of every turn in the path, and praying constantly that no other rock would be hurled against me from above. When, at long last, I reached the top of the path, I lay there completely exhausted and unable to take a further step. The old woman was nowhere to be seen.

As I lay there, worn out and riddled with fear, my mind strove vainly to grapple with accidents that were beyond all reasoning. I now knew definitely that I had not fallen asleep at the wheel of my car. I knew, too, that twice a fiend of an old woman had tried to send me to the shades from which I was convinced she herself had risen. I had had enough. If, all unwittingly, I had disturbed the haunts of some avenging 'ghost', the only answer was to leave her haunts forthwith. Call me a coward, if you like; and coward I certainly became! But, then and there, I determined to return to Edinburgh and the safety of its streets.

I limped slowly back to the hotel, intending to pack my bags and depart. Yet, as soon as I had reached the hotel, a new fear struck me. To leave forthwith would mean driving through Arisaig, and on to Glenfinnan, by night. I couldn't face it. I knew that even driving along that road by day I should be crawling at a snail's pace, and looking to the right and left of me all the time. I even had thoughts of driving the odd four miles into Mallaig and there putting myself and my car on the boat. In the end I decided to stay the night, and to leave on the Saturday morning.

After dinner I told the landlord of my decision to leave early the next morning. I excused myself by reference to some urgent business that had arisen from my mail; and, in expressing my appreciation of the comfort of my stay, murmured something of my regret at having to leave so soon, and before I had even made any attempt to trace my ancestors who had come from Morar about two hundred years ago.

'Have you seen Father MacWilliam?' came his unexpected reply.

'No,' I answered. 'Why do you ask?'

'Well, it will be this way,' he said. 'The Father knows the history of Morar. He's been at the books and the papers these many years. And he's the one who would be telling you about your own folks, way past, if, indeed, there is anything to be known of them at all.'

'Could I call upon him now?' I asked eagerly.

'Indeed you could; but he'd be out.'

I looked at him in surprise.

'He'd be out, for he's in my own parlour this very time. Come you with me, and you can have a talk with him before you go.'

Full of interest, I was led to the back of the hotel, where Father MacWilliam, a plump and rosy-faced priest, was snugly ensconced in an easy-chair, and deep in the pages of an enormous book.

'Father, I've brought you Mr John MacDonald,' said my host, without further ado. 'He's for leaving tomorrow, but he'd be glad if you could be telling him of his people who, it would seem, came from these parts maybe two hundred years ago. If I were to let the two of you talk together, maybe he'll be learning something of what he wants to know.'

The priest gave me a warm smile of welcome, and somehow managed to unfold himself out of his chair. The landlord gave us a nod, and left the two of us together.

'John MacDonald,' said the priest, looking at me. 'It tells me nothing. Everyone here is a MacDonald. Every man, woman and child. God bless them all. Could you tell me more?'

I had to confess that I couldn't. All I knew was that my forbears had left Morar, or some place in its vicinity, about the 1750s. That, and no more.

Father MacWilliam shook his head. ''Tis no use,' he said. 'I can be of no help to you, much as I would have liked. Too many MacDonalds have left these parts – and sometimes I think too many have stayed on. But there, you've had a good time for the few days you've been here. And that's aye something.'

'Yes,' I answered slowly, and then, with a sudden desire to unburden myself, 'a good enough time if it hadn't been for an old woman who has twice tried to stone me to death.'

'What?' shouted the priest, his eyes suddenly blazing. 'You will be telling me that! Were her clothes dripping with water? Did you see, man, did you see?'

'Yes,' I answered, quickly. 'They were dripping wet. And she glared at me with such hatred in her eyes that I knew she was trying to kill me. Who is she? Or what is she?'

'I know only too well what she is,' he replied, slowly and quietly. 'And I know now who you are, John MacDonald, and I can give you your forbears. I'm thinking 'tis well you'll be leaving when the morning comes. But tell me your tale, and I'll tell you mine.'

Briefly I told him of my two encounters – on the road from Glenfinnan, and on the path by the falls. I told him, too, of the feeling of fear that had come to me. 'But why,' I protested, 'why should this old hag – ghost or spirit or fiend or whatever she is – hate me, a complete stranger, and try to murder me?'

'Because you are no stranger,' answered the priest, gravely. 'You are a MacDonald of Grianan, and the curse is on you and all your kin. That's why. And there's more to it. The same curse made your own people sell all, pack up, and sail across the seas in the year 1754. And though I'd be the last man to be frightening you, I shall be glad when you're back in your own land again.'

'But the thing's impossible,' I burst out, even though my own experiences had told me the very contrary.

'Not at all,' he replied firmly. 'Doesn't the Holy Book itself speak of evil and foul spirits? And didn't an evil spirit attack the seven sons of Sceva, leaping upon them, and driving them away, wounded and naked?'

'Well, what is the curse?' I demanded impatiently.

'That the stones of the earth shall crush you and all your kin,' answered the priest, looking at me sadly. 'And I'd be glad to be seeing you escape.'

'But why should there be such a curse?' I pleaded.

'Listen, my son. Away back in the seventeenth century the MacDonalds of Grianan were big folk, holding their land by charter of the king and with a right of judging the people on

their land – even with a right of *furca et fossa,* a right of "gallows
and pit", a gallows for hanging guilty men, and a pit for drowning guilty women. And in that time, when many a poor woman
was put to death because she was reputed to be a witch, Angus
MacDonald of Grianan, you'll forgive me, was a cruel man. Then
it was that Isabel MacKenzie, a poor creature on his lands, was
accused of witchcraft because a neighbour's cow had sickened
and died. Isabel MacKenzie was condemned to death, and Angus
MacDonald the cruel man, decreed it should be death by drowning. Did not his own charter say so? That poor creature was tied
by her wrists to the length of a rope; the rope was tied to a boat;
and Angus himself, with the others of his house, rowed out into
the loch, dragging her behind them till at last she was drowned.

'Then, it is said, as the waters slowly ended her unhappy life,
she cursed Angus and all his kin. "The waters of the loch shall
drown me, but the stones of the earth shall crush you and all your
kin – *Pronnaidh clachan na talmhainn thu 's do chinneadh
uile.*" '

The priest paused, 'And so it has been,' he continued, with a
sigh. 'Angus laughed, as the years passed and he still lived. But
one night, in a storm of wind, the chimney of his house was
blown down and the stones of it fell through the roof and crushed
him to death where he lay in his bed.

'Alastair, his son, was of finer mould. I can find no word of his
doing wrong to man or beast. Yet he, too, was to die. There was a
jetty to be built – and this was maybe a full twenty years after his
father had died – and Alastair had gone down to see the men at
the work. There was a tackle of some kind for lifting the heavy
stones, and, somehow, a stone slipped from the tackle. It fell on
him and crushed him to death.

'Then it was that people began to look at Grianan and quietly,
among themselves, began to talk of the curse. And then it was
that the MacDonalds of Grianan began to die more quickly.
Always there was a stone of the earth in the way of their dying;
and some of them, with their last words, would be speaking of
strange things – of a woman with burning eyes, and whose
clothes were wet with the waters of the loch. And, in the end, one,
Roderick MacDonald, having seen his own father crushed to

death by a millstone that was firmly fixed and yet somehow broke loose, sold his lands and his cattle, and sailed to America with his wife and child.

'And you, my son,' said Father MacWilliam, laying his hand gently on my arm, 'you are come of Roderick's stock. Yet I see some comfort for you. In all the papers that I have read, Isabel MacKenzie's curse never failed before. Twice it has failed to touch you. To me it would seem that her evil power is on the wane. I shall pray for you. But I shall still be glad to see you gone.'

'And I can do nothing?' I asked lamely.

'Nothing, save to put your trust in God,' he answered. 'And to remember that the power of the Lord is greater than all the powers of evil.'

Again he touched me lightly on the arm, looked kindly at me, and went out.

To be quite frank, I do not remember very clearly how I passed the rest of that evening. I was already completely unnerved, and now the story of my own house, the house that had the curse upon it, occupied my mind to the exclusion of all else. I wanted company. I wanted to have people around me. And yet my mind was never on the talk that they made. I am ashamed to think how boorish and uncivil I must have seemed. I am ashamed, too, to think of the drink that I took. I freely admit that terror had taken hold of me. Terror of being left alone. Terror of going to my bed. I drank in the bar, trying to make friends with complete strangers and yet thinking always of an old woman and her curse on my kin. In the end, I am told, I had to be carried to bed by the local doctor and a guest at the hotel. For a time, drink had ousted terror.

I do not know what time it was when I awoke. It was already daylight – but daylight breaks early in the Highlands in summer time. My head ached violently. Then I remembered my heavy drinking, and, with that, I remembered its cause. But what had awakened me? The wind was blowing strongly and yet, I assured myself, not strongly enough to bring a chimney-stack crashing down. But what was that? My ears caught a strange noise that seemed to come from the corridor outside my room. At once all my terror returned. I sat up in bed. There was the noise again! A shuffling noise. And something more. A noise that came between each shuffle. What was it? A shuffle; a strange dull thump; a shuffle; a thump. And drawing nearer all the time.

I tried to shout, but I could only croak like a feeble frog. I jumped out of bed, trembling from head to foot. How could I escape? Outside, in the corridor, a hell-hag, dead three hundred years ago, was coming to me, coming to crush me to death with a stone. A stone! That was the noise I could hear! She was pushing it before her, pushing it up to my door!

I looked wildly round. Thank God! The window! Flinging it wide open, I climbed quickly out, and, hanging from the window-ledge by my hands, let myself drop. As I landed on the ground I fell over backwards and, at the same instant, there came a heavy thud at my feet and the soft garden-earth splashed over me. I lay there, paralyzed with fear.

Then, slowly, I raised my head to look. A large stone had embedded itself in the ground exactly where I had dropped and exactly where I would have been had I not fallen over on my back. The curse was still upon me, and my life was to end with a stone.

I sprang to my feet, and, strangely, found my voice again. With a wild cry I ran across the garden, my injured knee sending quivers of hot pain up my thigh. And immediately I was held in a fast grip. Trembling and overwrought, I whimpered like a beaten cur, only to be at once calmed and reassured. I had run straight into the arms of Father MacWilliam.

'You are safe, my son,' came his gentle voice, as he still held me in his arms. 'Safe and saved. The powers of darkness shall trouble you no more. I have wrestled, even as Jacob wrestled at Peniel. Come with me to my own house. The Lord forgive me: I should have taken you there before.'

Paying no attention to the confused hubbub that now came from the hotel, he led me gently across the road – its stones feeling smooth and cool to my bare feet – and over the open moorland to the church. There he took me into his house and put me in his own bed. On the instant, I fell into peaceful sleep.

Late the next morning I awoke to find my clothes on a chair by my bed. I washed and dressed, and went downstairs. A wise and gentle priest was awaiting me. He gave me breakfast, and then took me to my car which, with all my luggage packed and neatly stowed on the rear seat, was standing at his gate. 'There you are, my son,' he said. 'The curse is at an end. You can take any road and drive on it as freely as you wish – though,' he added, with a twinkle in his eye, 'always observing the laws that are enforced by the police.' He gave me his blessing, and wished me God-speed. With unashamed tears in my eyes, I thanked him again and again. At last I drove away.

Without a qualm, without fear of any kind, I drove back through Arisaig and Glenfinnan, ran back through Ballachulish and Callander, and so to Edinburgh.

Yet my tale has not quite ended.

On my way back, I stopped at Ballachulish for a very late lunch at the inn. As I ate alone in the dining-room, I heard two men talking outside by the open window.

'That was a mighty queer business last night, though I could get nothing out of the landlord when I tried to pump him this morning.'

'Yes, but the fellow was obviously drunk. He had to be carried to bed, you know.'

'I agree, old man. All the same, there was more to it than that. As you know, my room was next to his, and, just before he gave that awful yell which woke up everybody, I'd already been wakened by a strange kind of bumping noise which I couldn't fathom. I got up and looked out of the window, thinking the noise was probably coming from outside – and it may well have been that coping-stone, which had obviously worked loose, and which the wind may have been lifting slightly before it fell.

'However, that's not what I was going to say. As I looked out of the window, there, in the clear light of the early morning, I was astonished to see the local priest standing in the middle of the lawn, with one arm raised above his head, while a dishevelled old woman crouched and cowered before him. The very next second I saw this fellow climb out of his window and drop down. There was a crash as the coping-stone fell. And, with that, he jumped up, gave his appalling yell, and rushed straight into the arms of the priest. Where the old woman had gone to I don't know. She just seemed to disappear. And what she and the priest were doing ...'

'What an extraordinary ... Did you ...'

The men had moved away, and their voices were fading. I tip-toed as fast as I could to the window and strained my ears. But I could catch only a few more words.

'And another queer thing – when I dashed out into the corridor in my bare feet it seemed to be soaking wet all along its length.'

From *Dark Encounters* by William Croft Dickinson (Harvill Press, London).

THE EARLIER SERVICE

Margaret Irwin

Mrs Lacey and her eldest daughter Alice hurried through the diminutive gate that led from the Rectory garden into the churchyard. Alice paused to call: 'Jane, father's gone on,' under the window of her young sister's room. To her mother she added with a cluck of annoyance, 'What a time she takes to dress!'

But Jane was sitting, ready dressed for church, in the window-seat of her room. Close up to her window and a little to the right, stood the square church tower with gargoyles at each corner. She could see them every morning as she lay in her bed at the left of the window, their monstrous necks stretched out as though they were trying to get into her room.

The church bell stopped. Jane could hear the shuffle of feet as the congregation rose at the entrance of her father; then came silence, and then the drone of the General Confession. She jumped up, ran downstairs and into the churchyard. Right above her now hung the gargoyles, peering down at her. Behind them the sun was setting in clouds, soft and humid as winter sunsets can only be in Somerset. She was standing in front of a tiny door studded with nails. The doorway was the oldest part of the church of Cloud Martin. It dated back to Saxon days; and the shrivelled bits of blackened, leather-like stuff, still clinging to some of the nails, were said to be the skins of heathens flayed alive.

Jane paused a moment, her hands held outwards and a little behind her. Her face was paler than it had been in her room, her eyes were half shut, and her breath came a little quickly, but then she had been running. With the same sudden movement that she had jumped from the window-seat, she now jerked her hands forward, turned the great iron ring that served as a door-handle, and stole into the church.

The door opened into the corner just behind the Rectory pew. She was late. Mrs Lacey and Alice were standing up and chanting the monotone that had become a habitual and almost an unconscious part of their lives. Jane stole in past her mother, and knelt for an instant, her red pigtail, bright symbol of an old-fashioned upbringing, flopping sideways on to the dark wood. 'Please God, don't let me be afraid – don't, don't *don't* let me be afraid,' she whispered; then stood, and repeated the responses in clear and precise tones, her eyes fixed on the long stone figure of the Crusader against the wall in front of her.

He was in chain armour; the mesh of mail surrounded his face like the coif of a nun, and a high crown-like helmet came low down on his brows. His feet rested against a small lion, which Jane as a child had always thought was his favourite dog that had followed him to the Holy Wars. His huge mailed hand grasped the pommel of his sword, drawn an inch or two from its scabbard. Jane gazed at him as though she would draw into herself all the watchful stern repose of the sleeping giant. Behind the words of the responses, other words repeated themselves in her mind:

> The knight is dust,
> His good sword rust;
> His soul is with the saints, we trust.

'But he is *here*,' she told herself, 'you can't really be afraid with him here.'

There came the sudden silence before the hymn, and she wondered what nonsense she had been talking to herself. She knew the words of the service too well, that was what it was; how could she ever attend to them?

They settled down for the sermon, a safe twenty minutes at least, in the Rector's remote and dreamlike voice. Jane's mind raced off at a tangent, almost painfully agile, yet confined always somewhere between the walls of the church.

'You shouldn't think of other things in church,' was a maxim that had been often repeated to her. In spite of it she thought of

more other things in those two Sunday services than in the whole
week between.

'What a lot of Other Things other people must have thought
of too in this church,' she said to herself; the thought shifted
and changed a little; 'there are lots of Other Things in this
church; there are too many Other Things in this church.' Oh,
she *mustn't* say things like that to herself or she would begin to
be afraid again – she was not afraid yet – of course, she was not
afraid, there was nothing to be afraid of, and if there were, the
Crusader was before her, his hand on his sword, ready to draw it
at need. And what need could there be? Her mother was beside
her whose profile she could see without looking at it, *she* would
never be disturbed, and by nothing.

But at that moment Mrs Lacey shivered, and glanced behind
her at the little door by which Jane had entered. Jane passed her
fur to her, but Mrs Lacey shook her head. Presently she looked
round again, and kept her head turned for fully a minute. Jane
watched her mother until the familiar home-trimmed hat turned
again to the pulpit; she wondered then if her mother would indeed never be disturbed, and by nothing.

She looked up at the crooked angel in the tiny window of
medieval glass. His red halo was askew; his oblique face had been
a friend since her childhood. A little flat-nosed face in the carving
round the pillar grinned back at her and all but winked.

'How old are you?' asked Jane.

'Six hundred years odd,' he replied.

'Then you should know better than to wink in church, let
alone always grinning.'

But he only sang to a ballad tune:

> 'Oh, if you'd seen as much as I,
> It's often you would wink.'

'In the name of the Father and the Son and the Holy Ghost –'

Already! *Now* they would soon be outside again, out of the
church for a whole safe week. But they would have to go
through that door first.

She waited anxiously till her father went up to the altar to
give the blessing. After she was confirmed, she, too, would have to

go up to the altar. She would have to go. Now her father was
going. He took so long to get there, he seemed so much smaller
and darker as he turned his back on the congregation; it was
really impossible sometimes to see that he had on a white surplice
at all. What was he going to do up there at the altar, what was
that gleaming pointed thing in his hand? *Who* was that little
dark man going up to the altar? Her fingers closed tight on her
prayer book as the figure turned round.

'You idiot, of course it's father! There, you can see it's father.'

She stared at the benevolent nut-cracker face, distinct enough
now to her for all the obscurity of the chancel. How much taller
he seemed now he had turned round. And of course his surplice
was white – quite white. What *had* she been seeing?

'May the peace of God which passeth all understanding –'

She wished she could kneel under the spell of those words for
ever.

'Oh, yes,' said the little flat-nosed face as she rose from her
knees, 'but you'd find it dull, you know.' He was grinning atro-
ciously.

The two Rectory girls filed out after their mother, who carefully fastened the last button on her glove before she opened the
door on which hung the skins of men that had been flayed alive.
As she did so, she turned round and looked behind her, but went
out without stopping. Jane almost ran after her, and caught her
arm. Mrs Lacey was already taking off her gloves.

'Were you looking round for Tom Elroy, mother?' asked Alice.

'No, dear, not specially. I thought Tom or someone had come
up to our door, but the church does echo so. I think there must be
a draught from that door, but it's funny, I only feel it just at the
end of the evening service.'

'You oughtn't to sit at the end of the pew then, and with your
rheumatism. Janey, you always come in last. Why don't *you* sit at
the end?'

'I won't!' snapped Jane.

'Whatever's the matter, Jane?' asked her mother.

'Why should I sit at the end of the pew? Why can't we move
out of that pew altogether? I only wish we would.'

Nobody paid any attention to this final piece of blasphemy,

for they had reached the lighted hall of the Rectory by this time and were rapidly dispersing. Jane hung her coat and hat on the stand in the hall and went into the pantry to collect the cold meat and cheese. The maids were always out on Sunday evening. Alice was already making toast over the dining-room fire; she looked up as the Rector entered, and remarked severely: 'You shouldn't quote Latin in your sermons, father. Nobody in the church understands it.'

'Nobody understands my sermons,' said Mr Lacey, 'for nobody listens to them. So I may as well give myself the occasional pleasure of a Latin quotation, since only a dutiful daughter is likely to notice the lapse of manners. Alice, my dear, did I give out in church that next Friday is the last Confirmation class?'

'Friday!' cried Jane, in the doorway with the cheese. 'Next Friday the last class? Then the Confirmation's next week.'

'Of course it is, and high time, too,' said Alice, 'seeing that you were sixteen last summer. Only servant girls get confirmed *after* sixteen.'

That settled it then. In a spirit of gloomy resignation Jane engulfed herself in an orange.

There were bright stars above the church tower when she went to bed. She kept her head turned away as she drew the curtains, so that she should not see the gargoyles stretching their necks towards her window.

Friday evening found Jane at the last Confirmation class in the vestry with her father and three farmers' daughters, who talked in a curious mixture of broad Somerset and high school education and knew the catechism a great deal better than Jane.

After they had left, she followed closely at her father's elbow into the church to remove hymn books and other vestiges of the choir practice that had taken place just before the class. The lamp he carried made a little patch of light wherever they moved; the outlying walls of darkness shifted, but pressed hard upon it from different · quarters. The Rector was looking for his Plotinus, which he was certain he had put down somewhere in the church. He fumbled all over the Rectory pew while Jane tried on vain pretexts to drag him away.

'I have looked in that corner – thoroughly,' she said.

The Rector sighed.

> 'What shall I say
> Since Truth is dead?'

he inquired. 'So far from looking in that corner, Jane, you kept your head turned resolutely away from it.'

'Did I? I suppose I was looking at the list of Rectors. What a long one it is, and all dead but you, father.'

He at once forgot Plotinus and left the Rectory pew to pore with proud pleasure over the names that began with one Johannes de Martigny and ended with his own.

'A remarkably persistent list. Only two real gaps – in the Civil Wars and in the fourteenth century. That was at the time of the Black Death, when there was no rector of this parish for many years. You see, Jane? – 1349, and then there's no name till 1361 – Giraldus atte Welle. Do you remember when you were a little girl, very proud of knowing how to read, how you read through all the names to me, but refused to say that one? You said, "It's a dreadful name," and when I pressed you, you began to cry.'

'How silly! There's nothing dreadful in Giraldus atte Welle,' began Jane, but as she spoke she looked round her. She caught the Rector's arm. 'Father, there isn't anyone in the church besides us, is there?'

'My dear child, of course not. What's the matter? You're not nervous, are you?'

'No, not really. But we can find Plotinus much easier by daylight. Oh – and father – don't let's go out by the little door. Let's pretend we're the General Congregation and go out properly by the big door.'

She pulled him down the aisle, talking all the way until they were both in his study. 'Father doesn't *know*,' she said to herself – 'he knows less than mother. It's funny, when he would understand so much more.'

But he understood that she was troubled. He asked: 'Don't you want to get confirmed, Jane?' and then: 'You mustn't be if you don't want it.'

Jane grew frightened. There would be a great fuss if she backed out of it now after the very last class. Besides, there was the Crusader. Vague ideas of the initiation rites of knight and crusader crossed her mind in connexion with the rite of Confirmation. He had spent a night's vigil in a church, perhaps in this very church. One could never fear anything else after that. If only she didn't have to go right up to the altar at the Communion Service. But she would not think of that; she told the Rector that it was quite all right really, and at this moment they reached the hall door and met Mrs Lacey hurrying towards them with a letter from Hugh, now at Oxford, who was coming home for the vacation on Wednesday.

'He asks if he may bring an undergraduate friend for the first few days—a Mr York who is interested in old churches and Hugh thinks he would like to see ours. He must be clever – it is such a pity Elizabeth is away – she is the only one who could talk to him; of course, he will enjoy talking with you, father dear, but men seem to expect girls too to be clever now. And just as Janey's Confirmation is coming on – she isn't taking it seriously enough as it is.'

'*Mother!* Don't you want us to play dumb crambo like the last time Hugh brought friends down?'

'Nonsense,' said the Rector hastily. 'Dumb crambo requires so much attention that it should promote seriousness in all things. I am very glad the young man is coming, my love, and I will try my hardest to talk as cleverly as Elizabeth.'

He went upstairs with his wife, and said in a low voice: 'I think Jane is worrying rather too much about her Confirmation as it is. She seems quite jumpy sometimes.'

'Oh – *jumpy*, yes,' said Mrs Lacey, as though she refused to consider jumpiness the right qualification for Confirmation. The question of the curtains in the spare room, however, proved more immediately absorbing.

Hugh, who preferred people to talk shop, introduced his friend's hobby the first evening at dinner. 'He goes grubbing over churches with a pencil and a bit of paper and finds things scratched on the walls and takes rubbings of them and you call them *graffiti*. Now, then, father, any offers from our particular property?'

The Rector did not know of any specimens in his church. He asked what sort of things were scratched on the walls.

'Oh, anything,' said York, 'texts, scraps of dog Latin, aphorisms – once I found the beginning of a love song. When a monk, or anyone who was doing a job in the church, got bored, he'd begin to scratch words on the wall just as one does on a seat or log or anything today. Only we nearly always write our names and they hardly ever did.'

He showed some of the rubbings he had taken. Often, he explained, you couldn't see anything but a few vague scratches, and then in the rubbing they came out much clearer. 'The bottom of a pillar is a good place to look,' he said, 'and corners – anywhere where they're not likely to be too plainly seen.'

'There are some marks on the wall near our pew,' said Jane. 'Low down, nearly on the ground.'

He looked at her, pleased, and distinguishing her consciously for the first time from her rather sharp-voiced sister. He saw a gawky girl whose grave, beautiful eyes were marred by deep hollows under them, as though she did not sleep enough. And Jane looked back with satisfaction at a pleasant ugly, wide, good-humoured face.

She showed him the marks next morning, both squatting on their heels beside the wall. Hugh had strolled in with them, declaring that they were certain to find nothing better than the names of the present choir boys, and had retired to the organ loft for an improvization. York spread a piece of paper over the marks and rubbed his pencil all over it and asked polite questions about the church. Was it as haunted as it should be?

Jane, concerned for the honour of their church, replied that the villagers had sometimes seen lights in the windows at midnight; but York contemptuously dismissed that. 'You'd hear as much of any old church.' He pulled out an electric torch and switched it on to the wall.

'It's been cut in much more deeply at the top,' he remarked; 'I can read it even on the wall.' He spelt out slowly: ' "*Nemo potest duobus dominis servire.*" That's a text from the Vulgate. It means: "No man can serve two masters".'

'And did the same man write the rest underneath, too?'

'No, I should think that was written much later, about the end of the fourteenth century. Hartley will tell me exactly. He's a friend of mine in the British Museum, and I send him the rubbings and he finds out all about them.'

He examined the sentence on the paper by his torch, while Hugh's 'improvisation' sent horrible cacophonies reeling through the church.

'Latin again, and jolly bad – monkish Latin, you know. Can't make out that word. Oh!'

'Well?'

'It's in answer to the text above, I think. I say, this is the best find I've ever had. Look here, the first fellow wrote, "No man can serve two masters," and then, about a century after, number two squats down and writes – well, as far as I can make it out, it's like this: "Show service therefore to the good, but cleave unto the evil." Remarkable sentiments for a priest to leave in his church, for I'd imagine only the priest would be educated enough to write it. Now why did he say that, I wonder?'

'Because evil is more interesting than good,' murmured Jane.

'Hmph. You agree with him then? What kind of evil?'

'I don't know. It's just – don't you know how words and sentences stick in your head sometimes? It's as though I were always hearing it.'

'Do you think you'll hear it tomorrow?' asked York maliciously. He had been told that tomorrow was the day of her Confirmation. She tried to jump up, but as she was cramped from squatting so long on her heels she only sat down instead, and they both burst out laughing.

'I'm sorry,' said York, 'I didn't mean to be offensive. But I'd like to know what's bothering you.'

'What do you mean?'

'Oh, you know. But never mind. I dare say you can't say.' This at once caused an unusual flow of speech from Jane.

'Why should evil be interesting?' she gasped. 'It isn't in real life – when servants steal the spoons and the villagers quarrel with their neighbours. Mrs Elroy came round to father in a fearful stew the other day because old Mrs Croft had made a maukin of her.'

'A what?'

'An image – you know – out of clay, and she was sticking pins in it, and Mrs Elroy declared she knew every time a pin had gone in because she felt a stab right through her body.'

'What did your father say?'

'He said it was sciatica, but she wouldn't believe it, and he had to go round to Mrs Croft and talk about Christmas peace and good will, but she only leered and yammered at him in the awful way she does, and then Alice said that Christmas blessings only came to those who live at peace with their neighbours, and Mrs Croft knew that blessings meant puddings, so she took the pins out, and let the maukin be, and Mrs Elroy hasn't felt any more stabs.'

'Mrs Croft is a proper witch then?'

York stood up, looking rather curiously at her shining eyes.

'Cloud Martin has always been a terrible bad parish for witches,' said Jane proudly.

'You find *that* form of evil interesing,' he said.

Jane was puzzled and abashed by his tone. She peered at the wall again and thought she could make out another mark underneath the others. York quickly took a rubbing and, examining the paper, found it to be one word only, and probably of the same date as the last sentence, which had caused so much discussion about evil.

' "Ma – ma," ah, I have it. "*Maneo* – I remain", that's all.'

' "*I* remain?" Who remains?'

'Why, the same "I" who advises us to cleave to evil. Remembering, perhaps, though it hadn't been said then, that the evil that men do lives after them.'

She looked at him with startled eyes. He thought she was a nice child but took things too seriously.

Hugh's attempts at jazz on the organ had faded away. As Jane and York left the church by the little door, they met him coming out through the vestry.

'Lots of luck,' said York, handing him the paper. 'Did you turn on the verger or anyone to look as well?'

'No – why? Aren't the family enough for you?'

'Rather. I was only wondering what that little man was doing by the door as we went out. You must have seen him, too,' he said turning to Jane, 'he was quite close to us.'

But as she stared at him, he wished he had not spoken.

'Must have been the organist,' said Hugh, who was looking back at the church tower. 'Do you like gargoyles, York? There's a rather pretty one up there of a devil eating a child – see it?'

On the Sunday morning after the Confirmation, the day of her first Communion, Jane rose early, dressed by candlelight, met her mother and sister in the hall, and followed them through the raw, uncertain darkness of the garden and churchyard. The chancel windows were lighted up; the gargoyles on the church tower could just be seen, their distorted shapes a deeper black against the dark sky.

Jane slipped past her mother at the end of the pew. Except for the lights in the chancel, and the one small lamp that hung over the middle aisle, the church was dark and one could not see who was there. Mr Lacey was already in the chancel and the service began. Jane had been to this service before, but never when the morning was dark like this. Perhaps that was what made it so different. For it *was* different.

Her father was doing such odd things up there at the altar. Why was he pacing backwards and forwards so often, and waving his hands in that funny way? And what *was* he saying? She couldn't make out the words – she must have completely lost the place. She tried to find it in her prayer book, but the words to which she was listening gave her no clue; she could not recognize them at all, and presently she realized that not only were the words unknown to her, but so was the language in which they were spoken. Alice's rebuke came back to her: 'You shouldn't quote Latin in your sermons, father.' But this wasn't a sermon, it was the Communion Service. Only in the Roman Catholic Church they would have the Communion Service in Latin, and then it would be the Mass. Was father holding Mass? He would be turned out of the Church for being Roman. It was bewildering, it was dreadful. But her mother didn't seem to notice anything.

Did she notice that there were other people up there at the altar?

There was a brief pause. People came out of the darkness behind her, and went up to the chancel. Mrs Lacey slipped out of the pew and joined them. Jane sat back and let her sister go past her.

'You are coming, Janey?' whispered Alice as she passed.

Jane nodded, but she sat still. She had let her mother and sister leave her; she stared at the two rows of dark figures standing in the chancel behind the row of those who knelt; she could not see her mother and sister among them; she could see no one whom she knew.

She dared not look again at the figures by the altar; she kept her head bowed. The last time she had looked there had been two others standing by her father – that is, if that little dark figure had indeed been her father. If she looked now, would she see him there? Her head bent lower and sank into her hands. Instead of the one low voice murmuring the words of the Sacrament, a muffled chant of many voices came from the chancel.

She heard the scuffle of feet, but no steps came past her down into the church again. What were they doing up there? At last she had to look, and she saw that the two rows were standing facing each other across the chancel, instead of each behind the other. She tried to distinguish their faces, to recognize even one that she knew. Presently she became aware that why she could not do this was because they had no faces. The figures all wore dark cloaks with hoods and there were blank white spaces under the hoods.

'It is possible,' she said to herself, 'that those are masks.' She formed the words in her mind deliberately and with precision as though to distract her attention; for she felt in danger of screaming aloud with terror, and whatever happened she must not draw down on her the attention of those waiting figures. She knew now that they were waiting for her to go up to the altar.

She might slip out by the little door and escape, if only she dared to move. She stood up and saw the Crusader lying before her, armed, on guard, his sword half-drawn from its scabbard. Her breath was choking her. 'Crusader, Crusader, rise and help me,' she prayed very fast in her mind. But the Crusader stayed motionless. She must go out by herself. With a blind, rushing movement, she threw herself on to the little door, dragged it open, and got outside.

Mrs Lacey and Alice thought that Jane, wishing for solitude, must have returned from the Communion table to some other pew. Only Mr Lacey knew that she had not come up to the Communion table at all; and it troubled him still more when she did not appear at breakfast. Alice thought she had gone for a walk; Mrs Lacey said in her vague, late Victorian way that she thought it only natural Jane should wish to be alone for a little.

'I should say it was decidedly more natural that she should wish for sausages and coffee after being up for an hour on a raw December morning,' said her husband with unusual asperity.

It was York who found her half an hour later walking very fast through the fields. He took her hands, which felt frozen, and as he looked into her face he said, 'Look here, you know, this won't do. What are you so frightened of?' And then broke off his questions, told her not to bother to try to speak but to come back to breakfast, and half-pulled her with him through the thick, slimy mud, back to the Rectory. Suddenly she began to tell him that the Early Service that morning had all been different – the people, their clothes, even the language, it was all quite different.

He thought over what she stammered out, and wondered if she could somehow have had the power to go back in time and see and hear the Latin Mass as it used to be in that church.

'The old Latin Mass wasn't a horrible thing, was it?'

'Jane! Your father's daughter needn't ask that.'

'No. I see. Then it wasn't the Mass I saw this morning – it was –' She spoke very low so that he could hardly catch the words. 'There was something horrible going on up there by the altar – and they were waiting – waiting for me.'

Her hand trembled under his arm. He thrust it down into his pocket on the pretext of warming it. It seemed to him monstrous that this nice, straightforward little schoolgirl whom he liked best of the family, should be hag-ridden like this.

That evening he wrote a long letter to his antiquarian friend, Hartley, enclosing the pencil rubbings he had taken of the words scratched on the wall by the Rectory pew.

On Monday he was leaving them, to go and look at other churches in Somerset. He looked hard at Jane as he said good-bye. She seemed to have completely forgotten whatever it was that had so distressed her the day before, and at breakfast had been the jolliest of the party. But when she felt York's eyes upon her, the laughter died out of hers; she said, but not as though she had intended to say it: 'You will come back for Wednesday.'

'Why, what happens on Wednesday?'

'It is full moon then.'

'That's not this Wednesday then, it must be Wednesday week. Why do you want me to come back then?'

She could give no answer to that. She turned self-conscious and began an out-of-date jazz song about 'Wednesday week way down in old Bengal!'

It was plain she did not know why she had said it. But he promised himself that he would come back by then, and asked Mrs Lacey if he might look them up again on his way home.

In the intervening ten days he was able to piece together some surprising information which seemed to throw a light on the inscriptions he had found at Cloud Martin.

In the reports of certain trials for sorcery in the year 1474, one Giraldus atte Welle, priest of the parish of Cloud Martin in Somerset, confessed under torture to having held the Black Mass in his church at midnight on the very altar where he administered the Blessed Sacrament on Sundays. This was generally done on Wednesday or Thursday, the chief days of the Witches' Sabbath when they happened to fall on the night of the full moon. The priest would then enter the church by the little side door, and from the darkness in the body of the church those villagers who had followed his example and sworn themselves to Satan, would come up and join him, one by one, hooded and masked, that none might recognize the other. He was charged with having secretly decoyed young children in order to kill them on the altar as a sacrifice to Satan, and he was finally charged with attempting to murder a young virgin for that purpose.

All the accused made free confessions towards the end of their trial, especially in so far as they implicated other people. All however were agreed on a certain strange incident. That just as the priest was about to cut the throat of the girl on the altar, the tomb of the Crusader opened, and the knight who had lain there for two centuries arose and came upon them with drawn sword, so that they scattered and fled through the church, leaving the girl unharmed on the altar.

With these reports from Hartley in his pocket, York travelled back on the Wednesday week by slow cross-country trains that managed to miss their connexions and land him at Little Borridge, the station for Cloud Martin, at a quarter-past ten. The village cab had broken down, there was no other car to be had at that hour, it was a six-mile walk up to the Rectory, there was a station hotel where it would be far more reasonable to spend the night, and finish his journey next morning. Yet York refused to consider this alternative; all through the maddening and uncertain journey, he had kept saying to himself, 'I shall be late,' though he did not know for what. He had promised Jane he would be back this Wednesday, and back he must be. He left his luggage at the station and walked up. It was the night of the full moon, but the sky was so covered with cloud as to be almost dark. Once or twice he missed his way in following the elaborate instructions of the station-master, and had to retrace his steps a little. It was hard on twelve o'clock when at last he saw the square tower of Cloud Martin church, a solid blackness against the flying clouds.

He walked up to the little gate into the churchyard. There was a faint light from the chancel windows, and he thought he heard voices chanting. He paused to listen, and then he was certain of it, for he could hear the silence when they stopped. It might have been a minute or five minutes later, that he heard the most terrible shriek he had ever imagined, though faint, coming as it did from the closed church; and knew it for Jane's voice. He ran up to the little door and heard that scream again and again.

As he broke through the door he heard it cry: 'Crusader! Crusader!' The church was in utter darkness, there was no light in the chancel, he had to fumble in his pockets for his electric torch. The screams had stopped and the whole place was silent. He flashed his torch right and left, and saw a figure lying huddled against the altar. He knew that it was Jane; in an instant he had reached her. Her eyes were open, looking at him, but they did not know him, and she did not seem to understand him when he spoke. In a strange, rough accent of broad Somerset that he could scarcely distinguished, she said, 'It was my body on the altar.'

From *Madame Fears the Dark* by Margaret Irwin (Chatto & Windus Ltd, London).

FROM LIFE

'HERE I AM AGAIN!'

Copy of a letter dated July 10th, 1917 from Charles G. S. — Esq., to Lord Halifax.

DEAR LORD HALIFAX,

I send you herewith my plain, unvarnished tale, according to your kind request. I may say in confidence that the house was — —, Deal, but I would rather that my name and the name of the house should not be mentioned in case you care at any time to give publicity to the story. The only tales dealing with ghostly phenomena which seem to me to be of any value are those relating first-hand experiences. All others are so embroidered that the truth of them is merely a matter of surmise.

My experience was *horrible*, so much so that I have vowed never to have anything to do with spiritualism in any shape or form. I want no more materializations which seem to be the goal of all ardent spiritualists.

The house in question is an old Georgian house in Deal. It was built about 1740 and Nelson addressed many of his letters to Lady Hamilton from there, calling it 'dear — House'. My host and I had been yachting together, and on our arrival from the sea unexpectedly found the house full of relations who had come to stay. A bed was arranged for me in a dressing-room. On a previous visit I had heard that the house was haunted and that all the daughters had seen the figure of someone they called their great-grandmother gliding about. The servants had been terrified, and in consequence of what they saw had refused to stay. I had forgotten this. I was in rude health after my Channel cruise and nothing ghostly was discussed before I retired to bed.

In the middle of the night I awoke, feeling that something uncanny was about me. Suddenly, there appeared at my bedside the phantom of either an old man or woman, of dreadful aspect, who was bending over me. That I was wide awake is beyond all question. I at once became cataleptic, unable to move hand or foot. I could only gaze at this monstrosity, vowing mentally that if I ever recovered from this horrible experience I would never dabble in table-turning, planchette, etc., again, for here was a real materialization and the reality was too terrifying for description.

Next morning I told my host privately of what had occurred. He said he was not in the least surprised, as everybody living in the house except himself had, at one time or another, seen something of the sort.

Twenty years passed and I had almost forgotten the incident. I had frequently re-visited the house and had seen nothing. Then one day I was again invited and found my host alone. We played billiards together and retired rather late. I was suffering from toothache and on getting into bed was utterly unable to sleep. The room was in a different part of the house from the dressing-room in which I had slept on the occasion of my first visit.

Suddenly, although it was early summer, I began to feel very cold. I seemed literally to freeze from my feet upwards, and although I put on more clothes, the cold rapidly increased until I imagined that my heart must be failing and that this was death.

All at once a voice (unheard physically) appeared to be saying over and over again to me, 'Here I am again! Here I am again, after twenty years.' Once more, in an exact repetition of my feeling twenty years before, I pulled myself together and said to myself, 'This time I will see this thing through and definitely prove whether my former experience was an hallucination and whether there really is such a thing as a ghost. I am wide awake beyond all possibility of doubt and only too conscious of a raging toothache.'

The thing again spoke to me mentally: 'Look round. Look round.'

I now had that unaccountable feeling of horror which all accounts of such manifestations agree in declaring are produced on such occasions. Turning round, I saw in the corner of the room facing me a curious column of light revolving spirally like a whirlwind of dust on a windy day. It was white, and as I gazed, it slowly drew near to me.

'Here I am again!' the thing kept repeating.

I stretched out my hand for the matches at my bedside. As the thing got gradually closer and closer to me, it rapidly began to take human shape. Under my eyes and within my grasp it assumed that very figure I had seen twenty years before. There was no doubt whatever about this, and having reached the limit of my endurance, I shouted out, 'Who's that?' No answer coming, I hurriedly struck a match and lit a candle.

Next morning I told my host what had befallen me. He was greatly interested, and related two weird occurrences in the house, both of which had taken place during the three weeks previous to my visit.

On the first occasion he was in his dressing-room, when a servant came up to say that a friend had called to see him. He ran hurriedly downstairs and, as he turned on the landing for the next flight, he saw the figure of a man rushing upstairs. My friend, unable to stop himself, put up his hands to avert a collision and went right through the figure.

The second occasion had been when one evening an officer of Marines came to play billiards with him and brought his dog, which lay under the table. Suddenly the dog sprang up and began barking furiously at something invisible in the corner. It went on barking till its mouth foamed and its hair stood on end. They endeavoured in vain to calm it. From under the table it kept making violent rushes at the corner and then retreating again. Neither my friend nor the officer who was visiting saw anything.

From *Lord Halifax's Ghost Book* (Geoffrey Bles Ltd, London).

THE MAN WHO DIED AT SEA

Rosemary Sutcliff

My mother was not quite like most people's mothers. She came, as far as anybody knew, of good hard-headed North Country Saxon stock on both sides, but she should by rights have been Irish or Highland Scots. She had what people called the 'Celtic temperament', up one instant and down the next, and making sure that my father and I were up and down with her. When she was down, it was as though a brown fog hung over the whole house, and when she started going up again, it was as though the sun came out and the birds started singing. Living with her had never a dull moment, but it could be rather unnerving, for she had, unquestionably, a touch of the Second Sight, another thing which one expects of a Celt more than a Saxon.

She saw our beloved old dog lying in his accustomed place before the hall fire, six weeks or so after he died; and she heard things – the same old dog padding around the house, even years later; footsteps and voices that weren't there for other people; and occasionally she knew that certain things were going to happen. They didn't always happen, but they happened often enough for my father and I not to like it very much when she predicted something bad. (It generally seems to be future trouble and not rejoicings, that shows itself to the person with the Second Sight.)

The first time that she became aware of this uncanny gift it frightened her so badly and made such a deep impression on her that when she told me about it, thirty years later, she told it as freshly and in as much detail as though it had happened only the day before. It was indeed an unnerving experience for a young girl.

My mother was seventeen at the time, and she was going out to

India to stay with an elder brother in the Indian Civil. It was her first trip away from home, and by herself, and at the beginning she felt a little strange and lonely, but she soon got to know a few people and settled to life on board ship. Among the other passengers was a middle-aged man – I shall call him Mr X. One can't be a month or more in the same ship without coming to know the faces of all the other passengers, so she came to know this man by sight, and she heard other people speak to him by name. But he remained simply a middle-aged face with a name to it, among all the crowd of passengers that she didn't know.

The weeks went by, and she had a mild flirtation with one of the ship's officers; they were through the Suez Canal, and the *punkahs* (fans) came into use, and the nights as well as the days began to be very hot. And one night in the Indian Ocean, she woke from an uncomfortably vivid dream to find herself in the gangway outside her cabin on her way to fetch the ship's Doctor because Mr X was dying.

She had never walked in her sleep before, and she was bewildered and startled, but she pulled herself together and crept back into her bunk without waking her cabin mate, telling herself that it was probably the heat.

The next night exactly the same thing happened again. Only this time she was more than half way to the Doctor's cabin when she came to herself, and had quite a long walk back, hoping desperately that she wouldn't meet anybody on the way.

She still told herself it was the heat; but she began to be very worried in case it should happen a third time and that she actually got all the way to the Doctor's cabin: and finally she decided that the best thing would be to go and tell him the whole story.

So next morning, that was what she did. 'If you wake up in the night and find me flapping around your cabin in my nightie, it's because I've come to tell you that Mr X is dying. I've never walked in my sleep before, but last night and the night before, I woke up on my way here. I think it must be the heat.'

The Doctor said, 'Well I hope to God nobody *does* die this trip, because I've done the stupidest thing – I've forgotten to bring any death certificate forms with me.'

And it was when he said that, that my mother realized for the first time, the full, very frightening implication of this sleep-walking to fetch the Doctor. Whenever she caught sight of Mr X that day, she looked at him rather anxiously, but as far as she could judge, never having really *looked* at him before, he seemed just as usual.

That night she slept beautifully, no dreams, no sleep-walking: and when she woke in the morning it all seemed so comfortably in the past that she decided she had been rather silly and had made a fuss about nothing. Then, while she was dressing, the stewardess came in with a message from the Doctor. She was to go to him in the Sick Bay at once, and not to speak to anyone on the way.

In the Sick Bay she found the Doctor looking rather white. He said, 'I didn't want you to hear it from anyone else and get a shock – Mr X had a heart attack and died in the night.'

THE WISH HOUNDS

Kathleen Hunt

Of this story Mrs Hunt says: 'The Wish Hounds are an old tradition, akin to Gabriel's Hounds or the Wild Hunt of Scandinavia. I have written in the first person, because, although I have never encountered the Wish Hounds as closely as this, I have had several nasty moments. Dartmoor is an eerie place in bad weather and half light. All the places mentioned are real ones, and the route of the walk, which is about eighteen or twenty miles long, can be traced on a map.'

THE great bog which lies at the heart of Dartmoor is a silent place. Few birds fly there, and the streams flow quietly between banks of black peat, or lose themselves in morasses of moss and rushes. For many miles you can walk, and hear only the sound of the wind in the heather, and the sullen splash of your own feet in the black water. On a fine, sunny day, this silence is pleasant, a release from the noise of the world; under grey skies, or in a fog, it is grim and threatening. It is through this silence that the Wish Hounds hunt.

The Wish Hounds themselves run in silence, unable to give tongue, for they have no tongues, or indeed any heads at all, only a wisp of cold, bluish flame flickers at the end of their great black necks. Their heavy feet make no sound over the moss and heather.

I did not believe in the Wish Hounds that day when I set out from Chagford to walk to Cranmere Pool, in the heart of the moor. The day was fine, I had a map and a compass, and some pasties from the little shop in Chagford market place. As I took the deep lane to Gidleigh, and came out on to the moor by the stone circle, it seemed to me that all was well with the world, and

a good day's walk in front of me. I set my course for the Thirlstone, that strange waterworn tor that looks as if the sea had
raced through its arch, and ate my lunch sitting on top of it,
looking east away from the moor, over fields and woods for miles
upon miles, until the tower on Haldon Hill rears itself on the
very edge of sight.

It is when you go down from the Thirlstone into the moor that
the loneliness grows about you. The high shoulder of the hill behind cuts off all sight of the lands beyond the moor, and the
walking begins to get harder, less a walk than a series of jumps
from one tussock of heather to another, trying to avoid the black
peat mud lying between.

The sky began to cloud over as I crossed the valley between the
Thirlstone and Hangingstone Hill, and, as I breasted the hill and
swung left to avoid the marsh of Taw Head the first drops of
rain drove into my face on a westerly wind. Soon a mist, or
rather a low cloud, mingled with the rain, and visibility became
very poor. Nevertheless, I decided to carry on, and make for
Cranmere and the West Okement River, which I could follow
until I came out on to the army roads on the northern side of the
moor.

When I first became aware that something was following me I
cannot say. I was fully occupied in picking my way across the
bog, trying to keep my feet dry without deviating too far from the
line of the compass. Gradually I became nervous, and started to
look back over my shoulder. At first there was nothing to be seen
but bog and heather, veiled with rain and mist. Then I saw a rock
where no rock should be; at first I thought it was some trick of
my eyes in the deceptive weather, and resolutely started on again.
Soon, however, I felt myself constrained to glance behind me
again, and saw that there were now three of the dark objects, and
that they seemed to be nearer.

Then I knew that I was pursued, and, unreasoning at first, I
ran in terror. This was playing into the hands of my enemies, for
they could run faster than I could, moving easily over the hum-
mocks of peat, and leaving no footprints on the black mud. They
could not have harmed me, had they caught up with me, and that
was not their aim, rather they sought to drive me into a marsh, or

into one of the deep green holes called 'feather-beds' because of their softness, into which I could sink without trace.

So I was playing their game by running away, and yet terror drove me on as those black shapes plodded silently after me in the mist and the rain. My compass was now almost useless, for even in clear weather the high tors are not visible from the bog around Cranmere, and now I dared not stop to take the frequent bearings that were necessary. I ran, blindly, into the heart of the moor, heading into the wind, with the rain beating on my face, and the black hounds, now increasing in number to about ten or twelve, racing behind me.

As I ran my senses began to return to me, and after a while I realized that my best plan would be to turn right, and northwards, and so hope to strike one of the military roads that would bring me safe into civilization again. I swung round, but my pursuers forestalled me, and raced ahead to cut me off. Frustrated I turned back into my original course, no longer looking for Cranmere, but simply fleeing from the hounds.

I have said that I was not looking for Cranmere, but nevertheless I stumbled into it. It is not a pool, but a mere depression in the peat, with a post box and visitors' book in a little cairn, but I had no time to bother with them now. I was forced to halt to get my breath, and the hounds halted too, ranged along the rim of the 'pool', their bodies headed into the wind as if they were scenting the breeze with invisible noses.

Then the wind changed. It happened quite suddenly, swinging from West to North, and taking the rain away with it. The sun came out and sparkled in the drops of rain hanging on the heather. The hounds turned away, and began to vanish, melting away like the cloud wreaths upon the slopes of the hills. Soon I was alone once more, and free to walk in whatever direction I chose. The infant West Okement was running at my feet, and I followed it until it became a swift stream, gurgling and chuckling in its bed. Then I left it, and walked by compass once more until I struck the military road that was to lead me into Okehampton.

The sun was setting behind Yes Tor as I hurried on my way downhill, and I glanced fearfully at the shadows, expecting every moment to see them spring into life and pursue me. But they did not, and I reached the lights of Okehampton safe and sound. But it will be a long time before I walk alone on Dartmoor again, however promising the morning.

THE MAN IN THE ROAD

F. M. Pilkington

Miss Pilkington is of Scots and Irish parentage and is very much aware of the supernatural. This is her earliest ghostly experience.

WHEN I was about eleven, I went out one evening with my mother to take her dog for a walk before bedtime. We were then living in Kingstown, now known as Dun Laoghaire, some miles down the coast from Dublin.

There was a bit of road not far from where we lived which was said to be haunted, but none of my family had ever seen anything supernatural there. On this occasion it was dark, the gaslamps were lit, and we were just turning out of our road into this particular stretch, when the dog suddenly ran ahead, and then began barking furiously. My mother called to him to come back, but without success, and this was very unusual, for he was a well-trained and obedient animal. We went up to where the creature stood, growling and barking by turns, just by one of the lampposts, and saw, standing directly in the lamplight, a tallish man, wearing a hat with a pointed crown, and a small plume on one side, a dark cloak, and buckled shoes – we were not near enough to see his features clearly.

My mother went forward and gripped the dog's collar, saying as she did so, 'I must apologize for my dog's bad behaviour.' I was just behind her, and quite suddenly, as I looked at him waiting for him to speak, the man vanished completely. As it was a straight road, with a high wall on that side with no doors, there was no normal explanation for his disappearance.

My mother did not seem perturbed – it was not her first encounter with a ghost – but I must confess that my legs shook, and I was very glad when we got home. The dog was trembling all over, with the hair along his back standing straight up, and it was some while before he would stop growling. I suppose the shock for me was all the greater because I had quite thought the man must be going to a fancy-dress ball, and had not felt in the least frightened until he vanished so strangely.

MY HAUNTED HOUSES

M. Joyce Dixon

Miss Dixon writes: 'I am not psychic and although I tell fortunes for fun, I lay no claim to extra-sensory powers. But I *am* very sensitive to atmosphere: atmosphere in the relationship of persons one to another, and particularly the atmosphere of places. There are parts of the country and some houses which "speak" to me of evil and dark deeds; others which make me feel happy and confident. It is interesting (to me at any rate) that the last three houses I have lived in have ghostly associations of a pleasant sort.'

I HAD an interesting experience when, as a young woman, I spent a short holiday with an elderly aunt in a guest house in Winchester. This old house, Queen Anne or Georgian, was a perfect setting for a ghost story and even the aunt was not impervious to the atmosphere, as she confessed before we left. Nevertheless the subject was not mentioned and on the first night we went to our respective rooms. I went to sleep in a large double bed in a room large enough for the far corners to fade into gloom, and opposite the bed were clearly defined the outlines of a window which must have been bricked in when the old window tax was introduced.

I slept well and waked early as I usually do in summer. I felt very gay and fresh, for the sunlight was pouring into the room and I was looking out on to a beautiful flower-filled garden. It was some minutes before this vision faded and I realized that I was lying staring at the blocked-up window. I might have thought it was but a waking dream if it had not been followed by another odd experience.

I got up and dressed and went to find my aunt. She had had an unquiet night and said she nearly came to my room but found she lacked the courage. We went down to breakfast together. There were several people ahead of us on the broad staircase – a married couple, two maiden ladies and an old canon. Although the latter was a common enough sight in Winchester something incongruous about him caught my attention, perhaps the fact that he was wearing his clerical hat.

The staircase was wide and dark and near the bottom was a little square landing; a blank wall ahead and the flight of stairs turned at a right-angle to reach the ground. The canon was a few steps ahead of me when he reached the landing. To my amazement he walked straight through the blank wall leaving no trace, while everyone else made the turn and continued their descent unconcernedly.

These occurrences seemed to me of sufficient interest to call for a bit of research. I was able to confirm that the window in my bedroom had been blocked up and also, what was now a disused grave-yard, had once been the flower garden of the house. I also found out that an alteration had been made to the stairs which in former times went straight, without a turn, to the ground floor. There was a story that the house was in fact haunted by a canon who had lived there for many years; so what I had seen was the old man taking his accustomed way downstairs.

I was living with my sister in a large old house in Keats Grove in Hampstead. It had been divided into flats and we had taken what must have been the drawing-room floor. The room we used as our sitting room was large and beautifully proportioned with windows reaching almost from floor to ceiling.

One Sunday afternoon we were sitting reading quietly by the fire. Something made me look up and glance towards the door, and there was the daintiest little girl I have ever seen, wearing a white party frock of long ago. She came towards me, one arm outstretched and the other raised with a finger on her lips. She trod airily like a ballet dancer and smiled happily as she drew near. Then she was gone.

'I have just seen a ghost,' I said. I felt not the least bit of fear or even surprise – the 'appearance' was as natural as if a living child had come into the room – and gone again, intent upon her own affairs.

For some years I lived in a small and narrow Queen Anne house in old Hampstead where the atmosphere was exceptionally happy.

One day I was visited by an acquaintance with psychic gifts – she had been 'telling my fortune' and as she finished she said unexpectedly, 'Who are the dear old couple sitting by the fire place?' and before I could reply continued, 'They must be your father and mother who have passed on, they are so very fond of you.'

'No,' I said, 'you are mistaken there, because my mother was never old.'

'Well,' she said, 'at any rate I can assure you that they love you as if you were their own daughter.'

When I eventually sold the little house, it was bought by a young actor. He asked if there was a ghost, obviously regarding such a phenomenon as an attraction; so I told him my story. He proved to be more curious than myself and made inquiries. In fact a devoted old couple had lived there for many years.

The cottage where I now live in Wisbrough Green is blessed by the shade of Dame Venn. She lived here about a hundred years ago and I know quite a lot about her as I was privileged to meet a very old antiquarian and clockmaker who had been post boy in the village when she was still alive, and he told me all he knew, including the fact that she had been seen on occasion metamorphosed into a hare with a little red cloak floating behind her! Even if this seems hardly credible there is no doubt she was a very real person. She was known as a sorceress and people came in their coaches and carriages from as far away as London and Brighton to seek her advice.

But she was not feared. Everyone liked her and she was a familiar figure at all the local fairs selling nuts from the hedgerows at a farthing a bag.

During my early tenure of the cottage she was first seen by a teenage schoolboy who visited the cottage and insisted on going all over the house. On his way home he asked the friend who had brought him if the cottage was supposed to be haunted as he had seen an old lady sitting in my bedroom.

She is an unusual ghost for she has her own definite standards of behaviour. If one conforms to them she is quiescent and one is only conscious of a presence or occasionally one sees the steam rising from her magic brews. On the other hand I *have* had guests to whom she has justifiably taken exception and there is no limit to the stage effects she can turn on to frighten them.

I will give one memorable instance. During the War I admitted to the cottage certain paying guests at weekends. One weekend a mixed party of four came down from London. They were young and in most things immoderate, and their vibrations and behaviour were clearly out of tune with those of Dame Venn. I was very tired and after one night I absented myself and committed them to the charge of Dame Venn with a silent admonition that she was free to do as she chose by them.

I heard next day that as night fell, the peace of the cottage was disturbed by a succession of strange noises so alarming that the visitors dared not disperse to their bedrooms. At last, too weary to sit up any longer, they did go to bed. By this time the witch had apparently enlisted the help of my black cat, for as the first guest was about to climb into her bed, the cat leapt through the window and flung a dead rabbit on the pillow. Three people had no sleep that night and left first thing in the morning. On my return only one remained to greet me. Evidently she had escaped the witch's machinations, for when she finally retired, she had slept peacefully, and she could not resist waiting to tell me the story. As I said, Dame Venn does not approve of any laxity in behaviour, and makes her disapproval very clear .

IN SEARCH OF A GHOST

Eric Roberts

Although Eric Roberts has yet to see a ghost for himself, he is convinced that ghosts – and especially poltergeists – really do exist. He therefore never resists the opportunity of endeavouring to make a ghost's acquaintance in the hope that, one day, he will be presented with the final and irrefutable evidence of personal encounter.

He thought his chance had come when he spent an evening in a haunted house on Dartmoor – an experience that he broadcast on the B.B.C. programme *Home This Afternoon*.

IT was when I was in Devonshire on holiday that I was offered the opportunity of making the acquaintance of a ghost, a thing I had long wanted to do as I had always been a firm believer in ghosts, although only through second-hand experience.

Hence my interest when the owner of a large house in the wilds of Dartmoor informed me that, any time from about 10.30 onwards, a little lady in a grey cloak was in the habit of making a nightly perambulation along the corridors and into some of the rooms.

Not that the owner lived in the house herself. In fact, the place was uninhabited except on those occasions when people came down to fish the nearby river, and used the premises more for shelter than for comfort. For the rest of the time it stood empty, a tall, gaunt building exuding an inhospitable atmosphere, with its windows so tightly shut that they gave the impression of having been sealed.

I collected the key as night began to fall, and made my way up the weed-strewn narrow path that led to a heavy porch in whose dark recesses stood the front door like a bastion, defying entry. It was almost with a sense of guilt at my intrusion that I turned

the massive key in the lock that swung the door back on its
creaking hinges.

The house was without electric light, but I had been told that
I should find candles in the hall, and when I lit one the shape of
furniture gradually separated itself from the shadows – a hall-
stand, chairs, and a solid mahogany table all looking as if they
had been built into the floor, so long had it been since they were
last moved.

Before settling down to await the arrival of the ghost, I made
as swift an inspection of the house as my flickering candle would
allow, first negotiating some stone steps that led to a vast stone-
floored kitchen that occupied the whole of the basement. From
here I returned to the hall and made my way upstairs to peer
cautiously into several bedrooms where old iron bedsteads stood
like sentinels against the walls.

At one end of the landing, I found a room that had obviously
served as a study, although the only books that were now in evidence were a few paper-backs yellow with age. I found their titles
a trifle disturbing – *The Hangman's Noose, Death Under the
Stairs,* and *The Creeping Flesh* were typical examples.

But it was time for my vigil to start, so I steered my way
to a huge armchair whose upholstery had provided many a
banquet for the moths, put my candle on the floor, and
waited.

Nothing happened. Then, after a time, it occurred to me that
as the ghost only visited some of the rooms, she might be giving
this one a miss, so I decided to pay another visit to the bedrooms.

It was in the third of these that I saw her – at least, I thought I
did. In the feeble light of my candle a figure at the far end of the
room moved perceptibly towards me as I approached. My heart
thumped with excitement as I rather fatuously bade her good
evening, but as I drew nearer I saw that this was no little old lady
in a grey cloak but a middle-aged gentleman whose hair was beginning to recede at the temples, and who looked rather in need
of a shave.

It was me – staring wide-eyed at myself in the long mirror of a
tall wardrobe lurking in the gloom of the bedroom. Bitterly dis-
appointed, I returned to the landing, and was halfway towards

the next bedroom when a crash from the kitchen shattered the silence.

So that's where she was! And by the sound of it, the dear old thing had tripped over a bucket. So, with candle held aloft, I clattered helter-skelter down the stairs thinking that the sight of a ghost rubbing its shins and muttering spooky oaths as it dusted itself down would be something worth seeing.

But there was nothing there. I examined every corner of the vast kitchen, but all was exactly as it had been before, giving the impression that nothing had been moved for years.

I stayed a little while longer, and for a time even extinguished the candle so that the dense shadows thrown by the flame vanished into darkness as black as pitch. But the ghost failed to walk that night.

Or did it?

When I finally decided to leave, I locked the door from the outside, and then tried it to make sure it was secure. But the handle turned uselessly in my hand. So I unlocked the door again and tried to go back in, but the handle would not withdraw the catch. The door was held fast, so that any further entry was most effectively barred.

You may say this was just a normal failure of a lock. But was it?

A week or two later I heard from the owner that not even a locksmith had been able to discover what had gone wrong with the lock, and they had been obliged to get into the house through a downstairs window. Which makes me wonder if the ghost was really there all the time, and having seen me off the premises, took care that I didn't return to disturb her privacy again.

After all, *something* must have caused that crash in the kitchen, mustn't it?

THE LIMPING MAN OF
MAKIN-MEANG

Sir Arthur Grimble

Sir Arthur Grimble, a member of the Colonial Administrative Service, was sent out as a young man, in the Spring of 1914, to the
Gilbert and Ellice Islands Protectorate. He studied the local language
and from the first became intensely interested in the customs and
beliefs of the people. He wrote about his experiences in *A Pattern
of Islands* and it is from this book that what follows – just one of
his several encounters with spirits – is taken.

IT is clearly up to a District Officer to be listening and learning
all the time. But there is a mortal difference of spirit between
genuine research and prying. The danger is, the genuine thing
can deteriorate by such subtle and unconscious stages into mere
over-curiosity that a *bona-fide* student may find himself poised
on the very brink of fiddling before he wakes up to the horrid
change that has gone on inside him. That was what happened
to me on Makin-Meang.

Perhaps the eeriness of the island's reputation for ghosts,
added to the odd taciturnity of its villagers, had something to
do with my ineptitude. But I base no defence on that. The District Officer's job is to find ways through to his people, not to
leave them groping for ways through to himself.

I had heard of the ghosts of Makin-Meang before I got there.
The people of Tarawa and Maiana and Abaiang were full of
tales about them. They told me that the whole Gilbertese race,
for over thirty generations by their count (it was sixty or so by
mine), had looked on that most northerly island of the group
as their halfway house between the lands of the living and the
dead.

The story went that, when anyone died, his shade must first
travel up the line of islands to Makin-Meang. Going ashore

there on a southern beach, it must tread the length of the land
to a sandspit at the northern tip called the Place of Dread. This
was not an actual place-name, but simply a term of fearful reference to the locality – for there sat Nakaa, the Watcher at the
Gate, waiting to strangle all dead folk in his terrible net. The
ghost had no hope of winning through to paradise except by way
of the Gate, and no skill or cunning of its own could save it from
the Net. Only the anxious family rituals, done of its body,
could avail for that; and even these might fail if any outsider
were to break in upon their course.

The reasonableness or not of these beliefs is of no concern. It
was the age and intensity of them that weighed on Makin-
Meang. Every yard of the island was loaded with the terrors
and hopes that sixty generations of the living, and the dying,
and the long-dead, from end to end of the Gilbert group, had
focused upon it.

The impress of man's thought was as heavy as footfalls on
its paths. I wondered if that was why those silent villagers always
seemed to be listening inside their ears for some sound I could
never hear.

They were courteous and gentle, but they would not talk to
me about the place where Nakaa sat; they did not even try to
change the subject when I raised it; they simply dropped their
eyes and removed themselves into abysses of reserve. It was not
from them but from my orderly, a Tarawa man, that I learned
how best to avoid the horror of meeting a ghost face to face.
He lived in such open fear of doing so himself that the Native
Magistrate had let him know out of pity.

He told me that the shades of all the folk who died on the
other fifteen islands found their way to Nakaa by the road above
the western beach, whereas only those of local people used the
eastern path. There were therefore many more chances of meeting ghosts on the west side than on the east. Not that it mattered
greatly which way you chose going north, because you were
travelling with the stream anyhow, and the only thing you had
to remember was never, never to look behind you. But coming
back against the northbound traffic, you must take no road save
the eastern one. You could find out in advance when that was safe

or not by asking if any local death was expected the day you planned to use it.

When I had finished my routine work on the island, I naturally wanted to see the Place of Dread, so I called the Native Magistrate along one morning and asked him to find me a guide.

I have never seen a face change and darken as swiftly as his did at my request. He stood dumb for a while with downcast eyes; then, still looking at the ground, 'Do not go to that place,' he exclaimed, and again, on a higher note, passionately, 'Do not go!' The edge on his voice made it seem almost as if he had said, 'I order you not to go.'

'But why?' I said irritably. 'What's all this nonsense about Nakaa's place? What's all the mystery? Shall I offend anyone by going?'

'Nobody will be offended,' he replied, 'but do not go. The place is perilous.'

'But why perilous for me, a Man of Matang?'

His only reply was to wrap himself in a cloak of silence. So I tried another line: 'You're a member of a Christian church. You surely can't believe still that souls go that way to Heaven or Hell. Or do you?'

He lifted his eyes to mine, crossing himself. 'Not Christian souls,' he whispered, 'but pagan ones ... to Hell ... they still walk the island ... and Nakaa stays there ... and there is fear ...' His voice trailed off into mumbles; I got no more out of him.

I should of course have made up my mind in all decency then to find the place for myself. The island is a straight, lagoonless ribbon, and I could not possibly have missed its tapering northern end. But I was cussed: 'Please find a village constable who isn't afraid to be my guide,' I said, 'and send him to me here.'

He looked at me mutely, spread his hands in a hopeless little gesture, and left. The constable, a giant of a man with bushy eyebrows and a grimly smileless face, appeared within the next half-hour. He said before we started that, as I was a stranger, I must take the western path going northward, just as the ghosts of strangers did, and that I must be careful not to look back.

'And if I do look back?' I said.

'If you look back and see a ghost,' he replied, 'you will be dead within a year,' and marched off ahead of me without another word.

I followed him in silence, eyes front, for perhaps half an hour, when he stepped suddenly into the coconut forest on our right. 'Come in among the trees,' he called without turning his head: 'This is my land. There is a thing you must carry to Nakaa.'

The thing was a seed-coconut. It appeared that every stranger, on his first visit to the Place of Dread, must bring with him a sprouting nut to plant in Nakaa's grove. I thought well of the idea until he told me I must carry it myself. It had an enormous sprout. I am inclined to believe he chose that particular one with deliberate malice, seeing that the only correct way to carry it (or so he said) was upright in my cupped hands with elbows well against my ribs. I felt a complete ass sweating meekly behind him in that ridiculous attitude for the next five or six miles with my aspidistra-like trophy fluttering in the wind.

I planted the nut at his order where the trees petered out in a shady desolation at the island's tip. When it was done to his liking he just walked away into the forest.

'Here!' I called. 'Where are you going now?'

'I will wait here,' he replied; 'There in the north is the place you seek,' and was lost among the trees.

There was nothing in that empty waste to distinguish it from fifty other such promontories in the Gilbert group. It was merely a blazing acre or two of coral rock shaken by bellowing surf and strident with the shrieks of swarming sea-birds. I walked to the point where the meeting tide-rips boiled. It was from there that happy ghosts, the Net of Nakaa passed, fared forth across the sea to be gathered at last with their fathers. I knew that in that very flash of time, from somewhere down the chain of islands, the thoughts of dying folk might be winging their way in wistfulness and fear to the spot where I was standing. But somehow, my mind only played with the idea. There was no sense of reality. The place itself put me utterly out of tune with the old beliefs. Perhaps it was the noise. Death is so quiet, and there was nothing in Nakaa's domain but that din of birds and shattered waters and the trade wind's diapason booming in my ears.

Nevertheless, the brazen heat of rocks and sand that drove me out at last did have its importance, because it gave me the thirst that led to what followed. I went straight back to my guide among the trees and asked him in all innocence to pick me a drinking nut.

He sprang back as if I had struck him: 'I cannot do that,' he almost barked. 'I cannot do that. These trees are Nakaa's.' Fear oozed out of him, almost as tangible as sweat.

I could not press him to violate his belief; nor had I learned yet to scale a forty-foot tree for myself; so I had to sit down there in Nakaa's grove to a sickeningly dry lunch of bully-beef and biscuit. I remember muttering to myself, 'This is how the old devil strangles foreign ghosts, anyhow,' as I gulped the stuff down.

It was past two o'clock when we started for home down the eastern path. My friend told me that his proper place going south was in the rear, and dropped forty paces behind. Perhaps he just wanted to keep out of my sight as well as the sound of my voice; anyway, it was I who led the way against the traffic-stream of local ghosts.

After ten minutes' walking, with thirst at concert pitch, I stopped and croaked back at him (he would not come near), 'Are we out of Nakaa's grove yet?'

Not yet, he shouted back, there was still a mile or more of it. It was then that an unpleasant little worm within me turned. I made up my mind to disregard his scruples and ask anyone we met, anywhere, to pick me a nut. And there, in the midst of that peevish thought, was suddenly a man coming along the track to help me.

Across the arc of a curving beach, I saw him appear round a point. I could follow every yard of his course as he came nearer. My eyes never left him, because my intent was pinned on his getting me that drink. He walked with a strong limp (I thought that might make it hard for him to climb a tree). He was a stocky, grizzled man of about fifty, clad rather ceremoniously in a fine mat belted about his middle (a poor kit for climbing, commented my mind). As he came up on my left, I noticed that his left cheek was scored by a scar from jawbone to temple, and that his limp came from a twisted left foot and ankle. I can see the man still in memory.

But the question is – did he see me? He totally ignored the greeting I gave him. He did not even turn his eyes towards me. He went by as if I didn't exist. If anyone was a ghost on that pathway, I was – for him. He left me standing with one futile hand flapping in the air to stay him. I watched his dogged back receding towards my oncoming guide. I was shocked speechless. It was so grossly unlike the infallible courtesy of the islanders.

He was just about to pass the constable when I found voice again: 'Ask that chief to stop,' I called back, 'he may need some help from us.' It had struck me he might be a lunatic at large: possibly harmless, but we ought to make sure of that. But the din of the surf may have smothered my voice, for the constable didn't seem to hear. He passed the newcomer twenty yards from where I stood, without a sign of recognition.

I ran back to him. 'Who is that man?' I asked.

He stopped in his tracks, gazing at my pointed finger. 'How?' he murmured hesitantly, using the Gilbertese equivalent for 'Say it again'.

I said it again, sharply, still pointing. As we stood dumbly looking at each other, I saw swift beads of sweat – big, fat ones – start out of his forehead and lose themselves in his eyebrows.

Then it was as if something suddenly collapsed inside him. It was horrible. 'I am afraid in this place!' he screamed high in his head, like a woman, and, without another word, he bolted out on the beach with an arm guarding his eyes. He disappeared at a run round the point, and I didn't see him again until I got back to my quarters.

But there he was when I arrived, on the verandah with the Native Magistrate. I saw the two of them absorbed in talk, the constable violently gesturing now and then as I approached the house. But they stepped apart as soon as they heard my footsteps, and stood gravely collected when I entered, waiting for me to speak.

I plunged head-first into my petulant story. The sum of it was that the constable had witnessed the discourtesy of the man with the limp, and was now trying his silly best to shield him from censure. It might be very loyal, but did he take me for a fish-headed fool? To pretend he hadn't seen the fellow ... well ... really! And so on, I was very young.

The Native Magistrate waited with calm good manners for me to run down, and then asked what the man was like.

I told him of the twisted foot, and the belted mat, and the scar.

He turned to exchange nods with the constable: 'That was indeed Na Biria,' he murmured, and they nodded at each other again.

'Na Biria?' I echoed. 'Is he a lunatic?'

He dropped his eyelids, meaning, 'No.'

'Then bring him to me this evening.'

He looked me straight in the eyes: 'I cannot do that.'

'Cannot? What word is this ... cannot? Is everyone here dotty today? Why cannot you bring him?'

'He is dead,' said the Magistrate, and added as I stood dumb, 'He died this afternoon, soon before three o'clock.'

They were both so remote; the whole place was so secretive; my mind was as fagged as my body; everything in that moment conspired to weaken its resistance against the improbable. Perhaps I was being bluffed; I don't know; but I suddenly had the picture of Na Biria in the article of death projecting his dying thought, with sixty generations of fear behind it, along that path through Nakaa's grove to the Place of Dread beyond. Had I received the impact of his thought as it passed my way? Or if not, what was it I had seen?

I knew it was not only thirst that made my mouth so dry, and that angered me. 'If he only died at three, he is not yet buried, and I can see his body,' I exclaimed.

'His body lies in the village,' replied the Magistrate.

'And I can see it?' I insisted.

He paused a long time before bowing his head in assent. But brusquely the constable interrupted: 'No! The Man of Matang is a stranger! They are straightening the way of the dead. No stranger must break in ... No! ... No!'

The Magistrate silenced him with a gesture. 'I am a Christian,' he said solemnly to me: 'I will take you. Let us go at once.'

I followed him out of the house.

We heard the mourners wailing from a hundred yards off. I saw a dozen of them flogging the purlieus of the open-sided house with staves, to frighten away strange ghosts. I went near enough to see people sitting with raised arms at the head and feet of a body. But I halted outside the circle of beaters. It was finding them so earnestly at work that brought me back to the decencies. These folk believed utterly in what they were doing. For them, the dead man's whole eternity depended on their ritual. For them, the intrusion of me, a stranger, would send him to certain strangulation in Nakaa's Net. What earthly or heaven-born right had I, for a moment's peevishness, to condemn them for the rest of their days to that hideous conviction? I suddenly felt as small as I was. I could go no farther. I turned away from the house. The Native Magistrate followed me in silence.

From *A Pattern of Islands* by Sir Arthur Grimble (John Murray (Publishers) Ltd, London, and William Morrow & Co. Inc., New York).

ACKNOWLEDGEMENTS

EVERY effort has been made to trace the ownership of the copyright material in this book. It is the publisher's belief that the necessary permissions from publishers, authors and authorized agents have been obtained, but in the event of any question arising as to the use of any material, the publishers, while expressing regret for any error unconsciously made, will be pleased to make the necessary correction in future editions of the book.

Thanks are due to the following for permission to reprint copyright material: Brandt & Brandt for 'The House of the Nightmare' from *Lukandoo and Other Stories* by E. L. White; The Bodley Head Ltd, London, and E. P. Dutton & Co. Inc., New York, for 'The Hauntings at Thorhallstead' by Allen French, condensed from *Grettir the Strong*, Copyright © 1908 by E. P. Dutton & Co. Inc., Renewal 1936 by Allen French; Miss Susan Dickinson for 'His Own Number' and 'The Return of the Native' from *Dark Encounters* by William Croft Dickinson, Copyright © 1963 by William Croft Dickinson, published by The Harvill Press, London; The Bodley Head Ltd, London, for 'Gabriel-Ernest' by Saki (H. H. Munro) from *The Bodley Head Saki*; Curtis Brown Ltd, London, for 'Hand in Glove' from *A Day in the Dark* by Elizabeth Bowen, published by Jonathan Cape Ltd, London; the author for 'Curfew', Copyright © 1967 by L. M. Boston; The Citadel Press, New York, for 'John Bartine's Watch' and 'A Diagnosis of Death' from *Can Such Things Be?* by Ambrose Bierce; The Society of Authors as the Literary Representative of the Estate of the late W. W. Jacobs for 'The Monkey's Paw' from *The Lady of the Barge*, published by Methuen & Co. Ltd, London; J. M. Dent & Sons Ltd, London, and the Executrix of the Quiller-Couch Estate for 'My Grandfather Hendry Watty' from *The Wandering Heath* by Sir Arthur Quiller-Couch; Edward Arnold (Publishers) Ltd, London, for 'A School Story' from *Collected Ghost Stories* by M. R. James; the author for 'The Red Cane', Copyright © 1967 by E. F. Bozman; The Literary Trustees of Walter de la Mare, and

The Society of Authors as their Representative for 'Bad Company' from *A Beginning and Other Stories* by Walter de la Mare, published by Faber & Faber Ltd, London; Curtis Brown Ltd, London, and Harper & Row (Publishers) Inc., New York, for 'Proof' from *Portrait of a Judge and Other Stories* by Henry Cecil, Copyright © 1964 by Henry Cecil; the author for 'The Amulet' by Thomas H. Raddall; the Literary Executors of A. J. Alan, and Charles Lavel Ltd, London, for 'The Hair' from *The Best of A. J. Alan*; A. D. Peters & Co., London, for 'The Earlier Service' from *Madame Fears the Dark* by Margaret Irwin; Geoffrey Bles Ltd, London, for 'Here I am Again' fom *Lord Halifax's Ghost Book*; the author for 'The Man Who Died at Sea', Copyright © 1967 by Rosemary Sutcliff; the author for 'The Wish Hounds', Copyright © 1967 by Kathleen Hunt; the author for 'The Man in the Road', Copyright © 1967 by F. M. Pilkington; the author for 'My Haunted Houses', Copyright © 1967 by M. Joyce Dixon; the author for 'In Search of a Ghost', Copyright © 1967 by Eric Roberts; John Murray (Publishers) Ltd, London, and William Morrow and Company, Inc., New York, for 'The Limping Man of Makin-Meang' from *A Pattern of Islands* (*We Chose The Islands*) by Sir Arthur Grimble, Copyright © 1952 by Sir Arthur Grimble.

Some other Puffins

GHOSTLY GALLERY
Alfred Hitchcock

Eleven weird and uncanny ghost stories collected by Alfred Hitchcock, the master of mystery. They include really spooky spine-chilling stories, some fanciful ones, and some where the phantoms and apparitions are even treated humorously. Some of the phantoms are true shades of darkness, and others, stranger still, appear in the glare of the sun at noon or deep in the forest shadows – you may see a spook any day of your life.

For fearless readers of ten upwards.

THE WHISPERING MOUNTAIN
Joan Aiken

A boy was hesitating one sharp autumn evening inside the gateway of the Jones academy in the small town of Pennygaff in Wales. It was Owen Hughes, and he knew some of the other boys were going to attack him.

A few hours later he hardly cared, for he was deep in the most enormous adventure of his life. He had been kidnapped by two thieves, and with him they had stolen the legendary harp of Teirtu, which Owen had been guarding for his grandfather.

How could Owen escape from his captors? And how could he rescue the stolen harp?

For readers of ten and over.

EARTHFASTS
William Mayne

At the dusk of a summer's day, Keith Heseltine and David Wix were still out on Haw Bank, investigating something. There was a new mound in the grass, and it was getting bigger. Then the ground stirred, as if someone were getting out of bed. And with the movement came the sound of drumming. David was trembling all over, and so was Keith, and then they made sense of it. All that had come out of the hill was a boy about their own size, with a drum.

Two hundred years before, Nellie Jack John the drummer boy had gone to explore the passage under the castle, looking for King Arthur with his sleeping knights. Now he had come out again, but time had got mixed up, so that the ancient dead giants were walking about again, and domestic pigs were transformed into dangerous wild swine.

THE DOLPHIN CROSSING
Jill Paton Walsh

'Look, son,' said Crossman. 'This is no kids' game. You haven't any idea what it is like. You would be sailing into the middle of a battlefield. They are taking men off from right under the nose of enemy guns; sitting ducks those boats will be, and no defending them possible.'

This is the story of two boys and the friendship between them during the early days of the last world war – Pat and John, both knew the risks they were running, yet took a boat to help save the stranded British army from Dunkirk. For readers of ten and over, boys especially.

If you have enjoyed this book and would like to know about others which we publish, why not join the Puffin Club? You will be sent the Club magazine *Puffin Post* four times a year and a smart badge and membership book. You will also be able to enter all the competitions. For details of cost and an application form, send a stamped, addressed envelope to:

The Puffin Club, Dept A
Penguin Books
Bath Road
Harmondsworth
Middx